Sankofa

ALSO BY CHIBUNDU ONUZO

Welcome to Lagos

SANKOFA

A NOVEL

Chibundu Onuzo

Catapult  New York

Copyright © 2021 by Chibundu Onuzo

ISBN: 978-1-64622-083-0

Jacket design by Nicole Caputo
Book design by Jordan Koluch

Library of Congress Control Number: 2020948514

Printed in the United States of America
10 9 8 7 6 5 4 3 2 1

To Joseph Harker, for planting the seed.

Sankofa

1

My mother was six months dead when I opened the trunk I found under her bed. I opened the trunk on the same day her headstone was erected. Rose, my daughter, accompanied me to the cemetery. I wore black, like it was a second funeral. Grass had grown over her grave, the earth erasing all memory of its disturbance. The headstone was marble, paid for by my mother's funeral insurance. Rose chose the gold-lettered inscription.

Bronwen Elizabeth Bain
1951–2018
Beloved Mother, Grandmother, Daughter and Sister
Remember me when I am gone away,
Gone far away into the silent land.

The Rossetti quote was a touch melancholic, but so was my mother and, for that matter, so was Rose. We laid flowers, fresh white chrysanthemums. Rose said a few words, addressing my mother as if she were present. When she finished, she turned to me. I shook my head. The practice felt too foreign and fanciful.

Afterwards, we had lunch near Rose's office, in what my mother would have called a smart restaurant, a maître d' by the door, thick cloth napkins on the tables. Rose went back to work, and I returned home to retrieve my mother's trunk from the storage cupboard. The day's ritual had left me wanting to touch something that belonged to her.

The trunk looked old. Brass fastenings and studs. Rose would have called it vintage. I avoided it for a long time. I had not enjoyed my previous experience of sorting through my mother's things. There had been no catharsis, only a strange fatigue after holding the clothes she had worn and the books she had read. It became clear I did not know her very well. *Madame Bovary* was on her bedside table. In the recesses of a wardrobe, I found a pair of sequined gloves.

The trunk fastenings were stiff and took some force to spring open. I lifted the lid and took out what appeared to be a scrapbook. There was a copy of my birth certificate stuck to the first page; on the next, a photograph of me by the seaside. My skin was as brown as the sand. There was a clump of my hair glued in place. My mother had written under the cutting: *From little Anna's head. She cries when I brush it.*

The book was a sort of monument to my childhood, a small shrine of memories. In a picture from my confirmation aged thirteen, I wore a puff-sleeved dress. Plaits sprouted from my head like twigs and ribbons streamed from their ends, prayers knotted to branches. She had kept my letters from university, a swatch of red fabric, and a white rose, pressed yellow with age.

There were some loose pictures of my mother and her sister when they were girls. Aunt Caryl was tall, almost scrawny, with her red hair disguised by sepia. My mother was smaller and sleeker with shiny black curls. My mother looked like a Bain, dark hair and blue eyes, a winning combination that obscured the plainer family features of thin lips and a weak chin. Aunt Caryl was an alien, or adopted, or ask the milkman.

In the months I avoided the trunk, it occurred to me that information about my father might be inside. I was very curious about him in my childhood. I knew his name, Francis Aggrey. I knew that he had arrived in England in the late sixties to go to university. I knew he had lodged in the spare attic room of my grandfather's house, and that he and my mother had some sort of affair. When he returned to his country, Bamana, she didn't know she was pregnant with me. They never saw each other again.

Why didn't she write? She didn't have an address. Why didn't *he* write? How would she know? Why didn't she go to Bamana?

"I couldn't afford it," she would say. "We can barely afford to go to Blackpool."

What was he like?

"I don't know, Anna. It was so long ago. He was only here for a few months."

Her answers never changed. There was nothing more to tell. I didn't even know what he looked like.

By the time I was eighteen, I'd stopped trying to find out about him. Although, once in a while, I would daydream about traveling to Bamana, stopping strangers in the street and asking if they knew a Francis Aggrey. I don't remember when that dream died.

I'd gone through all the photographs. The box looked empty. I shook it and heard sliding, objects rubbing against each other. I turned the trunk upside down and banged it. A false cardboard bottom came loose. Two notebooks fell out along with a black-and-white photograph the size of a playing card.

The man in the picture was the darkest tint in the human spectrum. Clean-shaven, smooth-skinned, almost oiled. I had his jaw, that straight square jaw that no other Bain had. His suit was pale, either grey or light blue. A metal pin held his tie in place, a silk pocket square bloomed from his breast pocket. His hair was cropped close, freshly clipped, shining with hair oil. I turned the picture over. *To my white rose, with love, F.K.A., 1969.* The ink was faded, the letters cramped to fit into the small space, except his initials, which took up half the inscription. It could be my father. Francis K. Aggrey. What did the K stand for?

I opened the first notebook, cheaply bound and filled with the same tight script.

London is afraid of me. Black man cannibal. Black man rapist. Hide your fat wives and your dumpy virgin daughters. Shut your door in my face. Look out. Tollund Man is coming.

The author's voice was strong and alive, as if he had walked into the room and begun speaking. An intelligent black man, angry, humorous. Surely not my father, hidden away in this box by a woman who told me there was little to know but his name.

I do not know how to write in a book like this. I am not used to talking to myself, but where else will I keep my confidences? A student drowned himself last week. Ghanaian boy with mother and family back home in Accra, and he threw himself off a bridge because someone called him a nigger. One time is nothing. Nigger, coon, darkie—you hear it like a mosquito flying past your ear. But a year of traveling in a crowded bus with an empty seat next to you, of old landladies opening their doors and quivering at the sight of you, "Francis Aggrey? I thought you were a Scotsman,"

"Francis Aggrey, I thought you were white," and the bottom of the Thames might begin to look like home.

It *was* my father, Francis Aggrey, trapped between these pages for decades. I was suddenly cautious. What if this diary revealed something discreditable? Some crime he had committed, some fraudulent stain from which my mother thought it best to shield me.

I read on slowly. The next few entries were sketches of places I recognized. He was an accurate draftsman. On a double leaf he had drawn the façade of the British Museum with this caption:

> I go to the Africa Section to sit in the warmth. Masks, stolen from my ancestors, surround me. These masks are made grotesque by their setting, the sacred turned ridiculous under the gaze of the uninitiated. The British public glance at me often, eyes darting from fertility goddesses to my black face. One of these days, I'll climb into a glass case to oblige them.

I had enacted this scene several times in my youth. Young Anna walking into an affluent space, a jewelry store, for example, or a gallery. Cue side glances tracking my movement, nervous and on edge. I tried to explain it to my mother once. "Don't be so sensitive," she said.

> There is something unseemly in running home to tell tales in these blank pages instead of speaking my mind like a man. Just on the corner today, I was running late for a lecture and I asked a man for the time. "Twenty minutes to noon," he said, before adding, "You talk nice for a nigger, don't you?" In Fanti, my response would have been out before he finished speaking. "You talk nice for a fool." But in English, this language I learned from mission-

aries, linguistically trained to turn the other cheek, all I could manage was, "I wish you good day, sir."

Years from now, when I am back in the Diamond Coast, among my own people where I am most confident, to open these pages would be to release the sharp stink of unaired retorts.

I shut the diary. I did not want to meet my father in one sitting. I put the scrapbook and loose photos back in the box. I kept the books and Francis Aggrey's photograph. I double-locked my front door and checked the kitchen window was shut. I left the stair lights on to show I was awake and in lunging distance of a panic button. Next year, perhaps, I would sell the house and move to a flat with other families stacked like crates above and below me.

I went upstairs to my bedroom. I changed into my sexless pajamas and turned off the lights. I still slept on one side of the bed, pinned to my half of the sheets, facing the space my husband once occupied. In the mornings, one side was always ruffled, the other smooth as an egg: portrait of a single woman's bed.

2

woke up thinking about Francis Aggrey. I looked again at his picture, dated 1969. It was taken just after Enoch Powell's "Rivers of Blood" speech, the worst of times for my father and my mother to fall in love. Or perhaps they were never in love. I was merely the result of a hapless fling, conceived hastily in 1969 and born nine months later, in January 1970.

Surely my grandfather had been foolish to take on such a handsome lodger with a teenage daughter in the house. My mother was nineteen when she had me, which meant she was eighteen when they met. How had she dared look at Francis Aggrey, let alone sleep with him, creeping past Grandpa Owen's door and up to his bedroom?

I would never know. Her death was swift and unexpected. Light headaches had surged into blinding migraines, brought on by a brain tumor that was metastasizing. I sat by her while she lay under the standard-issue NHS blanket, shrouded to her neck, hiding the tangle of tubes that fed into her arms.

When she was in pain, her lips puckered like a purse drawn

tight. Her wrinkles became more pronounced, dark lines in pale skin, etching on porcelain. I often looked out the window on a view of a bare tree, roots buried under the asphalt of the parking lot.

While she was ill, I asked about Francis Aggrey only once. She grew agitated when I said his name.

"I was all the family you needed. Didn't I feed you and clothe you and love you? What else did you want?"

She tried to sit up and I eased her back down.

"I was just trying to make conversation," I said.

The doctor said my mother's personality might change as the tumor grew. I wondered whether her character had changed or merely revealed itself.

Towards the end, I moved her from the hospital to my guest bedroom.

"Where's Robert?" she would ask most mornings. I told her but she always forgot.

I learned how to sponge her clean and check for bedsores, to feed her and wipe her chin, to ask before I did any of these things because she was an adult. She died on a May morning, Rose and I by the headboard, my husband, Robert, briefly reinstated at the foot.

Perhaps there would be something in Francis Aggrey's diary about how he met my mother. She was often timid, unsure, almost fearful. From what I'd read so far, they didn't seem an obvious match. I opened to where I had stopped.

I have joined a union for African students. I came to England to bowl with the English, and dance around their Maypoles, but the English will not have me. Not for tea. Not for scones. I attended my first meeting today. It is all young Africans like myself in worn shoes, and carefully brushed suits and big talk about politics. Ghana, Nigeria, and Kenya have their independence. South Africa and Rhodesia must soon follow. Ghana has left the sterling standard and rightly so. Nigeria should align with the Communists. I sat in a corner and listened. They have had big men come out of this students' union: a president in Central Africa, I have heard, although you could not tell it from the building. Crumbling walls and damp. "Where are you from?" a Rhodesian called Thomas Phiri asked when I got up to leave.

"Diamond Coast," I said.

"That's a slave name. Named for what they stole from us."

It's the only one I know.

In the photograph, Francis looked young, not far from Rose's twenty-five. As I read his diary, my feelings were almost maternal. I was eager for my father to settle down, to make friends in his new playground, to stop feeling so rootless. I hoped this Thomas would be a good influence.

I have seen Thomas Phiri again. He is not so bad the second time around, a bit forward, but London does one of two things to a black man: cows him or turns him into a radical, which is what I think Thomas is. Compared to myself, at least. In the Diamond Coast, the politicians say we are too small for independence, that Ghana or Nigeria will try to swallow us up if we cut ourselves off from the British Empire. Nkrumah talks of a United States of Africa, but who will be the head of this United States? Not tiny D.C. Thomas does not agree with these arguments, which are not necessarily mine, but which I offer to counter his strong opinions.

The next page detailed Francis's run-in with his landlady and her son. First, the mother complained about the noise, and then the son came to put the unruly black tenant in his place, or that was how Francis saw it.

I knew well the hours of agonizing that could follow such an incident. A woman crossing the road to avoid you. A shopkeeper who did not notice that you were next in line. Was that racist? Was it not?

My mother mostly erred on the side of not. People were rude, people were ignorant, but only racist if they called you an ape outright.

I have had the flu. Two days in my room with no one to attend to me, eating bread and water and feeling sorry for myself. I am my mother's only child. I am used to being made much of when I am sick.

My mother never went to work when I was sick. She would sit by my bed and hold my hand, even when I was asleep. It was one of my earliest memories, waking up and feeling her hand in the dark.

Thomas has invited me for a meeting of the British Communist Party. I don't think I will go. It is illegal to be a Communist in the Diamond Coast, and while a meeting in Russell Square may not get one arrested, it is sure to come to the notice of the government authorities in London that are rumored to keep an eye on foreign students.

Francis Aggrey was cautious like me. I'd always avoided large groups of people swimming in the same direction with one mind. I could never agree with all the tenets of a movement and so I could not join, but merely sympathize with feminists, with socialists, with Christians, with atheists, with vegans.

I really cannot see what threat communism can pose to the world order, at least not as it has done in England. So much jargon, so much theory. Proletariat, bourgeoisie, hegemony: what do these words mean to the fisherman in Segu? I said this to Thomas afterwards and he replied that the meeting was a necessary part of my political education. All I saw was a gaggle of Englishmen playing revolutionaries. There were some members of the working class present, oil on their hands, straight from some factory job or the other, but for the most part, it seemed to be the bourgeoisie they are trying to destroy. One speaker said Labour is killing the movement with its cheap housing. The proletariat are being lulled into complacency with indoor plumbing and central heating.

It appeared Thomas was trying to politicize my father. I'd never seen the point of politics in Britain. There was no choice, only the same men who had gone to the same schools, pretending to believe in different things. I hoped Francis did not succumb.

It was already noon and I was still in bed with the diary. Francis Aggrey's writing was not always easy to read. When his tone was angry, his letters shrank into thin black strokes. I spent a quarter of an hour trying to decipher a paragraph.

I got out of bed but did not open the curtains. There was nothing to see in the room. I was hungry but I had no food in the house. There had been a flurry of resistance when the supermarket chain opened at the top of my street, but we all shop there now, grabbing the bargain cuts and combination deals. The store had made us all richer, pushing the value of our houses over two million pounds.

I stepped outside into the cold. I did not like the area much when we moved in. We were on the cusp of the countryside. In spring, when the wind changed direction, you could smell the manure. The street was like a car showroom now. Low, sleek sports cars that never went at full throttle, tethered birds in our suburbia. The neighborhood children didn't play on the streets anymore. I saw them strapped inside 4x4s but I rarely heard their voices.

I saw my neighbor Katherine by the shop entrance and swerved into the vegetable aisle. Of all my neighbors, she was the only one who came to knock on my door after the ambulance came home with my mother. She brought us food that was too rich for my taste. I did not know how to respond to her kindness. She invited me to her church, but I declined. It was too much to exchange for cream of mushroom.

I had only come for sausages, but I found apples and soup and ice cream in my basket. I had lost weight on a diet of takeaways or nothing. I did not like to eat by myself, hunched over a foil pack with a plastic fork, brittle enough to bite through. I must have appeared eccentric to the young Asian man I gave my twenty-pound note to. I had worn my coat over my pajamas and my hair was uncombed. He was already looking past me to the next customer, preparing his "How are you today?"

I fried two sausages when I got home. Their skins ruptured, hot mince spilling out like lava. I covered them in baked beans. I forgot to buy bread. I fetched Francis Aggrey from upstairs when I was done. He was familiar to me, a friend, almost.

I have been thrown out of my lodgings. Thomas came here the other day and made a racket. He turned up my record player and stomped around until my landlady herself came to knock. I felt chastised when I saw the old lady, not far from my grandmother's age, woken from sleep to ask us to keep it down. But Thomas shouted at her, "Ma'am, now you have a real complaint for your racist son!"

Reprisal was swift. The son came two days later with a tough behind him. He won't have any coons insulting his mother. Clear out or they'll break my bones. I made a meek protest, citing tenancy agreements and contracts. Then he decided to become violent. He pushed me in the chest and so I pushed him back. I have not wrestled with street boys in Segu to have an English midget shove me about. I was ready to fight them both when the useless back-up said, "If you give any trouble, we'll call the police and get you done for assault." I have chosen not to test the impartiality of the London police force. I am writing this from Thomas's flat. As he was the one who began my troubles, I will stay here until I find a new place.

I want to cheer for young Francis. He would have taught me how to fight, how to make a fist and throw a punch. Not like my mother, who raised me to have nice manners no matter the provocation. I was told to shrink from conflict even when it sought you out, even when it thrust its finger in your face and said, "Go back to your fucking country." Tell them this *is* your fucking country, Francis Aggrey would have said.

He wrote about living with Thomas, two young men in close quarters. My father was the tidier of the two, the more domestic. Thomas arranged their social affairs, dragging my father to meetings with what he termed the "British left." Francis was skeptical but he went. He had traveled some distance from the Francis sitting alone in the British Museum, ogled by strangers.

I have had a letter from home. It is my mother asking how my studies are. I have not set foot in a lecture hall in two weeks, while my poor mother is in Segu, trading fish up and down the coast so I can pay my fees and have a little spending money. Thomas is a bad influence. We are out till the early hours of the morning and we spend our days dissipated as drunks. I must find new lodgings.

Grandpa Owen was the only grandparent I knew. He taught me some chess strategies and called me Shirley Bassey when I sang off key. I would have liked Francis to write more about my grandmother, but he was too busy discovering London with Thomas.

Francis and Thomas attended a lecture on West African decolonization and Francis's tone grew fiercer. He bristled at an English woman being an expert on West Africa, and Thomas was pleased that his protégé was "waking up." It seemed my father had fallen prey to politics in the end.

I have been introduced to a man called Ras Menelik. He is Thomas's mentor, and I have been kept from meeting him because Thomas did not feel I was ready. Perhaps he is right. Had I met Menelik two months ago, I might have laughed in his face. No barber has touched his hair in years. He is like John the Baptist in the wilderness, or one of the mendicant men rooting for food in the rubbish of Segu. He has a bevy of young English girls around him, typing his ideas into articles and pamphlets and chapters. They are the secretaries of his movement, which is to emancipate Africa. I took two of his pamphlets away: "Africa: A New Dawn" and "Sunrise in Ethiop." I cannot tell if it is bombast or visionary. He sends his writings all over the world. People are reading his ideas as far as Tokyo, Thomas tells me.

I have been a few more times to Menelik's flat. It appears I am the first man from the Diamond Coast to join their circle. I was deliberately sought out because there are few students from the Diamond Coast in Britain. We are a poor colony. "Why is that?" Menelik asked me yesterday. "You say you are from the Diamond

Coast and yet you are poor?" The truth is, few of us in the D.C. have anything to do with diamonds. In my mother's tribe we are fishermen. We have no diamonds on our land and we pay little heed to what goes on in the diamond towns of the north. We fish as our ancestors have always done. Menelik showed me photographs of what he said were miners in Mion. They go down the mines in rags, Menelik says. They die in the tunnels and their bodies are left to rot, or they are blown up if the tunnel is still in use. They are paid too little to live on and are forever in debt to the mining companies for food and other basics. And what am I to do with this information, I wondered, as I stared at the bony limbs of my compatriots.

Run, you foolish boy, I thought. The world would always have people like this Menelik, trying to press guilt on you, forcing pamphlets with gory pictures into your hands, holding you personally responsible for wars, famines, genocides. Why not be of use to those around you? Why rile my father with atrocities he could do nothing about?

I have made friends with one of Menelik's secretaries. She is a bookkeeper during the week but comes to Menelik's flat on Saturdays to lend her hand to the liberation. She is the first *obroni* woman I have spoken to in any depth. Her hair is the color of ripened tomatoes, which makes her almost as rare as I am on the streets of London. I asked why she cares so much about Africans. She says she is from a colonized people herself. By that, she means she is Welsh.

A redheaded, radical Welsh bookkeeper. It must be Aunt Caryl! So absorbed was I in Francis's London life that I had almost forgotten that he must meet my mother at some point.

It seemed he had met Aunt Caryl first. She was always a few steps ahead of her younger sister. Four years older, a head taller, and first to Francis Aggrey, too. My mother was more beautiful, but Aunt Caryl had the glamour, a certain recklessness.

There were some more entries about her. They'd had a romance of sorts. Thomas, used to dalliances with white women, encouraged the match. He also had a wife in Rhodesia, a woman Francis was hearing of for the first time. I wonder what my father thought of his friend's philandering. The diary didn't say.

Francis's attachment to my aunt seemed shallow. He was curious about white women but cautious. He had a fear of being turned into a black sex object. He "walked out" a few times with her but there didn't seem to be more. Still, my aunt might have been my mother, or some other person like me, Bain and Aggrey mingled. She was better equipped perhaps to have a mixed-race child, but my mother was softer, the more maternal.

How did the sisters get on after sharing a man? How did they live with it? They were like the Boleyn girls, except Francis Aggrey was not a king, just a poor student living in a single room.

I wanted to speak to someone. I wanted to go out, but I no longer had places to go. I had shed my friends in the past eighteen months, more Robert's friends than mine. My mother was six months dead and I had been six months in the grave as well, or so it felt that evening when I was ready to rush out trailing my winding sheets. I called Rose.

"Mum! Hello. I was just wondering whether I should call to say bye."

It was not the first time she had traveled without telling me. My daughter had a life removed from mine. I glimpsed it on her social media pages: photographs with people I didn't know, in places I'd never been to. Her pose was always the same, legs angled to highlight her slim thighs, smile wide like a commercial. It was what you hoped for your child after twenty-one: independence. And yet, once in a while, the severance still came as a shock.

"Where are you off to now?" I asked.

"Mumbai, for work. I'm part of a team helping a car manufacturer get back on its feet. I know. I'm sorry. I should have mentioned it but it was decided at the last minute and I've been so busy. I have to switch off."

"I've been reading about Bamana," I said.

"What's that you said? Panama? Yes, I'm getting off. Just saying bye to my mum. Sorry about that. I have to go. We'll talk about Panama when I get back. I love you. I miss you."

My daughter had the strange habit of never saying bye. She said she preferred to leave things on a comma, not a full stop.

I put my phone down and set the kettle to boil. Where was Francis Aggrey now? Was he alive? Did he have another family? He was a handsome man. I couldn't imagine him still single.

I put a tea bag in a mug and poured boiling water over it. Steam rose. The water turned black. I took out the tea bag but I didn't throw it away. Aunt Caryl always said a woman and a tea bag were the same. No matter how many times you boiled one, there was always something left.

3

I t is a Sunday the next day and I go to the park. The sun is out, a
rare winter sun that raises a glare. There are families with small
children on leashes, tugging at the cords that bind them to their
parents. Dogs roam free, ranging far from their owners.

If Francis Aggrey had stayed in London we would have been a
colored family, welcome only in Notting Hill or Brixton. I saw the
marches on television in the seventies, the placards, KEEP BRIT-
AIN WHITE, the faces of the race warriors, bared to the cameras,
unashamed.

"Switch it off," my mother always said.

"Let her see it," Aunt Caryl would retort.

Grandpa Owen always concluded, "The English are shites."

A woman sits on the far end of my bench with a child clinging
to her. Her hair, done up in a bun this morning, is escaping from
the knot, falling down her face like wisps of dry grass. She holds a
cigarette in her free hand, unlit, poised.

Aunt Caryl was a smoker. My mother was not. My grandfather

had a pipe he lit occasionally. He was from a Welsh mining family. He showed me a picture of his father once, up from the mine with a dozen other men, faces covered in soot.

"Looked like a colored fella when he came home."

I was the only black child on our street. The shopkeeper called me Sambo and gave me free sweets, sherbets and cherry suckers that turned my tongue bright red. Jenny Jenkins was my neighbor and my best friend. When we quarreled, she called me a stinking wog.

"Can you watch him for me, please?"

It is the woman on the bench. She is speaking to me, leaning across the gap between us.

"Pardon?"

"Just for a moment. I need a smoke. Please. I'm just going across there." She points to a tree a few steps away. She props the child against the bench before I can answer. He is bundled in a red jacket stiff with padding, his arms sticking out like a scarecrow. She smokes and paces, watching us, turning her back on us. The child whimpers but does not cry. The wind picks up. Tar and nicotine invade our lungs. She drops the cigarette, only half smoked, and stamps out its spark.

"Thanks. I don't usually," she says. "I'm trying to quit." She picks up the child and is gone.

I remember my first year with Rose. The feeling of being watched and judged. I wanted someone to guide me through the rituals, someone who had been there before, any mother except mine. We couldn't talk—not about anything serious.

I watched a documentary after I had married and had Rose, in the nineties, when the personal trauma of ordinary people was becoming regular programming. It was about single mothers who had given up their children for adoption. The cameras tracked down the white mothers and the dark grown-up children. The producers staged meetings between the two parties then filmed the results: tears, anger, accusations, faux reconciliations, prime television. The next time I saw my mother, I asked, "Did you ever think of giving me up?"

"What do you mean?"

"For adoption."

"Of course not," she said.

"Didn't you mind? Being a white woman alone with a black child?"

"You're just the same as me, Anna. I didn't think about it."

We're just the same. It was her lie, her special fantasy. Francis Aggrey would have known I was different, would have been proud of it.

A couple walk past, holding gloved hands, leather on leather. They eye my bench but don't stop. I remember when Robert and I would rather have walked miles than have a third intrude. He was so direct, so relentless, so sure it was me and no one else. All I had to do was build my house on his assurances. Plus he knew about solid homes. His parents were thirty years married when I met him and are still married now. They have outlasted us with ease.

The sun is waning when I stand to go. I don't open my father's diary when I get back home. It is Sunday. I rest from Francis Aggrey.

I open my curtains when I wake up the next morning. I shower. I wash my hair and put on clothes that hang loose on me. Rose has booked an appointment with a divorce lawyer. Her office is on a high street with black letters stenciled on the display window: CAMPBELL AND HENSHAW FAMILY LAW. You can see into the waiting room, to the lone potted plant by the water dispenser, to the empty foam chairs. I am reluctant to go inside.

Rose does not approve of a two-year separation that tapers off into divorce. In her words, Robert has put my life on hold. I need the closure that a divorce will bring so I can heal and move on. I don't know where she has picked up this language, the wording of celebrity gurus tripping glibly out of her mouth.

I push open the door and a bell rings.

"Good morning," the receptionist says. She is about my age but she does not dye her hair.

"Morning. I have an appointment with Ms. Henshaw for eleven."

"Your name, please?"

"Anna Graham."

"Please take a seat. Ms. Henshaw will see you shortly."

Everything I have read says children should be kept out of a divorce, and yet I am here because I want my daughter's approval. I do not want to appear weak or passive to Rose. I know what it is to find a mother wanting.

There is a range of bland magazines fanned across the coffee table, neutral so as not to upset or remind people why they are here. Healthy, smiling faces but nothing sultry or semi-nude, no reminders of clandestine sex.

"Ms. Graham?"

The receptionist is standing in front of me.

"Yes?"

"Ms. Henshaw is ready now, if you'll follow me."

We climb up a flight of stairs. There are three doors, one with a WC sign. The receptionist knocks.

"Come in."

The room is spacious with large windows. Ms. Henshaw rises from behind her desk. She is married, I see, when she puts out her hand to shake me.

"Anna," I say.

"You can call me Anna also. Although if you do become my client we might find things a little confusing."

She looks like an Anna. Her hair is light brown and her eyes are blue. Her coloring is the type that flushes after a glass of wine.

"Please, let's sit where it's more comfortable."

She ushers me to the sofa. I would prefer her to remain behind the table, unseen below the waist, a professional torso.

"Can I get you anything to drink?" she asks.

"I'm fine, thank you."

A notepad and pen lie still in her lap. She is wearing lavender perfume. It wafts off her like scent from a plug-in air freshener.

"I always start by asking: do you want a divorce?"

"Well I—I've come to see a divorce lawyer."

"I know, but do you *want* a divorce?"

"I have grounds for it. My husband slept with another woman."

"That isn't what I asked."

There is a pause. Her questions are direct but her manner is gentle. She sweeps her hair back from her forehead. It is cut to graze her shoulders and she has styled it without a parting. It is the only impractical thing about her. Her trousers are black, her shoes are flat, and in her ears are discreet silver studs.

I feel the need to convince this sleek Anna.

"We've been separated for a year. A divorce is the next obvious step," I say.

"Have you tried counseling?"

"We went for a few sessions."

"And?"

"We stopped."

That was all there was to it. I wasn't suited for the probing questions of a stranger.

"What is your husband's profession?" she asks.

"Investment banker. Boutique firm. Things changed a bit for us after the crash. A few bad investments."

"And yours?"

"Housewife," I say. "But my mother died and left me her flat in Islington. It's been on the market for three months. Ex-council, unrefurbished, so proving a bit difficult to sell, but still, it's in a coveted area."

"And where are you living at the moment?"

"In our home. He moved out."

"And would you like to go on living there after the divorce?"

"I don't know. Sometimes I think I'd like something much smaller and more central, if I can afford it, and other times I think I would prefer a cottage in the countryside."

It was the effect of daytime television and all those people who felt they could reinvent their lives by escaping to green fields and the scent of manure.

"Any children under the age of eighteen?" she asks.

"I just have the one daughter. She's twenty-five."

"Do you still love your husband?"

She is auditioning me with these impertinent questions, weighing whether or not I am a worthy client. "Does it matter?" I ask.

"It can make the divorce process a lot harder."

"I'm here because my daughter booked this meeting. She thinks finalizing a divorce will give me closure."

"And you? What do you think?"

"It's a bit simplistic. You can't end twenty-six years with a piece of paper."

"No, but that piece of paper can be the first step towards a new life. If you want a new life."

There is another pause. She hasn't written anything on her sheet except my name: *Anna Graham.*

"I like my clients to give a firm yes to the question I asked at the start before we proceed," she says.

I attempt my own bluntness. "How do you make money, then?" I ask.

"I always get what my clients want, but I like to make sure that they really want it first."

She twists her wedding band. It is slim and studded with diamonds.

"All right, Anna. Shall we say we have begun the conversation? And you'll get back to me once you have a firm yes. I'll open a file for you. If we don't hear back within another three months, I'll assume that you've made other arrangements. Do you have any travel plans or family circumstances that mean you might need a little more time?"

"I want to go to Bamana," I say. "It's a small country in West Africa."

"Sounds nice. Beaches?"

"I have family there, but I've never been."

Once I say it, I know this is what I want. I want to meet my father more than I want to finalize my divorce. From this office stretches paperwork and itemization of my belongings, and the breaking up of my marriage piece by piece. Or I could go to Bamana and see if Francis Aggrey is still alive.

"I'll walk you out."

On the bus home I sit on the upper deck and I am level with the trees. The meeting has stirred up memories of Robert.

We first met in a bar, the type in the City that was quiet in the afternoon and closed on weekends. I sat, hemmed in between my colleagues, fellow trainee architects, waiting until it was my turn to buy someone a drink. Robert was at the counter when I was getting a gin and tonic.

"What are you having?" he asked. He had a pleasant voice. It cut through the background noise.

"It's not mine," I said. I was too concerned with making a good impression on my colleagues. I didn't have time to be chatted up by a stranger with a light baritone.

I took the order back to my table and slotted into my space. I concentrated on the conversation and tried to keep my hands still. There were two other female trainees, privately educated and more assured than me, I thought, although perhaps I misinterpreted things. They also ended up quitting soon after they married. Later, when I made my way to the loo, Robert stopped me.

"I just wanted to say I think you're absolutely beautiful. I've been watching you all evening."

"Thank you," I said, and walked past. When I came out, he was still there.

"Would you like to go for dinner? There's an Italian restaurant a few minutes from here. The pasta's great. I'm Robert, by the way." He put out his hand. At the counter I'd only seen his profile. He was handsome straight on, or, more accurately, he was well-groomed: tall, clean-shaven, trim in his suit. I shook his hand. Our grips were matched.

"Anna. I'll get my bag."

My mother liked Robert. He was tall. He spoke like a BBC announcer. She was a little awed by these shallow trappings. "You've done well for yourself, Anna," she said when she saw my engagement ring. I pestered her for weeks after. What exactly did she mean? She turned on me in a rare show of spirit and said, "Stop trying to turn me into a women's activist."

The only thing Aunt Caryl asked was "What's he like in bed?"

How much would I have made of my life if we'd never met? I wasn't suited to architecture: the hours were too long, the opportunities to express myself too few. Only a precious few rose high enough to stamp their point of view on a building. The rest of us were sketch-drawing props to someone else's grand vision.

I look up and see I have gone past my stop. I press the bell and walk home, thinking now of my last words to the lawyer. Somewhere in the world, Francis Aggrey may be alive, may have only a few months to live, may be dead. To find out, I must go to Bamana, and to go to Bamana I need money.

The fastest route is to either sell my mother's flat or divorce Robert. The monthly allowance he gives me is not enough to fund a trip. I was in a foolish financial position for a woman my age. Rose has more money than me.

When I got home, my eyes rested on a jade Buddha cross-legged in the hallway, brought back from Thailand in my hand luggage. It must be worth something. Perhaps I would end up auctioning the contents of my house to fund a trip to Bamana.

4

The next day I continue with Francis Aggrey's diary. His voice is familiar to me now—his dry wit, his flashes of anger, the pride that keeps him aloof despite his longing to make friends. He moved through London with this rich inner life hidden from all who passed him and concluded he was just another wog.

He writes of his parting with Aunt Caryl. I am relieved that there is no overlap with my mother, who is yet to make an appearance.

As for Francis and my aunt, he concludes that there is no spark between them. I am not surprised. The men in Aunt Caryl's life were transient, migratory birds that shed a few feathers in their passing. She was the opposite of my mother. She loved change. I imagine that Francis had been something new that fast grew old.

Menelik has given me another pamphlet about the diamonds in D.C. There is a small white settler population in Mion, which owns all the mines, and the indigenous Ba people are forced into their labor, the pamphlet says. Little is heard of their plight. The

Ba were the last to come into contact with Europeans and only a handful are educated. They have few spokespersons and their chiefs are in the pay of the mine owners. I will go to Mion one day and see for myself.

There are a few half sentences, fragments of thoughts.

Pan-Africanism or socialism?

Negro advancement in the twentieth century cannot be judged on . . .

We face neither east nor west.

My exams are in two weeks. I am buried in the library most days, cramming. I have not been to Menelik's flat.

Perhaps Francis's exams will break Menelik's hold over him. I was always good at exams. I could learn things and unlearn them once the test was over. It's how I got into grammar school.

My first exam is tomorrow. I have prayed to Christ and sprinkled some gin on my carpet for Bimba because I am a fisherman's son.

The last paper is done and I am free for a month. I would like to travel to Wales, or perhaps even Scotland, but as always I am low on funds. There are no jobs going for black men of my education, only work as diggers and bellboys, cringing for tips from some white patron or another.

It was a fine day and I wandered into Hyde Park. Menelik was at Speakers' Corner, denouncing imperialism. A small crowd had gathered. He paces when he speaks, like an animal in a tight cage. He talks in threes: Debt, Disease, and Death to imperialism. The English shuffled their feet and laughed. They do not take him seriously. I went back to his flat afterwards. We discussed socialism in Ghana with the newest member of our circle, Adrian Bennett. Bennett is a young lecturer at the LSE. He is the first *obroni* man I have seen in Menelik's flat. He gave me another book. This time on ancient African kingdoms. It is the size of a dictionary. I don't know when I shall have time to read it.

My dislike for Menelik increases. He seems both dangerous and charismatic, a personality to attract a vulnerable and lonely young man like Francis.

In a week's time I will be homeless. As I write this, Blessing is on her way to London in a ship and she will arrive in seven days. She says Thomas is taking too long to be called to the bar and she is tired of playing the abandoned wife in Salisbury. She has been saving the money Thomas sends home from the articles he writes for the press here sometimes. "She was meant to buy dresses with that," he said to me with his head in his hands.

I am unprepared for renting in London. I have lost my carapace.

It is like reading a play. The arrival of one character spells doom for another.

I have spoken to Caryl of my situation. I do not like to ask assistance from a woman I have walked out with but I am desperate.

Where was my mother? It was like her to be missing from her own story, blocked out by Aunt Caryl.

Caryl has found a place for me. If I take it, my new landlord will be her father. He has done up her old bedroom and is looking for his first lodger. It seems an improper suggestion. "Don't be silly,

Francis," she said to me. We were hardly a serious item. How quickly these *obroni* women dispatch a man's ego.

Well, I am in Mr. Bain's house now. It is a narrow Victorian dwelling on a modest street. Lower middle class, but tidily so. It is two floors high. Kitchen and parlor on the ground floor, two bedrooms on the first and my small room in what is almost an attic. I have a sink but I must share the bathroom with Mr. Bain and his second daughter.

I recognized this house from my childhood. We lived there until I was eight, when Grandpa Owen died.

Mr. Bain goes to work at a factory at 6 a.m. and his younger daughter leaves not long after for a job at a clothes store. I carefully time my ablutions so we do not meet. Yet I have caught a few glimpses of Caryl's sister. She is petite and pale with long black hair and eyes the shade of the Atlantic at noon. She is more conventional-looking than Caryl. That is my own proud way of saying I find her beautiful.

At last, my mother appears, and I am glad Francis Aggrey found her beautiful. She *was* beautiful, although she carried her beauty with downward looks and a hesitant manner that somewhat effaced her features.

Yet Francis had noticed her and picked the shy sister. Perhaps my mother hid this diary to protect me. It was better to know nothing of my father than to discover him on the first page and lose him again by the end.

I set my alarm and wake up early. I am going to the British Museum. I went for the first time as a teenager to sketch the Elgin

Marbles. Ms. Rendell, my art teacher, took a small group of us on a Saturday. I remember the stone rippling like cloth, the lithe torsos of centaurs, the naked display of muscle.

The morning rush has passed and the street is deserted. My tube carriage is empty apart from an elderly couple in tweed. The man holds a large, folded umbrella the height of a small child. I have forgotten mine. I sit on a newly upholstered seat, holding a fresh copy of a free newspaper. It is mostly adverts interlaced with gossip for the commuters before they plunge into the grey haze of office work. The carriage sways as it moves through the tunnels, tons of earth above us, Londoners walking on our grave. I feel ill. I stare out the window, counting the stops to Russell Square.

There are arrows in the station pointing to the museum. Even in November, the tourists are here: the orderly pack of Japanese, the elastic sprawl of Americans. The museum's façade is Grecian, built in rational lines. Inside, the glass ceiling is curved and modern, crisscrossed with steel, held up by a thousand minute calculations.

The Africa collection is in the basement. The noise from outside melts into a hush of spotlights and glass. A cloth of gold is mounted on a wall, draped in glittering folds, ceremonial robes of a great chief. It is an illusion, I see, when I draw closer—not cloth but tiny strips of metal, joined close until they look like fabric. *El Anatsui,* the placard says. *Ghanaian. 2001.* Francis Aggrey did not see this.

I move towards a display of sculptures. There is a small wooden man who has come from Bamana, an idol in a boat with a tiny pipe in his mouth. He is to bring fishermen luck. Francis Aggrey's mother dealt in fish. She might have prayed to this Bimba.

I stand in front of a wall of masks. There are masks for death here, jumbled with masks for love and weddings and fertility. The placards do not explain much. *Birth mask. Twin mask.* How were they used? For sacrifice? For blood?

I bring out my notebook to sketch a pair of nineteenth-century ivory leopardesses. A ring of coral encircles each waist, the haunches caught in motion, padding to their prey. I am shading in the hind-most spots when an American couple walks in.

"Well, aren't these creepy?" the wife says. She is sheathed in a grey puffer coat. Her blond hair straggles around her face like tassels of corn.

"Wouldn't want to wake up to that, would you, honey?"

They are standing in front of the wall of masks.

"They are not meant to be stared at," I call out from my bench.

They turn. There are only three of us in the room. The wife steps towards me.

"Are you a guide?"

"My father is from West Africa."

"So what are they for?" It is the husband asking.

"I don't know."

I return to my leopardesses and they move on to another part of the exhibition. I have drawn the waist of one leopardess too thick. Even in pencil, I cannot replicate the litheness the artist has rendered in ivory. By the time I have penciled in the whiskers the couple is gone. There is something domestic in the cats I have drawn, suburban tabbies not jungle creatures.

It is lunchtime and I venture outside to the main road. The shops are selling Union Jack kitsch: mugs, clothing, stuffed bears. There is a bunting of international flags on the Italian restaurant I choose. A bell goes off. A waiter approaches.

"Table for one, madam?"

I am ushered to a table for two and Robert's place is cleared away, napkin, knife, and fork. The menu is placed before me. It is written in green flourishes, curling vines on white stone. I order pasta. I have brought Francis Aggrey's diary with me. I bring him out. Lunch with my father.

He writes of meeting Blessing for the first time. She is unimpressed by her husband's politicking. I like the sound of her. She seems the first practical person that Francis has met. Perhaps she will be the one to finally break Menelik's hold over him.

Menelik has gone on a speaking tour of the country, attempting to set revolutionary fires in damp hedges and lanes. My father is left alone in the attic room. On some evenings, he hears my mother play the flute. I remember the mournful airs in minor keys. She tried to teach me but I hated the way spit bubbled through the notes and had to be drained after each piece.

I spoke with Bronwen for some length today before she went off to her noon shift. Her name means "the white one," a fitting description. She is only eighteen and says she will not work in a shop forever. She plans to design and sell her own clothes on Bond Street. She has made the red dress, the one I admire.

My mother wanted to design clothes and sell them on Bond Street. I never knew. I did know the meaning of her name. My grandfather named her Bronwen and gave me the middle name Brangwen, which meant "pure and dark," my mother's opposite. There was a darkness that shone, he used to say, the gleam of an onyx, the luster of black marble.

Grandpa Owen was a kind landlord. He invited my father to a Sunday roast with Aunt Caryl and my mother. He included Francis briefly, perhaps dangerously, in their family.

I have dishonored myself. I chose to stay home this Friday, instead of joining Mr. Bain at the pub. Around 9 p.m., needing to relieve myself, I went down to the toilet. The door was unlocked and I found Bronwen sitting on the rim of the bathtub with her feet soaking in a bucket of water. She was wearing a dressing gown that stopped at her knees. She blushed.

"Sorry. I should have locked the door. I'll be out now."

And like an experienced seducer, I asked, "Might a massage help?"

Before she could reply, I had knelt and lifted her foot out of the bucket. It was small and slender, the length of my palm, the width of four fingers. I began. I have seen it done in Segu. First the arch is bent back and forth, then the heel squeezed, then the toes splayed, fingers pushing in and out of the gaps.

"Does it hurt?" I asked. She shook her head and so I took out the next foot. My hands slid to her leg. It was slim and strong, the muscles firm from walking miles of shop floor. I inched to her knee, wondering at my daring. There was a graze, a dark line not fully healed. I touched it with the tip of my tongue. The flesh was cool and salty, the taste of the sea. Black man cannibal. My hand crawled under her dressing gown. She was naked underneath. When I touched her part, she gasped.

For the first time, I looked in her face.

"Shall I stop?" I asked, suddenly unsure of myself.

"Yes," she said. There were tears in her eyes. I withdrew my hand. Black man rapist. The evidence of my ministrations was already apparent. My fingers had left marks on her pale skin.

"I beg your pardon," I said.

I heard a key turning in the front door and I fled. I have abused Mr. Bain's trust. I have taken advantage of Caryl's young sister. Me, a grown man of twenty-five. I will give my notice tomorrow and start looking for new accommodation.

She was only eighteen, I want to shout. Predatory is what you would call Francis today. I'd guessed already that he was "an older man," but still, I had hoped the story of their romance would be less sordid, less entangled in the grey area of consent. I wished I could read my mother's version of events.

"Madam, shall I take this?" the waiter asks with his hand on the edge of my bowl. The restaurant has emptied. The lunch crowd is gone. The evening patrons are anticipated. A corner of my pasta remains uneaten, cold and congealed. I am bent over the diary, my nose almost touching the page.

"Yes, please."

"Shall I bring the bill?"

"Coffee, please," I say.

I am still in the Bain household. I go out early and return late. Menelik has returned from his speaking tour. We went on a march against neo-imperialism today. I shouted myself hoarse against predatory capitalism, but afterwards I wondered to what end? Losing my voice will not displace Western business interests in Africa. Perhaps it is time I began thinking of what I, personally, can do when I return home after my studies.

Coming in tonight, I saw Bronwen's back in the kitchen but I hurried past her. The holiday will be over in ten days and then I will be too busy to dwell on that embarrassing episode.

How did she feel living in the same house with him? Had she tried to avoid him too?

Things have fallen apart. Menelik has been arrested and charged with treason. They say he bought arms illegally from a Russian dealer and plans to sell them to the ANC in South Africa. His flat was ransacked and sealed, his papers seized. They are looking for his contacts. "It is best to stay low," Thomas said. Blessing is angry that Thomas has put them in danger by associating with what she calls riff-raff. Menelik is from Guyana. His real name is George Hamilton.

Riff-raff fraud.

Thomas advised me to burn you. His words. "Burn that book you're always snitching into."

Another thing Thomas said to me before we parted. Never marry.

With my mother, Francis was predator. With Menelik, he was prey. He had naively fallen in with a dangerous crowd. Was this why he had left England? To escape arrest?

I have found a note slipped into my room. It says:

I didn't want you to stop.

This is what I have drafted in reply:

Dear Miss Bain, You must forgive my taking advantage of you. I am seven years your senior but alas lacking in both wisdom and common sense. It was an abuse of the hospitality your father has shown me. Please let us not speak of that evening again.

I still felt she was too young, too easily swept away by attention from this urbane, older man. He would have seemed that way to her, a teenage department-store attendant with no university education. At least the relationship appeared to be consensual.

We have kissed. I am playing with fire.

And my mother had gotten burned. A single mother before she was twenty.

The matter is done, through no working of mine. Friday evening. Mr. Bain was out. I climbed up to my room and discovered the door ajar. I turned on the light and found her inside, barefoot in her dressing gown, the belt of the robe untied. I am a man like—

Two thirds of the page has been blacked out. My mother had wielded the censor's pen and erased the details of their first night together. She was always mildly prudish. She said intercourse instead of sex.

She was a virgin. This I discovered after the deed was done. In Segu a man does not take a woman's maidenhead lightly. The family can force the culprit to marry her.

Francis's writing about the affair is feverish. He is distracted from his studies. He is infatuated with my mother. He is ashamed of the secrecy and yet the affair continues. They fantasize about what their child might look like. He wanted a boy. Despite his revolutionary politics, he was still a traditional man.

I have had a telegram from Segu. It is from my uncle. It says my mother is very sick and I must come home. I fear she is dead. The Akan people do not announce death directly.

Bronwen came tonight, but it is a day she must avoid me. We spoke instead of my mother. I am her only child by my father, a man many years older, who died and left her a widow when she was still young. I do not remember much of my father. He seemed always sick to me. My sharpest memory is of him hawking up blood and sputum into a calabash cupped in my mother's hands. She is both parents to me and I have never felt the lack. She bought her first fishing boat at twenty-five and now owns a small fleet. I cannot bring myself to talk of her in the past tense.

Francis is now an orphan, alone in the world. I am sorry for his loss, my loss also, a grandmother I never met.

I have paid for my passage and gone to bid Thomas farewell, who I found calculating the cost of a pram. Blessing is pregnant and they are happy despite the curtailment of his freedom. He is now almost absent from the circles of the British left. "I have moved to the outer radius," he said. Bronwen has a premonition that I will not return. She dreamed that I drowned at sea. I told her it is not so easy to sink ships these days. I will leave this diary in her keeping. I do not want her to read it, but I will like her to hold it until I return.

The remaining pages are blank. I flip through them twice. It is the end of my father. Francis Aggrey is gone and I don't know if we will ever meet again. This is a portion of the grief my mother must have felt.

I settle the bill, tip my waiter, and step into the cold. The streets are full and the evening lights are on. I join the throng of workers marching in step, trying to still my thoughts and loosen the constriction in my chest.

Why had he not come back? I imagine him in Segu, writing off his affair with the *obroni* and moving on with his life, while my mother waited in London, frantic and disgraced. Did he find out my mother was pregnant? Did Thomas or Blessing get news to him? Did he reject me before I was born?

What difference will it make if Francis Aggrey knew of me? With or without Francis Aggrey, my life has run to this moment where I am standing in front of the London School of Economics struggling to breathe with tears on my cheeks.

London sidesteps me, the stream of workers flowing around an obstacle. A woman crying in the street is nothing new. I call Robert. He does not pick up.

Rose is in Mumbai. I call my neighbor Katherine. She had left her number on my kitchen table, alongside a Tupperware box of pasta, with the words: *Call me if you need anything.*

"Hello, Katherine speaking. Hello?"

"It's Anna from Windsor Street."

"Anna. How lovely to hear from you."

"I still have your Tupperware. I've been meaning to bring it back."

"I didn't even notice. How are you?"

"I'm in front of the LSE building in Holborn. I think I'm having a panic attack."

"Right," she says. "Are you close to the station?"

"Yes."

"Do you think you can get on the tube or will it aggravate things?"

"I don't know."

"Can you walk to the station?"

"Yes, I think so."

"What did you get up to today?"

"I went to the British Museum."

"That's nice. Did you go to see anything in particular?"

"Some African artefacts. A couple of masks. Some beautiful leopardesses."

"Are you walking now?"

"Yes, I am," I say.

"What else did you do?"

"I ate alone in an Italian restaurant."

"What did you have?"

"Pasta."

"Nice?"

"A little dry. I'm at the station now," I say.

"How long do you think it will take you to get home?"

"Forty minutes."

"I'll see you on the other end, then."

"No, I couldn't possibly ask that of you."

"Get on the train. I'll see you soon."

There are no free seats. I stand with strangers packed close, holding on to a bar drenched in germs. A passenger rises to leave; another slides into his place. It is a game for the young and agile. I stand all the way to my stop. I feel numb. The whirlwind has passed. When I get outside Katherine is waiting with a flask.

"I thought you might like some tea. Did you manage all right?"

5

Katherine sits opposite me in my kitchen. Her hair is tied-back brown that is going grey. She is older than me but slimmer, with the rangy physique of a runner. Her clothes are casual: sweater and jeans, but expensive. Cashmere. I have nothing to offer except expired crackers and chocolate ice cream.

"I'll have the crackers, thank you. The date's always a suggestion." In the familiar space of my blue tiles and granite worktops, I wonder if I have made it all up.

"Do you want to talk about it?" she asks.

"I don't know if I have the words. I've never felt that way before. I don't feel that way now."

The urge to confide in someone presses. I would rather Rose or even Robert were here, but this kind stranger is all I have.

"I found a diary that belonged to my father among my mother's things," I say. "She died six months back, if you remember. Francis, my father, returned to West Africa before I was born. I don't think he knew about the pregnancy. He may not even be alive."

"Are you sure it's his diary? Your mother never mentioned it?"

"I'm sure, and for whatever reason—maybe a good one—she kept it from me."

I do not want her to think ill of my mother. Already I feel I have shared too much.

"Did you like what you read in his diary?" Katherine asks.

"Yes. I liked his writing voice very much."

"You'll want to find out more, then."

Of course. I may not be able to go to Bamana immediately, but some of the dramatis personae may be somewhere in London this very moment: Thomas Phiri, Blessing, perhaps even Menelik, if he ever got out of jail. Katherine's suggestion is sound.

"What do you do?" I ask her.

"Full-time home manager or housewife, according to the census. I worked in banking until my third child. I hung on for as long as I could."

"I was an architect. Gave it up not long after I married. A mistake," I say.

"Everything happens for a reason."

"You believe that?"

"Yes. During the crisis, my husband, Simon, lost his job in the City and he couldn't find work for two years."

"I'm sorry to hear that."

"No need," she says. "That's when we started going to church. Before then we were always playing keep-up, always one step behind someone. We sold our boat. We didn't need one. I'm scared of the open sea."

I don't know how to respond to this edited version of life. In a few years I might be sitting across from a stranger, telling of how my husband cheated, and of how my mother died, and it might be the best thing that happened to me.

"I should leave you to get some rest," she says. "Call me if you need anything."

After she is gone, I take out my phone. Robert has returned my call and left a message.

"Hi, Anna. Sorry I was out. Everything all right? I hope it's not the boiler. Sometimes the start button can get a bit fiddly. Do you remember when we first bought the house and the heating broke down in winter and we all slept in the same bed? Anyway, I can come and have a look if you want . . . Rose texted me she's in Mumbai. We always wanted to go to India, didn't we—?"

I cut the line and go upstairs. The second book from my mother's box is in better condition than Francis Aggrey's diary. The spine is smooth. The cardboard cover is dark green, almost black. I open it. My mother's hand has glued a press clipping to the first page, a short piece from *The Times*.

"MASTERMIND" IN MION KIDNAPS IS EX–UNIVERSITY OF LONDON STUDENT

Police in the Diamond Coast are seeking the whereabouts of Kofi Adjei, who is suspected of planning the kidnap of three English mine owners in Mion. Two years ago, Adjei (formerly known as Francis Aggrey) was a student at University College London, although he did not succeed in taking a degree. A former lecturer described Adjei as "quiet and reserved." The mine owners were released last Friday after a ransom of £30,000 was paid. [March 12, 1971]

The articles got longer, the headlines more alarming

KOFI ADJEI ESTABLISHES DIAMOND COAST LIBERATION GROUP FROM HIDING [June 4, 1971]

MION POLICE STATION ATTACK CLAIMED BY DIAMOND COAST LIBERATION GROUP [September 16, 1971]

MION MINE OWNER SHOT AND IN CRITICAL CONDITION [December 3, 1971]

My father was a terrorist and he had been radicalized in England by Menelik.

INSIDE THE BARBARISM OF THE DCLG [February 2, 1972]

KOFI ADJEI, DCLG LEADER, ARRESTED [August 17, 1972]

For the first time there was a photograph accompanying one of the articles. It was Francis Aggrey, unrecognizable from the dandy in London. They had stripped him to the waist, and he was seated on the ground with his legs stretched before him. He was thin and unshaven, his hair wild and uncombed.

They tried the "Terror of Mion," on January 13, 1973, two days after my third birthday. In April 1973 they sentenced him to twenty years in prison.

They had planned it all in Menelik's flat and here it was: the liberation of Africa, Francis Aggrey brought low, sitting in the dust. Did his old friends read of it? Did Thomas and Blessing Phiri sitting in some suburb in London see him in the news? The clippings continued.

In September 1975, Amnesty International protested my father's inhuman treatment in jail. The following year, peace talks began with the Diamond Coast Liberation Group. The turnaround was swift. My father was released in 1977 after serving five years of his sentence. Elections were scheduled. By November 1977 Kofi Adjei was the front-runner.

KOFI ADJEI SWEEPS TO VICTORY IN DIAMOND COAST
   On Tuesday morning more than three hundred thousand Diamond Coasters went peacefully to the polls, and yesterday night the results were announced. Kofi Adjei, once the Terror of Mion, has won the first general election in the Diamond Coast and shall become the first prime minister. In June he will be sworn in as leader of a new country: Bamana. [January 11, 1978]

It was Francis Aggrey, transformed from the fugitive of a few years ago. He was bare-chested and powerful, a cloth worn over his shoulder like a toga. In an outstretched hand, he was holding a fly whisk, the tip pointing triumphantly at the sky: an image of a great chief. My father was the first prime minister of Bamana.

6

This was what my mother had hidden from me, buried in this box and locked away. It was not a secret I could have kept in my childhood. I was too hard-pressed on every side to not draw out this trump when I was called a wog or a nigger, to not shout back, "My father's a prime minister."

And who would have believed me? Who had heard of Bamana anyway?

Kofi Adjei Prime Minister Bamana I typed into Google. I'd never searched for Francis Aggrey's name on the Internet before. By the time the technology was available, I no longer thought about him much. Kofi's Wikipedia entry was long.

> Kofi Adjei was the first president of Bamana, serving from 1984 to 2008.

The dates didn't match the newspaper articles, although the man in the picture could be him: clean-shaven, elderly, with a tuft of mustache on his upper lip. He was more weathered than the young Francis Aggrey but it was a good likeness.

Kofi Adjei was born in Segu in 1944 to Clara and Peter Aggrey. Adjei was christened Francis Kofi Adjei Aggrey but changed his name to Kofi Adjei when he began the liberation struggle.

It was him. Much of the biography was now familiar. I had a grandfather who died when Francis Aggrey was young. My grandmother was a businesswoman. There was a sentence for the missionary schooling at CMS Segu; a paragraph for his time at UCL. I knew of his friendship with Ras Menelik. There was no mention of Thomas Phiri.

In later life, Adjei reflected on the racial prejudice he received from landlords in London.

That was all there was in possible reference to the Bains.

Adjei was sworn in as the country's first prime minister in June 1978. After a constitutional change in 1984, he became the first president of Bamana. In 2008, after thirty years in office, Adjei stepped down.

Thirty years in office was too long. I did not know much about African politics, but to remain for three decades in power would surely make him some sort of dictator.

There was an African family: Elizabeth, his wife, a nurse who smuggled bandages and penicillin during the liberation struggle; Afua, Kweku, Kwabena, and Benita Adjei, my half siblings. It seemed presumptuous to claim them as such. To find out at forty-eight that my father was alive and a six-hour flight away. I felt giddy, like I had stood up too fast after sitting down for hours.

I am going to church with Katherine. She rang to ask me this morning if I wanted to come and I had no plausible excuse. I did not want to sit at home brooding over my discoveries about Francis Aggrey, and church seemed as good a diversion as any. When I was younger, I had faith, a flickering thing that came on in times of great need.

When my bell buzzed at 11:45, I was ready by the door in boots and gloves, a sweater and a coat. In the daylight I saw the wrinkles around her eyes and the brown spots on her hands. She was greyer in the sun, and gaunter. Her jeans could be a size smaller. The fabric sagged around her knees like loose skin.

"I'm so glad you're coming."

She walked like a runner, bouncing and trotting. Fog streamed from my mouth and I grew warm under my layers.

"So, how's the search going? Have you found anything new about your father?"

"Not really," I said.

I don't mean to make a secret of my discovery, but I am not yet ready to share, not even with this kind stranger.

"That's surprising. It's almost impossible to hide with the Internet these days. Have you tried Facebook?"

"Not yet."

"You should. Even my mum's on it and she's in her seventies."

It was a stone church with stained-glass windows and a tended cemetery bereft of flowers. Inside was modern and warm: padded chairs instead of the long, bony pews I remembered from childhood. The cross hanging behind the altar was made of lightbulbs: art installation rather than sacred object. The flagstones were covered in rugs.

"Modern."

"Yes, our vicar used to be an artist."

Katherine knew a lot of people.

"This is my neighbor Anna," she said, introducing me to each one. I was a prize. A possible new convert. Everyone was in jeans and trainers and hoodies, except a few elderly women holding fast in twinsets and pearls. I was surprised by their youth, their slim vigor. They hugged Katherine and smiled widely when they grasped my hand.

The vicar was black. Perhaps this was why Katherine had brought me. He was tall and spare, and welcomed us in an accent that I could not place. All that was priestly was the white collar that glinted in the open V of his fleece. Two boys and a girl got on stage, the girl with a guitar, the boys with their hands empty. They led us in song. The lyrics appeared on a screen, a few lines at a time, karaoke-style. There was a man working the projector at the back, clicking to the next slide a second before we needed it.

Jesus is alive, amen,
Jesus is alive.
Yesterday, today, forever,
Jesus is alive.

Around me eyes began to close. An old lady, the most proper in the bunch, was the first to raise her hands. I thought she was signaling someone. Then slowly it spread through the room. A man bent till his torso lay parallel to the floor. A woman twirled once. Her skirts rose and settled. Katherine neither raised her hands nor danced. She was not the only one standing still but I wondered if my presence was inhibiting. I closed my eyes too, but the music had taken them to a place I could not follow. I could sneer at it all, their suspension of rationality, their gullible thirst for the supernatural, but Katherine had been kind to me and her kindness came from this place.

There was a segment for prayer. They prayed for nations at war, for the Amazon rain forest, for children in the inner city, and then a tiny window to pray for ourselves. I, too, decided to suspend disbelief.

"Please let my mother's flat sell so I won't have to ask Robert for money to go to Bamana."

It was a selfish prayer. Its chances of success were therefore limited. When it was over the vicar returned to the stage. This was more familiar. There was no lectern nor was he using notes, but it was a sermon, this much I recognized. Love is patient. Love is kind. Love does not boast. The mic was clipped on, barely visible as he moved from one side of the stage to the other, pacing and stopping. His manner was engaging, funny even, when he told a story about the first time he changed a nappy. We moved from this bouncing sermon to the solemnity of Communion. The chalice was raised to the light. Violence was done to the host. It was snapped in two—the sound of breaking, the wafer brittle as bone. It was theater, as all religion was theater, but it was well done. When the velvet collection bag was passed around, I placed a five-pound note inside.

"You don't have to," Katherine whispered to me.

"I know."

Katherine was in charge of the refreshment table afterwards. There were tea, coffee, hot chocolate, biscuits, and store-bought muffins. Perhaps this was why she was so popular. I stood by the table with my coffee and biscuits, watching as she spooned sugar with one hand and wiped spills with another. I could imagine her trotting up and down a banking floor, efficient but distant. The children were back from their Sunday school. They ran in between the legs of the adults.

"Hello, there." It was the vicar, descended from the stage and walking now, amid his flock. He put out his hand to shake me.

"Carl Offor."

I motioned that my hands were full.

"Anna Graham."

"Pleasure to meet you."

"It's my first time." I felt the need to offer some confession. "I haven't been in a while."

"You are welcome."

"Thank you."

I expected him to turn away, but he remained by my side.

"I hope you enjoyed the service."

"It was lovely, really. Short and sweet. Things used to go on a bit when I was a child."

"There's been reform in the Church of England."

"I can see."

He snorted, and I glimpsed the gap in his teeth.

"Well, I hope you come again, Anna. This is your home."

"Thank you."

It was trite, but in a sense true. The Church doesn't pay tax.

He moved on. A woman who must be his wife came up to him. She touched his arm and said something into his ear. She had dreadlocks that fell down her back in thin ropes. The ends had been dipped in honey dye. Of course he was married. The pool dwindled with age.

Later, I helped Katherine clear the refreshment table and fold its stiff metal legs. We were among the last to leave.

"So, what did you think?"

"The vicar asked as well."

"He's new. Only been here about a year."

"It was a good sermon," I said. "He seems nice and his wife is pretty."

"Yes, very pretty. So, same time next week?"

"A lot of it was familiar."

"Except the biscuits, surely? We never had such good biscuits at mine."

"Except the biscuits," I say.

"So, you'll come next week, then?"

"Maybe."

"And you'll let me know if you find out more about your father. Imagine meeting him after all these years. It would be a wonderful experience."

"I hope so."

I unlocked my front door and stepped on a folded sheet of paper. It was a note pushed through my letterbox while I was in church. My name was on the flap. The handwriting was Robert's, large letters all the same size, perfectly formed as though with a stencil.

My breath was uneven from Katherine's brisk pace or from the latent excitement my husband could still arouse. I flicked his note open.

> Just wanted to make sure everything was all right. I returned your call and left a message. You've changed the locks or else I'd have waited for you to come home. Let me know you're okay.
>
> All my love, Robert

I found out about his affair by chance. He went on holiday with his mistress but told me he was traveling for work, to Brussels or some other bland decoy. They'd taken pictures together. Afterwards, she sent a photo while I was texting Rose from his phone.

At first, I'd admired the woman in the bikini, the muscle definition in her stomach, the large sunglasses perched on her head. And then I wondered why a bare-chested Robert was next to her, arm around her hip, lips pressed to her blond weave.

You think it can never happen to you. It is the hubris that makes daily life possible. The bomb explodes for someone else; the sky always crashes on their head, until the ticking parcel stops with you.

Self-pity threatened to sweep away the pleasant residue of the church service. All Robert's love. How trite. I tore the note into pieces.

7

A bronze Isaac Newton sat naked and bent over a compass in the British Library courtyard. The building was overwhelmingly brick. A child might have put it together with pieces of toy blocks. Inside were pale marble and white columns, airy and light, a surprise after the dense exterior. Registration was on the second floor.

"Good morning. How may I help?" asked a man with a row of black pens in his breast pocket. His shirt was white, his suit navy blue. A pair of glasses hung from his neck by a rainbow cord, a sharp burst of personality.

"I'm researching Kofi Adjei, the first president of Bamana."

"And are you a PhD research student or an academic?"

"Do I have to be? The website didn't mention that."

"No, but we'd like to know for our records."

"No."

"Do you know what books you'd like to view?"

I read out the titles: *Memoirs of a Freedom Fighter* and *Bamana: The First Hundred Days.*

"May I see your ID and proof of address?"

He lowered his eyes to my passport and then raised them to me. The Anna Brangwen Graham in the photograph was plumper and, to her knowledge, adequately married.

"If you'd just look into the camera."

My startled face was printed on a plastic card, along with a bar code and my full name.

"There you are, Ms. Graham. All set."

"Bain."

"Pardon?"

"Bain. I'm thinking of changing my surname back to my maiden name."

"Right. Well, if you do, let us know so we can update your details. Next, please."

The Asia and Africa Reading Room brought to mind neither Asia nor Africa. Rows of heads bent in quiet study, feet resting on hushed grey carpet, eyes flicking to muted cream walls. There were no windows. All the light in the room was artificial, giving no sense of passing time.

Memoirs of a Freedom Fighter by Kofi Adjei was a slight volume, thinner than I had expected. *Bamana: The First Hundred Days* by Adrian Bennett, the LSE lecturer in Menelik's circle, was three times its size. I sat down at desk number 129 and began with my father.

I was born in Segu, the son of a humble fish trader and the lowest grade of civil servant the British imperial machine could create. My father, Peter Aggrey, had his first contact with the British as a young man. He was pressed into the labor gang that built the railway from the diamond mines of Mion to the port city of Segu. The British called this kind of work "forced labor" but it was really slavery because it was a job one could not quit. Living conditions were very poor for forced laborers. They often died of malaria, snakebites, and a combination of overwork and malnutrition. One night, my father escaped, taking with him the damaged lungs that would plague him for the rest of his life.

He could not go back to his village of Yabo because the chief, a collaborator, would have him whipped and sent back. So he set off from his family and kinsmen for the city of Segu, a young man on his own. Nowadays, this is a journey many rural youth take with little trepidation, but for my father it would have been like setting off to the moon on foot. He arrived in Segu with little English and fell into the hands of some Irish missionaries.

They stole his name of Kwabena, drizzled river water over him, and baptized him Peter. They taught him enough reading, writing, and 'rithmetic to make a catechist out of him, but my father, although nominally a convert, did not much care for the celibacy of the Irish brothers. He became a manservant or "boy" to an English commissioner, one John Aggrey, whose surname my father adopted. The new name was a sign of his connection to a powerful white man and also a symbol of how far he had come from that village boy. In the Yabo of that time, they did not care much for surnames. A man was known by his deeds, not his ancestors.

When John Aggrey was posted to Ceylon, he helped my father secure a clerkship in the railway office, and there he remained for the rest of his life. He married a girl his parents sent him from Yabo, but she was sickly and bore him sickly children that died one after the other. European science, I am sure, can offer many explanations for those infant deaths but the Akan also have an explanation: *kwasamba* or spirit children, who are sent to the world to torment their parents by living and dying over and over again.

The wife eventually went the way of her children and my father was a widower for many years until he met my mother, Clara, a fisherman's daughter and, at sixteen, twenty years younger than him. She was unschooled and could not even write the English name her mother had borrowed from a popular cosmetic powder, but she was beautiful. He married her and they had one son, whom they called Francis Kofi Adjei Aggrey.

He did not add, "and thus a legend was born," but he meant it. Only a vain man could write an autobiography at forty, in the middle of an active life. Kofi had traveled very far from the thoughtful, introspective Francis.

I still thought of my father as Francis, although I could guess at why he changed his name. It was a historic reversal. Kwabena to Peter, Francis to Kofi. I wonder what my grandparents would have made of Francis's mixed-race daughter. He wrote of my grandfather's death.

I don't remember him ever being in good health. He was always a coughing presence in a back room and I had to play quietly so as not to disturb. He died of tuberculosis probably, even though this is only an educated guess. He was never admitted into a hospital, as the "colored" hospitals of the time were badly run and unhygienic.

He was a kind man. At his funeral there were many relatives whose school fees he had helped pay from his meager clerk's salary. As his only son, I led the procession to the grave in red and black robes, and my mother, walking behind me, had to pinch me in the back to stop me smiling so broadly.

He wrote of his time at school in a manner that seemed geared to highlight the latent greatness in young Francis.

I was a bright but restless student. My teachers would often send me home with top marks and torn clothing. On such days my mother would lament the death of my father. What I needed was a strong hand to give me a firm beating. Sometimes she would send me to her brother for a thrashing, but he, too, also felt pity for the poor fatherless child and often let me off with a stern talking-to.

I led my peers in both sports and academics. They used to call me "Boy Wonder."

I did not know what my mother was like at school. I never thought to ask. She was probably not a girl wonder.

Francis made his way through school in the Diamond Coast and worked as a railway clerk before he made the great leap to England for further studies in engineering, a move that he said won him great admiration.

I did not expect the cold nor the blandness of English food. I was also not popular with the ladies. Some of them expected an African man to be a sort of tour guide, a whistle-stop cultural exchange. Mr. Aggrey, how is the weather in your country? How is the food? I preferred a woman I did not always have to be explaining myself to. Why do you, Why do you . . .

He wrote briefly of the political scene in London. Menelik was given a lesser role in my father's life. He was portrayed as a curious figure that Francis had come across rather than the mentor he had seemed in the diary. My father wished it to appear that he had engineered his political awakening on his own.

There was no mention of Thomas Phiri or, for that matter, my mother or Aunt Caryl. Instead, a few chapters later, was a wholesome account of the romance with his wife, Elizabeth, begun when he returned home.

I noticed Sister Elizabeth right away. Even in the plain lines of her nursing uniform, you could see her small waist and shapely ankles. I was sad that I was only admitted for one week. Once I set eyes on her, I would have been happy to lie in that hospital bed for a year.

My father first tried to join more orthodox politics when he returned to the Diamond Coast in 1969. He secured a railway job in the north, the diamond region that Menelik had once challenged him for knowing so little about. The role was mundane and there was a ceiling to his progress, as he had not completed his degree. He joined the Diamond Coast Congress Party, but found its northern leaders snobbish and more interested in socializing with British officials than in seeking independence.

Next, he joined the National Union of Railway Workers and quickly rose to the position of secretary general. It was a more radical organization but still not radical enough for Francis. The British must go, and they must go immediately. And so in 1971 he founded the Diamond Coast Liberation Group.

I am often asked how freedom fighters passed the time while waiting for a window of opportunity to strike. A cell could spend weeks roving in the bush before a plan could be put into action. We thought of freedom and our families, but mostly what we thought of was food.

There is much in the bush that is edible if one would let go of finicky Western prejudices. The first time I was presented with a mopane worm, I considered downing arms and returning home.

Me, the only son of my mother, who was only ever fed the choicest cuts of meat, to eat a grub dug out from the ground. Yet I grew to appreciate these worms that we would snack on during the day. They could be eaten raw or slightly roasted. There were also some excellent hunters in our group, skilled at setting traps for bush rodents and other smaller creatures. Once in a glorious while, someone would trap an antelope and we would eat chunks of meat, whose fat and gristle would stoke our memories for weeks.

It was lunchtime and, one by one, the other readers drifted out, and I followed them. The café was an open space of mushroom-top tables with the muted buzz of people who could not forget they were in a library. I was too shy to join anyone. I bought a salad and circled until an empty table appeared. I set my tray down and speared a beetroot with my plastic fork. Opposite me was a wall of books trapped behind glass. I tried to read the gold lettering on the spines while I ate, but the print was too small. They were objects, carefully chosen for their style, like the lamp fittings.

"May I join you?"

"Yes, of course," I said.

The stranger was over fifty, going grey but with unlined skin. Not handsome, but large and at ease in his frame. A thick musk of cologne billowed out from him. My eyes roved to his left hand and caught a gold band. He put his tray down. He was eating a proper meal—rice and curry with peas on the side. I looked into the leaves of my salad. I was suddenly aware of the bovine crunch of vegetables in my mouth. I chewed faster, eager to leave.

"So, what are you researching?" His voice was deep and attractive.

"Me?" I asked.

He nodded.

"Francis Aggrey. Or Kofi Adjei, as he is better known. He was the first prime minister of Bamana."

"I know him," he said.

"Personally?"

"I mean I know of him. I was in secondary school when he became prime minister. In Nigeria we sent money for the liberation struggle in what was then the Diamond Coast."

I dated a few African men at university—the type that had a knee-jerk attraction to my skin tone, dark when placed next to my mother's, light when placed beside theirs. There was a Nigerian boyfriend whose mother did not like me. I didn't like her, either.

"I'm researching the Aba Women's Riot," he said. "Eastern Nigeria, early twentieth century. It's a leisure project. My great-grandmother was one of the so-called rioters."

The thirty minutes I had allotted for lunch were almost over. "I hate to be rude, but I must get back inside."

"Of course. It was nice to meet you—?"

"Anna," I said.

"Alex. Alex Obosi. All the best with Adjei. It's a shame how he turned out."

"How?"

"Badly. The crocodile, that's what they called him in Bamana when I was there. He was ruthless, cold-blooded, deadly."

"When did you go?"

"Oh, over twenty years ago now. Beautiful country. Beautiful women," he said. His eyes flickered to my breasts.

"Interesting." I stood up to leave.

"Take my card," he said. "Let's stay in touch. You're a lecturer, you said?"

"No. Leisure researcher also."

"Even better. We should have coffee one day we're both in."

Alex Obosi, Consultant, the square of cardboard said. To reduce this hulking man to a name, job description, and telephone number seemed a shame. I remembered the lawyer's words. There was life after divorce, although not with Alex Obosi. Too married. I put his card in the bin on the way out.

I turned to Adrian's book when I got back to my desk. I had gotten a feel for Francis Aggrey's memoirs. There was nothing of my mother, but there was also nothing of the man I knew from the diary. He had bared himself in those pages and now he hid his real self in these, crouching behind a legend of his own construction.

Adrian's book was also written in the first person. It was a travel memoir, a white man on a motorcycle, gunning his way through Africa. It would have been fresh in the seventies, but it had been done so often since then that it all seemed a cliché. There were chapters on food and women and dances and rituals, but the book was really about the Bamanaian Camelot that Francis Aggrey was trying to build in those first hundred days.

My father was a man of action according to Bennett. He was popular with the people, some of whom ascribed godlike powers to him. He was popular with foreign investors who flocked to Segu, filling the hotels, desperate to be part of the Bamanaian miracle my father was promising.

There were only five thousand registered automobiles in the country, but there would be more. Only four hundred qualified doctors, but there would be more. There would be more of everything, more for everyone. "Switzerland in West Africa," those were Bennett's words.

My father hated committees, and long meetings and civil servants. He was always leaving Segu to tour the rural areas, to show the people his face, a retinue of young men trailing after him. Few women, not even his wife followed him. Elizabeth Adjei stayed in the capital, cutting ribbons for the new government buildings that her husband was erecting.

The photo insert showed a series of black-and-white photographs of Bamana. In the rural areas were huts with thatched roofs, half-naked children, women fetching water from a stream, the Africa of charity appeals and Comic Relief. In the capital, Segu, were grandiose buildings, columns of concrete and glass, gleaming automobiles, nightclubs, jazz bands, stylish young women with trim waists and full skirts, glamorous as film stars.

There were pictures of my father, dressed in a suit, dressed in kente, dressed in overalls on a construction site, and always smiling; not pensive like the Francis Aggrey in my mother's photograph but smiling, smiling, smiling at the new world he was building.

Around me, the other readers were gathering their things, limbs unbending after hours sitting in the same position.

"The library will be closing in fifteen minutes," a voice said over the PA system.

I was seeing Rose tomorrow for the first time in two weeks. If I left now there was still time to go grocery shopping.

I closed Adrian Bennett's book. Why had he written it? He believed in the legend, it seemed, an early European convert, but the Messiah had morphed into the Crocodile. The religion had failed.

8

I smacked Rose in public once when she was a child. She was willful, always on the verge of those rages that toddlers pitch themselves into without warning. She screamed and beat her fists on the ground. Strangers threw glances. Finally, I pulled her to her feet and swiped her bottom. Most of the blow glanced off her nappy but the surprise was enough to quiet her.

"Does her mother know you hit her?" a woman said, marching up to me with her own matching blond child in tow.

"Yes, she does," I replied, too stunned to claim my daughter.

I am reminded of that incident now, as she sits opposite me in my kitchen. In most lights, Rose looks white, although it is obvious to me that she is my child. Her loose light-brown curls, when all of Robert's family is lank-haired, her full lips, even her blue eyes, are from my mother—Bain blue.

Lamb and potatoes lie roasting in an oven that has lain cold all these months. We wait at the kitchen table, studying each other.

"Mum, you look beautiful. You've lost weight."

"You look beautiful as well," I say, squeezing her hand.

She is bronzed from her trip to India and she, too, has lost weight. "Delhi belly," she says, when she sees me looking at her wrist, which my thumb and forefinger could encircle easily.

"And stress. God, there was so much work."

"Smells delicious," she says when I place a plate in front of her. She tells me about India, of a festival in the streets that she could only watch from her balcony because of a deadline. I am relieved when she asks for seconds. Maybe it is just stress.

"Enough about me, Mum," she says. "What did the lawyer say?"

"We had a good conversation. Where did you find her?"

"Imogen. She came here a few times when I was at Wickham. Her parents got divorced and she told me Anna got her mum half of everything. You gave up your career for Dad so he's going to owe you shedloads in spousal support. Also, how weird is it that you'll have the same name as your lawyer?"

"She's not my lawyer yet," I say, ready to move the conversation along. "By the way, I went to church the other Sunday."

"Really? Why?"

"A neighbor invited me. Do you remember Katherine? She came around once or twice when Nan was ill."

"How was it?"

"Different."

"Dad texted me," she says, circling back. "He wants me to visit his new place."

"What did you say?"

"Of course not."

I expected Rose's support. She was a woman before she was anyone's daughter. "How could he?" we echoed over and over to each other, like a choir singing in the round. And then I was tired of the chorus and Rose was not.

"I called him the other day," I say.

"Why? If you need to speak to anyone, call me."

"You were in India."

"You could have skyped. I've shown you how."

"You might have been in a meeting."

"Of course, in this big house by yourself, you're lonely so you call Dad. I could come visit more or you could move in with me for a while. I have the spare room just sitting empty."

Robert gave her half the down payment for her flat in Fulham.

"I'd be lonely there, too," I say. "You'd either be at work or with Arthur."

"We broke up."

Rose's boyfriends never last. She meets them in the countryside in the homes of the girls she went to school with. She shoots on the weekends, wearing gear that she bought secondhand. She skis. She can pass in these places and perhaps she does. A part of me envies her this. Her passage through the world is smoother because her skin is a few shades paler than mine.

"Aren't you going to ask why?" Rose says.

"Why, then?"

"It wasn't working. I've been feeling so restless lately. Remember you mentioned Panama. That's all I could think of on my trip. Just rent the flat and go traveling with Mum."

"Actually, it was Bamana."

"Really? Where's that?"

"West Africa. Where your grandfather is from," I say.

"Dad's father is white and English."

"Your other grandfather."

"Oh, the shite who left Nan when she was pregnant. Is he even still alive?"

I am not yet ready to tell Rose who Francis/Kofi really is. It has been a while since I've had any secrets, any air of mystery around my person.

"Yes, he's alive, and I believe living in Bamana," I say. "I'm going to try to find him. I've always wanted to see the country."

"Good luck, I guess. It might be fun to go back to your roots. Very on trend."

"I'm not trying to follow a trend, and they're your roots as well," I say. Her phrasing annoys me.

"Okay."

"Are you eating?" I ask.

"Pardon?"

"Are you getting enough to eat? With work and everything. It sounds like you've been busy."

"Yes. I am eating, Mum. Is that all you've been thinking about since I got here?"

"No, of course not."

Robert says we shouldn't confront Rose about food. It makes her feel cornered, flushed out into the open like the pheasants she shoots.

She left soon after. There was an important presentation to be prepared, or an important spreadsheet to be filled by an important deadline. I had lost track of the finer details.

Once she was gone, I checked my in-box. It was the fifth time that day. No new messages. I checked my sent folder again. The e-mail was there.

Dear Professor Bennett,

I hope you don't mind my contacting you out of the blue. My name is Anna Bain and I am researching the life of Kofi Adjei. I recently came across a diary that he may have written while he was a student in London. I would like your assistance in authenticating the diary. Thank you for your time.

Best wishes,
Anna

9

Evenings on my street are quiet. People stay indoors with their families. I stand by a window facing the road. The bins are wheeled out for collection in the morning: brown for food, blue for recyclables, black for everything else, a necessary infringement of our free will. My house is the only one without the plastic bin sentinels up front. A single woman makes little rubbish.

My bell rings after eight o'clock—too late for either Rose or Katherine. I go downstairs and look through the peephole. Robert is outside. He knows I'm home. Even with the curtains drawn you can see our bedroom lights from the street. I open the door.

"Robert," I say.

"Anna. I thought I'd stop by. I was in the area. I brought you some flowers."

He thrusts the bouquet at me and our fingers brush. The flowers are expensive. Not the limp supermarket variety, wilting from the shop. These have come from a florist. There are none in our neighborhood.

"Can I come in? Please?"

I step aside and we go to the kitchen.

"Would you like some tea?" I ask.

"Yes, please."

When he tries to open a cupboard, I stop him.

"It's fine. I'll do it," I say. I put on the kettle. "Sugar?"

"One teaspoon. Same as always."

People change, I almost reply, but I am done with my barbed one-liners. I know how much sugar he takes, and how much milk and how long the bag should sit in the hot water.

"You didn't call back and you didn't respond to my note. I was worried."

I saw the woman at his office Christmas party. It was my single sighting of her in person. She worked hard on her appearance. Pencil skirt, stilettos, toned calves from squats or some other repetitive exercise. I was the frumpy wife by then. Overweight. She was the only other black woman in the room. I'd asked about her. She was junior to Robert. Out of his sphere. They'd never met, he told me.

"You're looking well," he says.

"I'm wearing pajamas."

"Still the best thing I've seen this week."

"It's only Tuesday."

I turn my back to him. His compliments are a sort of tool to bend people to his will. Store attendants gave him discounts. Air stewardesses upgraded us. I always thought it was a harmless use of his charm. Now I wonder if he did more than charm some of those listless women.

"I remember this."

He is by the fridge pointing at a family photo of the three of us on holiday. We're facing the sun and smiling with squinting eyes. This photograph, for some reason, escaped the cull. Perhaps because most of Robert is out of focus.

"Do you remember? We ate so many gelatos that day. It was perfect, wasn't it?"

"Your tea's ready."

"Thanks," he says, but he does not leave the photograph. "The three musketeers."

I can feel myself being pulled into Robert's version of events.

"I had a meeting with a divorce lawyer."

"I see."

We sit at the kitchen table opposite each other. I should have made some tea for myself. I lace my fingers together and unlace them.

"Rose is right. We can't stay in limbo forever," I say.

"It was Rose's idea?"

"It's a good idea," I say, steering him back to the point.

"Is it? You know how I like my tea. I know how you like your boiled eggs, rock-solid yolk. I know you still don't sleep on my side of the bed because you hate sleeping next to the window. You can't just throw away twenty-six years, Anna. You're making a mistake."

"*You* made a mistake," I say.

I've produced it. The barbed one-liner. Silence except for the sound of Robert swallowing his tea.

"Yes, I made the mistake," he says, and cracks his knuckles, a habit I detest. "I'm sorry, Anna. I've been sorry for the last year. What do you want me to do?"

"I don't want you to do anything. I want you to have not done something. To have not slept with your colleague." My delivery is harsh and staccato. I can feel anger threatening my equilibrium. "I don't want to talk about it," I say.

"All right. I'm sorry I brought it up. How are you? The last time we saw each other was after the funeral."

"I'm fine," I say. "You're growing a beard."

"No. Just haven't shaved in a week. Nobody to impress."

He's still handsome, still has a job, still roughly the same weight as when we met. It will be easier for him to find another partner.

In counseling, Robert had said I was emotionally distant.

"Don't blame me for your infidelity," I replied at the time.

"It's true. You push everyone away. Me, Rose, your mother."

"Can I leave now?"

"There you go. Always running."

The session ended soon after.

The kitchen is warm. I get up to open the window and stay by the sink.

"Look, I don't want us to argue," he says.

"We're not arguing. I just said I went to see a divorce lawyer."

"I don't want lawyers."

"It's not your choice."

"You're right. I'm sorry. How are things? How've you been keeping busy?"

I want to tell him about Francis Aggrey. He is the only person I've wanted to tell since I discovered the diary. I am used to him making the plans for us. It began on our first date when he chose the restaurant. I'd never met anyone so sure about art, wine, or subjects he could know nothing about, like pig farming.

I've met more men like Robert since. The confidence is inherited, along with all their other ideas. Robert's father worked in the City, as did his father before him. What seemed like ambition was only deep passivity. I was the pioneer, not Robert. I had crossed every barrier to end up in that pub in the City, a tremulous trainee architect who none of her colleagues could place—not black, not white, not male, not posh.

But at twenty-two, it was Robert's assurance that was attractive. I let him choose and choose, until I became like one of those religious people with their mantra tattooed on their wrist: What would Robert do? This instinct to confide in him, where will it go when we are divorced?

"I found my father," I say, against my better instincts. "He's alive and he lives in Bamana. It's a small country in West Africa."

"I didn't know you were looking for him. That's great, Anna."

"Is it? You never asked about him," I say.

"I thought he and your mother lost touch after he left England."

"But you never asked me. We could have tried to find him."

"I didn't know it was something you wanted," he says.

"Or you didn't want a black father-in-law?"

"That's not fair, Anna. I love that our family is diverse."

His phrasing is odd. Diverse, like a family in a brochure, strangers assembled and told to smile.

"All right. We could go there to meet him," he says. "I could take the time off work. The next two months are pretty busy, but after that my schedule is light. I've always wanted to go to Africa."

"No," I say, puncturing his excitement before it overwhelms me. "I need to decide things for myself."

"Of course."

I feel churlish. It is Robert's way to rush to the center of things. He does not always mean harm.

"Thank you for the offer," I say.

"How's Rose? She still won't really speak to me. Do you see her?"

"Sometimes," I say.

"How's she looking?"

"Fine," I say. "A bit peaky after her trip to India. Food poisoning, I think, but fine."

"Right. Maybe I'll pop by her flat this weekend."

It was Robert who noticed Rose's eating. She was sixteen the first time she stopped. It was like a virus sweeping through her school, a plague of eating disorders: all those young, striving girls determined to starve. It was Robert who pointed out the slimness that slid into thinness, Robert who took her to the hospital, Robert who wanted to be married, wanted to be a father.

"I should go," Robert says. His tea is finished, and our conversation has dried up. I should offer protest, but I am ready for him to leave. He has unbalanced the mood of my house.

"Thank you for the flowers."

He has been drinking. I smell it when he hugs me. Not in the past hour, and I hope not alone, but it is no longer my concern. I am becoming someone apart from Robert, a process from which I now believe I will emerge mostly upright.

When he is gone, I check my in-box and see a new message.

Dear Ms. Bain,

Thank you for getting in touch. That would certainly be a historical find. Kofi, or Francis, as he was known then, was privy to the inner circle of prominent black intellectuals and nationalists living in London at the time. I myself knew him while he was a student.

I would have to read the contents of the diary to judge if it were an original. Even then, it might be a carefully doctored fake. These hoaxes have been known to exist.

Perhaps we could arrange a meeting, if you were willing to visit Edinburgh? Where are you based?

Regards,
Adrian

10

My train was scheduled to depart at 7:00 a.m. I left home at 5:30, when the street was still dark. There were sensors outside most houses and lights flashed on as I walked past, set off by my movement. On the tube workmen slumped in a row, orange high-vis jackets powdered with construction dust. Two were awake and speaking softly in Polish.

In King's Cross Station travelers stood with their heads tilted up to the electronic boards. My platform was not displayed. I bought a coffee and a pastry. Still no platform. I hovered in the aisles of WHSmith, stepping aside for more decisive customers. Finally, I chose a magazine with a maturing cover girl, more vigorous than youthful. Platform 7.

The carriage was warm, my window seat narrow. At 7:00 the train jerked forward. We sped past empty glass buildings, open-plan floors, vacant desks. There were apartment blocks painted in primary colors, designed by architects who obviously enjoyed playing with Lego. I saw bicycles on balconies, a naked face at a bathroom window, stacks of council housing, shopkeepers rolling up metal grilles, a boy in a hoodie pedaling sharply around a corner. Moments later, we burst out of London and into brown fields where trees and pylons dominated the skyline.

I searched flights to Bamana on my phone; prices began at seven hundred pounds with an eight-hour layover in Istanbul. Decent hotels—hotels with clean bathrooms and fresh linen, hotels with three-star reviews and above—started at a hundred pounds a night. I might be able to afford it all with a credit card. Three weeks was how long I imagined I would need to find Francis/Kofi, to meet him, to establish some sort of relationship.

I looked down at the magazine. It was wrapped in a plastic film that would choke a dolphin in six months. For every page of content, there were at least two of adverts. Mixed-race models abounded, our khaki skin *en vogue* now. I was once as pretty as these girls, prettier perhaps, but without knowing it. I was born before my time.

The cover woman was a pop star from the eighties, now retired to the countryside. They had photographed her in her garden with loose clothing and minimal makeup. Beside this was a smaller picture of her on stage, twenty years younger and wearing a leotard. Even with no one watching, she was still reinventing herself.

I leaned my head against the glass. The windowpane would flatten one side of my hair. I would need to fluff it up with my fingers before we reached Edinburgh.

I had stopped straightening my hair when Rose went to secondary school. Robert was shocked by my new curls, not quite an afro in the round mushroom style, but still too thick for him to run his hands through when we had sex. He grew to love it, he said, even though it meant people stopped asking if his wife was Mediterranean.

I woke to rain falling soundlessly. Droplets raced across the window. The view of scraped fields was blurred. I had a one o'clock appointment with Adrian Bennett, professor of postcolonial history at the University of Edinburgh. He had written other books. He had married and had two children. He had taught at Harvard and spent a year at Makarere in Uganda. There was a photograph of him on the university website, squinting and silver-haired, and an e-mail address.

After his first response, I suggested a meeting time. He replied by asking about my university affiliation. Professor Bennett, it seemed, had become cautious in his old age: not the Adrian of his memoir, held at gunpoint by a Bamanaian police officer on suspicion of being a spy. I told him I was an "independent researcher of Welsh and Bamanaian origin." I hinted at a possible family connection to Kofi. The date and time were fixed.

In the week leading up to our meeting, I returned to the British Library. I went to church with Katherine but left before the sermon. I watched a YouTube video of Kofi Adjei speaking at some sort of rally in 1988, a decade into his rule. He was flamboyantly dressed: gold buttons, silk pocket square, and a leopard-skin hat angled forward. The crowd cheered after almost every sentence, stopping only when he raised his hands to quiet them.

I read Amnesty International reports and looked at its human rights rankings. Bamana's position was nearer North Korea's than Sweden's. Freedom of speech was a flexible concept. Outspoken journalists were regularly detained. I reread Kofi's Wikipedia page and lingered at the section titled "Controversies."

In May 1988 five student activists, known as the Kinnakro Five, were shot dead on the campus of the Kinnakro University of Science and Technology after agitating for President Adjei to resign. It has been alleged that Adjei is linked to their deaths, although he has never been charged and no evidence has been brought forward.

I clicked on *Kinnakro Five*. Their brief entry began with a disclaimer: *Additional citations required for verification.* Someone had pasted their head shots into one photograph: five close-ups that looked like mug shots. They seemed young to have been in university—only one had a beard, the rest as hairless as my palms. They were shot at close range in the dorm room of Patrick Dumelo, their leader. Three of them had bullet wounds to the head, faces mutilated, closed-casket funerals. The authorities said it was an armed robbery. Nothing was stolen, not even the brand-new Walkman that Patrick's uncle had sent him from Hamburg.

The man in the diary was my father and the man on Wikipedia was also my father. If he had done what the internet alleged, then he was to be feared, not sought out. I was repelled by Kofi and drawn to Francis.

Eighteen months ago, I would not have traveled so far to meet a man who had known Francis Aggrey. Eighteen months ago, I was Robert's wife, and that came with its own preoccupations, an entire set of people and holidays and activities that I now see had everything to do with Robert and nothing to do with me. But there was an Anna Bain before there was an Anna Graham, perhaps the real Anna, the interrupted Anna who had always been curious about her father, maybe even desperate for him. And who was this Anna, hurtling towards Edinburgh? Anna unrooted and untethered, free and lost as a balloon in the sky.

The train broke into some sunshine. We were by the coast. A lone figure walked on a beach. A dog ran ahead. Beside me the snacks trolley rolled past in the aisle.

"Welcome to Edinburgh Waverley. Please remember to take all your belongings with you as you leave the train. We wish you a pleasant onward journey."

The station is named for a novel by Sir Walter Scott, a historical romance. The streets are paved with cobblestones: beautiful to look at, impractical for modern transport. I bounce in the back of my taxi. I cannot understand my driver's accent. I let him keep the change.

I stand at the cafeteria entrance watching the student life drift in and out. The fare is better than I remember from my own time at university—a salad bar, five dessert options, gluten-free, Halal, vegan, and the price of all this choice written in bold. Everyone knows what to do. They pick up trays, read menus, queue and pay, only briefly looking up from their phones. I walk around until I see Adrian seated in a window booth. I recognize the silver hair. I draw closer.

"Anna?" he asks.

I can still walk past.

"I beg your pardon. I'm expecting an Anna Bain."

"I'm Anna. Are you Professor Bennett?"

"Adrian is fine."

He stands to shake my hand. He is tall and his belly is flat under the checked shirt tucked into his dark jeans. He rises with ease and his grip is strong.

"I hope you had a pleasant trip from London. Will you be staying long?"

"I leave this evening," I say.

"In your e-mail you mentioned some family business?"

"This is it."

"Of course. You have a family connection to Francis," he says. "Can I offer you anything? A cup of tea or a coffee?"

"No, thank you."

A herd of students walk past, braying at a joke. I bring out the diary and place it on the table. His eyes shift to the book. He leans forward but does not touch it.

"So you found this in your mother's possession? What was your mother's relation to Francis, if you don't mind my asking?"

"He was a lodger. My grandfather was his landlord," I say.

"Does Francis mention me in the diary? Is that why you contacted me?"

"Partly. And I read your book on Bamana."

"May I?"

I nod, and he picks up Francis Aggrey's book. He opens it gently, like it might crumble. I look around. In an opposite booth, a boy and girl eat hunched forward, watching a single screen.

"This is remarkable." He is scanning those arresting opening lines. "How did you say your mother came by it?"

"They were friends."

"May I take photographs? I'll need more than a glance to make a judgment. I would not reproduce it, or even allude to it, without your express permission."

I will have to trust Adrian because he knew my father both as a student and as prime minister. He can tell me more than I can tell him.

"Yes. That should be fine," I say.

We take the lift to his office. It is a large box on the fourth floor. There are books on the shelves, on the carpet, on his table, even on the windowsill, blocking out the sunlight.

"Excuse the mess. Please have a seat. Now, where did I put my camera?"

I sit, and he moves around me, opening and shutting drawers, crouching to look under the table. His haunches are firm against his jeans but when he tries to rise from all fours, he falters and his knees stay on the ground. I look away until he stands.

"I'm so sorry. It must be at home. Will you wait while I go and look? Or perhaps you could come with me and have some tea. It's only a ten-minute walk and it would be more comfortable there than here." His manner is scrupulously polite. A gentleman, my mother would have called him. "A toff" would have been Aunt Caryl's description.

I am surprised that he is so trusting. The diary might be fake, a trap to lure him to some disaster. But he is male. He ignored all those warnings about strangers.

"Sure," I say.

Outside, it is cold but the sun has come out.

"Edinburgh is an ancient city. There have been people living here for thousands of years."

He speaks like a tour guide projecting to the back of the group.

"This street is called Cowgate, because in the old days farmers used to bring their cattle to the city via this road."

He has assumed that I am interested, and I am, in his obvious enthusiasm. I look at the street properly and see it is not meant for human proportions but for cattle, marching ten-deep, raising dust as they pass on their way to slaughter.

He lives in a town house behind a red door, the brightest one on the street. We step into a faint must of old paper. In the hallway there are shoes piled in a small pyramid.

"Shall I take off my shoes?" I ask.

"No, never mind that. Please. This way."

The living room is south-facing and flooded with light. There are books here also, enough to run a small lending library. Logs are cut and stacked by the fireplace. An entire wall is lined with wooden masks. They should be seen by a steady procession of guests. Perhaps this is why he has brought me to his home, to admire his collection. He follows my gaze.

"Mostly from West Africa," he says. "Some even from Bamana."

"Which ones?"

"This one here." He steps forward and touches it. I remember Francis Aggrey's words about sacred objects handled by the uninitiated. "Harvest mask, circa 1940," he continues, his fingers pale against the dark grain of the wood. "Look at the mouth, the deep 'o' for hunger that is about to be filled . . . and this is a wedding mask; same group that made it. Notice the eyes, the slits not so narrow, almost semicircles, happy eyes. They are very complex. Small movements in the wood can change the expression. This is what Picasso grasped immediately. Please, do sit down."

I choose a leather armchair that seems perfect for reading.

"What was Francis like?" I ask, before Adrian can launch into another lecture.

"I knew him better as a student. He was reserved back then. Obviously intelligent, but almost shy. When I met him again in Bamana, after he had become prime minister, I was surprised by how outgoing he had become. It made me wonder: which was the real person?" he says. "Let's get you something to drink."

He is a practiced host. He offers tea, biscuits, and serves them on a tray. The teacup matches its saucer; the biscuits are arranged on a gold-rimmed plate and there are silver tongs for the small, white sugar cubes. These are feminine details, but there has been no mention of a wife. He forgets his search for a camera and sits by a desk in the corner. There is a notepad and a pen already set out, and as he turns the pages of the diary, he jots things down.

There is no television in the room. When my tea grows cold, I walk to a shelf that touches the ceiling and read the titles. African books by African authors: *One Man, One Machete, The Joys of Motherhood, God's Bits of Wood.* I stop at Bessie Head because the name sounds English. *When Rain Clouds Gather.* I read the introduction. She was like me. White mother, black father, but in a worse place to be colored. The opening pages are strong so I take the book back to the sofa.

"I don't believe this," Adrian says.

"What?"

"I think I was present at this lecture. Listen."

"Yesterday, I heard Margery Perham lecturing on decolonization in West Africa at the Royal African Society. There were a few other Africans in attendance and afterwards they clustered around her. She is a collector of African students, Thomas tells me. Nkrumah, Kenyatta, Danquah, Appiah: she knew them all when they were ambitious young men in London and, even now, can call the state house in Accra and ask for a favor. I don't care for the Margery Perhams of this world. My maternal great-grandfather was a sheikh who walked from Togo to Mecca and, on the way home, stopped in Segu and never left. It is he who should be lecturing here, explaining West Africa to these *obroni*. I said this to Thomas and he replied, 'Finally. You are waking up.'"

"I was there," he says. "I was in the room. Incredible. And who knew Thomas Phiri was so important to Francis."

"What do you mean?" I ask.

"Well, Thomas was rather a second-rate fellow. Pompous, a bit of a hanger-on really, but I suppose Francis, as a newcomer to our circle, wouldn't have been able to tell."

"Your circle?" I ask.

"Yes, the British left. Socialists. A few Communists."

"Who else was important to him? Did he have any lovers?"

"Lovers?" He is puzzled by the question. As if I have asked for Francis's shoe size. "I wouldn't know about that. I doubt it. He was a very buttoned-up fellow in England. Although, you never know. He *was* handsome."

Adrian returns to the diary and I return to my novel, set in an arid place, dotted with dry bushes and thirsty cattle. Time passes until I look up and see the sun is setting. Adrian has not moved. There is no camera. Perhaps there never was. All he wanted was to work at his desk.

"I'm sorry to stop you but I must catch the train back to London. Will you take photographs of what's left?" I say.

"To be honest, I hate those things. You take the pictures and then work out how to get them onto your laptop, before finally opening the thing up and discovering you can't read the fine print no matter how much you zoom in. You could spend the night, if you wish. I'll have finished by tomorrow morning. I'm just about halfway."

"I don't have any nightclothes," I say.

"There are spares."

I do not want to disappoint him after his excess hospitality, but I have not planned to spend the night in Edinburgh. My deliberation is obvious.

"I'm sorry, I got carried away. Reading Francis's diary has reminded me of my first time in Bamana. Nineteen seventy-eight. I traveled alone for the most part when I was outside the capital. Sleeping in strangers' homes was the norm. I would ride till evening and stop when I saw huts. Every night I thought my luck would run out and the villagers would leave me out in the bush . . . but it never happened. There was always room for one more."

"I'll go tomorrow morning," I say.

"No, please. You mustn't do anything you don't feel comfortable with."

"I'm very comfortable sitting here with Bessie Head."

Adrian makes dinner. The kitchen is warm, heated by underfloor pipes. His pots and pans hang on the wall, copper finish, gleaming like parts of a gamelan. He works from scratch, filleting the fish, peeling the potatoes, dicing the vegetables. It is like watching a cookery show. He moves around with practiced ease, using sharp tools and chatting at the same time. Steam rises and fogs the windows. Oil sizzles when the plaice is laid in the pan, skin down. I offer to help. He shrugs me away.

"Tell me about your life in London," he says.

"I live alone. I have a daughter who is very busy with her work. My husband and I are separated. Is there a Mrs. Bennett?"

"She died last year."

"I'm sorry to hear that," I say. "Have you been back to Bamana since you wrote the book?"

"Just once. In 1984 Francis invited me to be part of a government-sponsored arts festival. Music, dancing, culture, literature—everything and nothing. I hardly saw him. There were too many rings of bureaucracy by then. Bear in mind, on my first visit, I stayed with him and his wife whenever I was in the capital."

We eat at the kitchen table. The fish flakes. The sauce has depth of flavor. We talk of the mundane, the weather in Edinburgh, the annual festival that brings a crush of people.

"I regret my book," he says, when we are almost done. "It came from an honest place. You should have read the press around Bamana. Some of the African countries that gained independence in the sixties were already faltering, and so the media was just waiting for Bamana to fall apart. How long before the military topples Adjei? How long before he loots the place? And so I decided to travel there and prove them wrong. I really believed I was documenting the first hundred days of something truly remarkable. An African miracle. I wrote that book in 1978. By 1984, when I returned, I had already changed my mind." It is a long speech given with almost no pause, but he is a professor, used to delivering lectures.

"What made you change your mind?" I ask.

"Well, the murder of the Kinnakro Five was still four years away. You know of them?"

"Yes, the student activists."

"Rather grim affair. That was still in the future, but the seeds were already sown. Six years after independence, no one could challenge the great leader Kofi. Power corrupts, but nowhere more than a small African state." I notice that he has called my father Kofi for the first time. I take my empty plate to the sink.

"Don't worry, I'll clear up," he says.

"No, let me. The meal was delicious." I pick up a sponge. "Are you still in touch?"

He does not answer. I turn and catch him watching me.

"What exactly is your family connection to Francis?"

"You'll have to read to the end of the diary," I say.

"I see. Well, to answer your question, we lost contact years ago. How shall I put it? We stopped moving in the same circles."

The bed in the guest room is laid with fresh sheets. There is an empty blue vase on the window. The night garments Adrian has laid out for me are nunnish, with long sleeves and buttons that stop at the base of my throat. I change and climb into the single bed. He has left a hot-water bottle under the sheets and I feel like a slice of bread slotted into a toaster. I close my eyes, expecting to be restless in this strange room, but I edge seamlessly into sleep.

11

I come down the next morning and find Adrian sitting at the kitchen table with his arms folded.

"You're Francis's love child," he says. His tone is flat, almost hostile.

"Yes, I suppose I am."

"So, what do you intend?"

"What do you mean?" I ask.

"Now that you've found out you're his daughter, what next? You've come all the way to Edinburgh. You must have a plan."

I do not know him well enough to be sure of his exact mood. I sit opposite him.

"Is the diary real?" I say.

"From what I can tell, yes, it seems original, although unfortunately he hasn't dated any of the entries. But what he writes about Menelik's circle, only someone who was there would know."

"Let's say I did want to meet him . . ."

"Almost certainly you'd have to go to Bamana. He doesn't travel

out of the country often these days. *If*, and that's a big if, if you secured a meeting with him, you'd have to reveal your claim—"

"My claim?"

"It is a claim until there's been a DNA test. You must realize
that."

"Is there a resemblance?" I ask.

"In the guile with which you approached me? Yes, certainly."

It is humor, but of the biting, caustic kind, not the good nature
of last evening.

"I haven't seen him in many years," he continues, "but there
might also be a slight physical resemblance. Do you intend to ask
him for money?" There lies the nub of his suspicions.

"Of course not," I say. I am almost indignant, but I remind myself I am a stranger to him, despite my expensive handbag.

"I'm sorry. I don't mean to pry. It's just how, perhaps, the
case might be viewed from outside." He stands and walks to the
fridge. "Right. Well, that settles things, then. Shall we have some
breakfast?"

The ease from last night's meal is gone. I am now allegedly a
president's daughter. We eat quickly and leave his house. On our
walk to the station we pass a large building, desperately trendy with
bare stone walls and steel trimmings. "Scottish Parliament" is all
the description Adrian gives. I have abused his trust. He has opened
his home to me, while I have concealed who I am till the last possible
moment. At the station, we stand by the barriers.

"Do keep in touch and tell me how you get on. You have my
e-mail address." He is dismissing me, like he has dismissed many
students, ushering them out of his office before throwing their es-
says in the bin.

"I was hoping for a lead," I say.

"As I said, Francis and I have lost touch."

"But someone else in Menelik's circle. Surely there must be at least one person you still talk to."

"Old age. It separates."

A whistle sounds, cutting through the noise of the station. Around us travelers surge forward. The trains wait for no one. I have met a man who knew my father, who shook his hand, who sees in my face a slight resemblance. I am further along than when I arrived in Edinburgh yesterday.

"You do look like him," he says. "Why didn't you just tell me who you were?"

"Would you have believed me without reading it in the diary first? A strange woman, out of the blue, telling you she's Francis Aggrey's daughter, a man you thought was too cold to take a lover. Wouldn't you have thought me mad?"

He smiles, his first honest smile of the day.

"Your father's gift of persuasion. I have an old address for Thomas Phiri. We haven't been in contact for over a decade. It's a long shot, but you can start there. I've written down my number as well. You can call if you need anything else."

He brings out a folded piece of paper from his left pocket. He has carried it all the way here, swinging between trust and suspicion.

"Your father was a remarkable man when I knew him. If you do get to meet him, don't be too disappointed that he is no longer the man who wrote that diary."

"Thank you."

I step through the barriers and head to Platform 7.

12

Outside Colindale Station was a sign pointing to the RAF Museum. There were no signs for Grahame Park Estate, but it was a more obvious landmark than a warehouse full of model planes. A five-minute walk from the station, the estate sprawled in every direction like a brick cancer. On Thomas's side of the estate, the buildings looked inward on a quadrangle of shops and restaurants. In one store, the attendant was trapped in a clear Perspex box with air holes for breathing and a letterbox opening for cash. A sign by the door said: NO CREDIT, NO GROUPS, NO KNIVES.

It was too sunny to feel threatened. Two Somali women walked past. Their feet were covered by their abayas. They glided, tall black swans that had learned to swim in concrete. I found Thomas Phiri's block. I leaned against the wall in the stairwell and waited for the boy at the top to descend. He should have been at school. He was trainered, tracksuited, hoodied, the uniform of the urban army I read about in the news.

"No, miss. After you."

"Thank you."

I climbed the stairs ashamed but still cautious, pressing against the wall when I drew abreast of him. I found the green door of apartment 404. If Thomas had moved, perhaps the new resident might pass on a forwarding address, or a phone number. I knocked.

"Yes?"

A black woman's face appeared with a scarf tied around her head, one stockinged and slippered foot also visible. The door covered the rest of her body.

"Good morning. I'm looking for Mr. Thomas Phiri," I said.

"And you are?"

"Anna Bain."

"Thomas doesn't live here anymore," she said, withdrawing her face.

"Are you Blessing?" I asked.

"How do you know my name?"

"I'm so sorry to turn up at your doorstep, but I only had your address. I wasn't given a phone number."

Her eyes narrowed. "Who gave you my address?"

"An old friend of yours—Adrian."

"I don't know any Adrian."

"He was a lecturer at the LSE when your husband was a student in London. Adrian Bennett."

"The white spy who used to sniff around us?"

Adrian, a spy? What could she mean by that?

"Why'd he send you to me?" She asked with some impatience. She would shut the door if I didn't say something.

"I think I might be Francis Aggrey's child," I blurted.

"That became Kofi Adjei?"

"Yes."

"Are you a journalist? Is this a hoax?"

"No."

There was nothing more I could say to convince her. She would either believe me or turn me away. I met her direct gaze, trying to appear as guileless as possible.

"Come in, then," she said.

Blessing was heavyset and tall. Menthol fragrance wafted from the folds of her green and orange *boubou*. She walked with her right hand against the wall, dragging herself forward along an invisible rope. I followed her into a living room heated to tropical temperatures. Water damage spread across the ceiling in brown discolored patches. She motioned me to a sofa too big for the room.

"Thomas is dead. He died two years ago," she said. "Would you like a cup of tea?"

"No, thank you."

"Died of stroke."

"I'm sorry to hear that."

She studied my face. I waited for the examination to end, fixing my eyes on a photograph of a young Blessing and Thomas on their wedding day. She was a head taller than her husband but her chin was lowered meekly. A pose.

"You say you're Francis's child . . . with a white woman?" she said.

"Yes. He met my mother when he was a student."

"It's possible. There were many cases like that we knew of. Irresponsible men. Not like Francis, though. Are you sure?" she asked.

"My mother was Bronwen Bain. Francis lived in her house as a lodger. My grandfather was his landlord. Owen Bain."

"How did you find out?"

"He left a diary. I found it among my mother's things after she died. I also found this photograph."

I gave her the signed photograph of Francis. She held it close to her face.

"Yes, that's Francis. Always was a sharp dresser. So how can I help you?"

"I want to meet him," I said.

"I'm sorry, I won't be of much assistance. We haven't spoken for almost forty years."

So that was it. Another brick wall. She was sliding to the edge of the sofa, preparing to stand and usher me out.

"He wrote about you and Thomas in his diary."

"Is that so? What did he say?"

"Here," I said, holding up the diary.

"Read it for me, please. My eyes."

"This is from when he moved in with Thomas."

"Yes, I remember that. I was still in Rhodesia. Go on."

"Thomas lives a rather interesting life. We are hardly ever in his flat, which is a mercy as the place is a pigsty. He steps out of his clothes and leaves them where they fall. He eats and dumps his plates on the windowsills. I cannot live in such conditions and I am constantly cleaning up after him.

Thomas knows a great many members of what he calls the British left. They are an odd assortment. Duchesses and dustmen rubbing shoulders. We are all equal at the meetings we attend— Thomas Phiri and Sir Henry Norris, shake hands and be friends, no difference between black and white—but step out on the street to hail a cab and you'll soon know the real story."

"That's right. That was Thomas. Untidy and too political for his own good. At least until I arrived. You said Francis wrote about me."

"Yes."

"I have met Thomas's wife. She is a formidable woman. He seemed rather diminished in his newly spick-and-span flat. She is determined that he be called to the bar this year. Blessing has been to Menelik's flat and is unimpressed. 'If you want to fight imperialism go back and join the Chimurenga.'

'We are strategizing,' Thomas said weakly.

'Strategize on the boat home.'"

"Interesting. I didn't know he noticed me enough to make such an observation. I *was* unimpressed by Thomas's friends. A bunch of radical posers. Although I didn't mind Francis. He was kind. Never came round to our flat without a small gift. Milk, apples, and so on."

"Did Thomas ever get called to the bar?" I asked.

"No. He couldn't pass the exams. He became a librarian," she said. "What else from those days?"

"He wrote about Menelik."

"He was a Caribbean, you know? Calling himself Menelik like some Ethiopian prince. They didn't take slaves from Ethiopia. Read it."

"Menelik has gone on a speaking tour of the North of England. His flat is closed and I am left unoccupied. I try my old haunts, the British Museum, the National Portrait Gallery, but I am thrown into those first days when I was a lonely Londoner. The other African students have scattered to their holiday jobs or the homes of their classmates. I have received no invitations. I do not know how to make myself amenable to the English.

I have begun the book Menelik gave me on African kingdoms. It is arranged in order of the alphabet. I have read through Adal, Aksum, Alodia, Asante, and am now on Bamana. It will be the end of the holidays before I reach Zulu."

We were silent for a moment, as if a prayer had just been read.

"So that's where he got the name Bamana from. You're holding history in your hands," she said.

"What was he like?"

"I didn't know him that well. He was Thomas's friend, not mine. There was something about him that made people want to impress him, something cool and aloof, like he was condescending. But I suppose he was just thinking things through as that book has shown, making note of everything. He was never one for a quick response," she said. "Does he know about your birth?"

"I don't think so. He went back to Bamana before my mother discovered she was pregnant."

"Why do you want to meet him, then? You seem to have done all right for yourself. Are you married? Children?"

"I have one daughter. I'm in the process of getting a divorce."

"Shame," she said.

Her pity made me suddenly spiteful. "The diary—it says Thomas had other women."

She leaned forward.

"You think you can come here and shock me with anything you read in that book?"

"I'm sorry, I spoke out of turn."

"No, you spoke to wound me because you're ashamed of this divorce, although I can't see why. People get divorced all the time. And Thomas was here for five years without me. What do you expect? I'm just glad I didn't arrive to find a half-caste bastard."

"I should go," I said.

"Now I'm the one who has spoken out of turn."

"No, really. I've kept you too long."

"Your father came here once in a motorcade of three black Benzes. Just after he was elected. His bodyguards stood in the hallway with their guns or whatever was under those big coats and we sat here, three of us in this room." She pointed at the spaces her husband and my father had occupied.

"He ate. One of his men insisted on tasting the food first, as if my sadza could be poisoned," she said with a small smile. "For months, the neighbors were talking about the African prince that came to see us. It left Thomas feeling small. My husband wouldn't have been president if he'd gone back to Zimbabwe, wouldn't have been a cabinet minister, probably wouldn't even have been a school principal. But seeing Francis made him feel like we should have gone home. That was the last time we saw him."

She stood. The interview was at an end.

"Are you sure I can't offer you a cup of tea?"

I dialed Adrian once I got home.

"Blessing said you were a spy," I said, bypassing a greeting.

"Did she?"

"I was expecting a more straightforward denial."

"I wasn't a spy, but I was invited in by the Home Office once or twice because of my friendship with some members of the black left."

"And you went?" I asked.

"I was curious. It was all a little James Bond. I didn't tell them anything of use. I didn't *know* anything of use. I certainly didn't know about Menelik's guns."

"You should have told me."

"And you should have told me you were Francis's daughter before spending a night in my home," he said. "I spoke to the Bamanaian high commissioner today. He was my chaperone in Segu when I was researching the book. He wasn't a diplomat then, just one of

Kofi's numerous lackeys. I told him I was thinking of returning to Bamana one last time and that I'd like to meet Kofi again if it were possible. He gave me a contact."

"You have my father's number?"

"Hold on. I have a contact for his personal assistant. There might be another six people between this assistant and Kofi, but it's a start."

"I want to meet him."

"I know. I hope you're ready. Have you told your family?" he asked.

"Do you think I should?"

"It's up to you. Nothing has come of it yet, but I'm sure they'd like to know."

"Well, I told my daughter that I've found my father, but I haven't said much about who he is."

"That may be best. Until we've fixed a concrete meeting."

"I agree," I said.

When the call ended, I put my keys in my pocket and left the house. It was dark outside and I was the only person on the street.

Was I ready to meet my father? In the documentary, just before the black children met their white birth mothers, they would have a moment alone with the camera. Their insecurities would surface. Sometimes they would cry from the anticipation. Will she recognize me? Will she like me?

I wanted Francis to like me, but Francis was gone. It was Kofi I would meet. The former president. The alleged murderer who was now a philanthropist in his old age. The Internet had recorded his good deeds too—orphanages, scholarships. He smiled in his recent photographs. His eyes twinkled at the viewer.

I walked past my neighbor and his dog, a small brown terrier, kept close on a leash. We had been neighbors for years but I didn't know his name. Robert would know.

"Evening," we mumbled at each other.

In some houses, the blinds were drawn and the front rooms were arranged, it seemed, for actors to weave around the furniture. You could stage a domestic drama in one of them, a daughter looking for a father who was not looking for her. Sometimes, someone would come on set, peer out into the night, and close the curtains.

13

My answering machine was blinking when I got home. I put down my shopping bags and pressed play.

"Hi, Anna. It's Shola here. Good news. We've got an offer for the flat. The couple had another seller pull out at the last minute. They're ready with all their paperwork, down payment, everything's ready. We can expect to close in about a month's time. Congratulations. Call me when you get this."

I braced myself against the wall. I was going to Bamana. I was going to meet my father. I called Shola back.

"Hello. Shola Ajayi speaking."

"It's Anna," I said.

"Oh, hello. You must be very excited. Congratulations."

"I can't believe it. How much?"

"Well, they started at three-ninety but I pushed them up to four hundred. It's ten thousand below our asking price, but remember, I said this property sits around the four hundred thousand mark because it hasn't been modernized."

Four hundred thousand pounds.

"So what do I do need to do now?"

"Nothing. I'll draw up the paperwork and when everything's ready, I'll ask you to come in and sign."

"What's the couple like?"

"Lovely. Young. They got married two years ago."

"Children?"

"Not yet," she said. "Well, I thought I should call you straight away with the good news. I'll get started on the paperwork and I'll see you in about a month."

"Can I still go to the flat?"

"Of course. It's yours until we sign the papers. All right. Bye for now."

I've met Shola only once. She was dressed immaculately—overdressed, it seemed—for a high-street estate agent. Her weave was long and expensive, human hair, the tips flipped with a tong. She was British Nigerian, more British than Nigerian, I thought, until she picked up a call from her father.

"Sorry, I'll have to take this. It's my dad and he's in hospital."

When she put the phone to her ear, she stopped speaking English. Her voice was deeper in the other language. She was more animated. She covered her mouth to laugh.

"What language was that?" I asked when she dropped the call.

"Yoruba. That's my tribe in Nigeria. Again, sorry about that. As I was saying—"

My mother's flat was in a low-rise council block in Islington and it was a stand-alone unit, unattached to a housing estate. These features slightly increased its value. On the walk from the station, I passed a bakery, two estate agents, an independent coffee shop, a gym, a massage therapist's with white pebbles and green succulents in the display window, all of which had opened in the last five years.

I had always thought she rented the flat from the council until the executor read out her will. "Left to my beloved daughter, Anna." She was a sales manager in a department store, watching other women step in and out of clothes, rehearsing for their lives in her dressing room. I was impatient with the size of her life, disdainful of it. And yet, somehow, she had amassed the money for a down payment. My mother, with no financial education and no university degree, had worked out how to own property in London. The paperwork showed she applied successfully for a mortgage in 1984 and completed her payments in October 2009.

I let myself into the building. Almost no one was left from the old days. The Sharmas moved to Willesden, to a house with a garden. Mrs. Levstein died. The Okoyes went back to Nigeria. The changes were gradual. At first, there were clashes between the old and new. Skirmishes were waged on the cork noticeboard: PLEASE KEEP THE NOISE DOWN AFTER 10PM. THE COOKING OF CERTAIN FOODS CAUSES THE BLOCK TO STINK. And then only the new tribe remained, with their parsley and olive oil. The old were all gone.

I unlocked the door of flat 7 and walked into the hallway. I was twelve again, letting myself in after school. I put my bag down. I took off my shoes from habit. We had a beige carpet. My mother was very careful of it. On the right was her double room. Her taste ran to clutter: framed family photographs on the walls, porcelain figures on the window ledge, too many cushions on her bed. My room was plain in comparison. I had a single bed, a double wardrobe, and a shelf of worn books that she bought secondhand. Adrian Mole came of age at the same time as me. It was all bare now, cleared out after she died.

Our rooms were on one side of the hallway, the toilet and bathroom were on the other. We could hear each other's pee striking the water. Sometimes at night, I would knock on the adjoining wall and she would knock back. We would pretend we were signaling in Morse code.

"Did you ever wish I was white?" I asked her when I was an adult.

"What do you mean? Of course not."

"But you always said, 'You're just the same as me, Anna.'"

"I didn't mean it that way. It was just when you came home and some kids had been mean about your hair being a bit different from theirs."

"A lot different. You can see that, can't you. It's very different. There's nothing wrong with it being different."

"I never said there was."

We couldn't speak about my childhood without me getting angry. It puzzled her. What had she not done? What had she not given? A sense of rightness, a sense of self. It was nothing when you had it. You hardly noticed. But once it was missing, it was like a sliver of fruit on a long sea voyage, the difference between bleeding gums and survival.

At the end of the hallway, a left turn took you to the living room and kitchen. The kitchen was small, functional. Our food was sound but plain—potatoes, meat, and green vegetables. She sewed in the living room. There was a cloth mannequin, a torso on a stick, smooth and flat-chested, riddled with pins. She adjusted our neighbor's clothes and made dresses for herself from patterns. She sewed all my clothes until I staged a teenage rebellion. I didn't smoke, I didn't drink, but I was not going to look like something out of a Laura Ashley catalogue. Even then, all she would concede to buying was jeans.

We didn't always get on in my teenage years. It was my snobbery, not any fault of hers. Grammar school made our home life suddenly seem mean and small. Why did we watch so much television? Why didn't we speak French?

I spent as much time outside of our flat as I could, in the homes of girls I envied. It wasn't like my local primary school. Nobody called me a wog or a darkie, but they always wanted to touch my hair. They wanted to know if I tanned, if food tasted different with thicker lips, if my hearing was sharper than theirs. I watched their parents, the father always a professional, the mother sometimes working but rarely. I thought to myself, one day I'll have a nice house, and a husband and a child, in that order.

I stepped out onto the balcony. It was empty now, like the rest of the flat. Once it had been filled with potted plants and flowers. My mother hung birdhouses there stuffed with seeds. In the summer we dried our laundry on it, and our clothes would smell of meadows. There was no laundry on the balconies in the block now.

The couple buying the flat would probably rip up the carpets and tear off the wallpaper. They'd knock down the wall between the kitchen and the living room. They'd lay wooden flooring and they'd give me more money than I'd ever earned in my life.

I could go to Bamana now, thanks to them, thanks to my mother. At her funeral I stood by her graveside dry-eyed. She was a good mother, hardworking, kind, quiet, timid, too timid to have raised a black child in the seventies. She was a very good grandmother. Rose cried as the earth covered the coffin.

Below, a line of cyclists darted past, trilling their bells. It would soon be evening. I left my mother's flat for the last time.

14

Aunt Caryl lived in a Jewish nursing home in North London. She chose it herself when she was diagnosed with Alzheimer's. She was admitted on the technicality that my great-grandmother Esther was believed to have been a Jew. According to Aunt Caryl's research, Jewish homes had the lowest incidence of bed sores.

I waited in the lobby. There was one other name in the guest-book. Under *Purpose of visit*, they had written, *Light bulbs*. Some renovation had been done since my last visit. The faded carpet and fringed lampshades were gone, replaced by clinical lights and laminate flooring.

Aunt Caryl wasn't in the common area where residents were arranged in armchairs like large potted plants—the closer to the TV, the more alert. Each step away from *Homes Under the Hammer* was a shade deeper into senility. On good days, Aunty Caryl was in hearing distance of the television. On bad days, she was by the door. On terrible days, she was in her room.

"Mrs. Graham." It was Maria, a petite Filipina carer.

"Hello, Maria. How are you today?"

"Very well, thank you. Follow me, please."

In the corridors, we passed other carers dressed in pale blue scrubs. I recognized faces: Daniel from Uganda, who was studying to become an accountant; Moses from South Africa, who filled out his scrubs like a body builder.

"Where's Tina?" I asked.

"She went back to Bulgaria."

Tina had a masters in communication. She also had three teenage sons who ate like horses.

Aunty Caryl's door was shut. Maria knocked but didn't wait for a response.

"Hello, love. Haven't seen you in a while."

She was looking at Maria.

"All right, Mrs. Graham. I'll leave the two of you for half an hour. I think that's all she can take today."

I stood at the foot of Aunt Caryl's single bed. Her hair was freshly cut and dyed the brick red it had always been. When they let it go grey, her reflection shocked her. There was a card on the windowsill from her birthday two months ago. They remembered the details. The Bethel Home for the Elderly was better than most. There was no smell of neglect, no fog of urine.

I had not visited since my mother's death. The bereavement, the separation from Robert, monitoring Rose's eating: it was all too overwhelming. I knew Aunt Caryl was no longer capable of missing me, yet I still felt guilt.

"Who's that?" she said.

"It's Anna, Aunt Caryl."

"Have you come to give me the paper?"

"No. I just came to see you."

"I'm fine. You can go now unless there's something special you want to tell me."

"I'm going to see Francis."

"About time. I always told your mother to tell you about him. I didn't mind her having my leftovers. I had enough attention from the boys back then. If you press that button someone will come and pour you a cup of tea."

"I'm all right, thank you."

"You don't want any tea?"

"No, thanks."

"Then you can fuck off." When I was younger, Aunt Caryl was the only one who understood that I was a black child living with a white family. My mother and grandfather's denial was farcical, almost sinister.

"You're Welsh," my mother would say, when I came home with grit in my hair.

"There've been Bains in and around the Wye Valley for generations," my grandfather would add.

Aunt Caryl took me to the Notting Hill Carnival when I was six. She held my hand as we moved through the throng of black people, more black people than I had ever seen in my life.

"Are we in Africa?" I asked.

"Not quite, love."

There was music, feathers, sequins, drumming. There were black women with white gauze wings, gold paste crowns, mirrors and face paint, floats and thrones, transformed for a day into carnival kings and queens before they sank back to earth at midnight. The crowd responded to the rhythm, swaying, bending, stamping, except the two of us, who stood as still as oak trees in the wind.

That was also the year of a riot at the carnival. Small and contained, so we only saw it on the news when we got home, but neither my mother nor Grandpa Owen thought it appropriate for a child after that. I don't know why I never went as an adult. I felt I had to go with someone, perhaps, and it didn't seem Robert's thing.

Aunt Caryl was growing restless now. Her bottom lip appeared from and disappeared into her mouth. Her eyes darted around the room, resting on everything but me. I stepped back from the bed and sat on the armchair in the corner.

"Do you remember Francis?"

"Yes. The butcher's boy," she said.

"Not that Francis. Francis Aggrey?"

"I'd have gone to Africa if I'd been the one who was pregnant." Her moments of lucidity were brief, flighty as a sparrow perching.

"Did he know about me?" I asked, keeping my voice casual.

"About who, love?"

"Did Francis Aggrey know Bronwen had a baby?"

"I've never met a Bronwen in my life. Pretty name, though."

The moment was gone. Her mind had flitted off into confusion again.

"I found his diary." I said.

"Whose diary?"

"Francis's."

"That must have been a surprise."

"I can read you a passage."

"Go on, then."

I picked a passage that might jolt her.

"I have walked out a few times with Caryl. Thomas congratulates me for finally finding an *obroni* woman. He says it is about time I know that a woman's secret place tastes the same, no matter what color hair surrounds it. I do not believe all Thomas's tales of conquest. One man cannot have such stamina, but he undoubtedly has an effect on *obroni* women. He is bold with them, leaning close when he talks, touching them lightly for emphasis. They appear receptive. Without immodesty, I am taller than Thomas and have often been called handsome, whereas even the kindest would not describe Thomas in that way. I, too, might have such an effect if I wished, but I am suspicious of *obroni* women. I think it is not attraction but curiosity that makes them follow Thomas.

On the MV *Aureole* to England, a district officer's wife stumbled against me in a deserted passage. I steadied her, and she must have taken this as encouragement for she slid her hand down my trousers like a common wharf whore. We remained in this position for a few moments. There was alcohol on her breath and the fug of her sweat repelled me, but I am a curious man. I kissed her, my first *obroni* kiss, and her tongue barreled past my teeth, filling my mouth with the taste of rum. 'Let me see,' she said dragging at my belt. 'I want to see what size it is on a nigger.'

Never was a man so fast deflated."

"You should never say that word, Anna."

"Which word?"

"Rhymes with 'bigger.'"

We smiled and for a moment she was Aunt Caryl again.

"Go on. What else did he say about me?"

Francis Aggrey's words were almost mystical in their power. For a few minutes they had pulled my aunt back from senility.

"Caryl and I have chosen to remain friends. There is no spark between us and I am uncomfortable with her in public. Whenever she reaches for my hand, I wonder if I am a romantic extension of the political work she does in Menelik's flat. A man called her a nigger lover in the street. 'And what if I am,' she replied. I do not wish that my person be used as a statement for racial equality. We never slept together: a black mark against me, Thomas says. He finds my objections absurd. 'Nobody's saying marry a white woman. Just find out what they're hiding under those wide skirts.' Thomas himself is married. His wife, Blessing, is in Rhodesia. What would she think of his escapades? 'I'm a man,' he said. 'No woman can chain me.'"

"That's a nice story. Please pass me my knitting."

"Do you remember this?" I asked.

"My knitting."

It was too early to tell what she what she was making out of the ball of green wool that lay on her dressing table. When she got to the end, a carer would unravel it and she would start again. It was cruelly efficient.

"Why won't you pass me my knitting? It's just there."

I didn't know where Maria had kept the needles, and she wasn't allowed to knit unsupervised. She had poked herself in the eye once.

"I think you're very unkind. I want you to leave now."

"Don't you want to hear any more?" I asked.

"Just leave."

I sang to her.

"*Huna blentyn ar fy mynwes, Clyd a chynnes ydyw hon.*"

The first few lines of "Suo Gân" could always quiet her. When Maria came back, she had fallen asleep.

"Poor dear," she said.

"How is she? I'm sorry I've been away for so long. We had a family bereavement. My mother died suddenly."

"Sorry to hear that, Mrs. Graham. She's been well. Just some days she wakes up and doesn't want to get out of bed. I don't blame her. I feel like that sometimes."

There were red scratches on Maria's arm. Carers mopped up pee and wiped anuses. They gave showers, trimmed nose hairs, clipped fingernails, endured the shit pay. And for this, they were hit and spat on by some of their charges, pinched and groped, called niggers and monkeys and chinks. I had complained to the manager, a white male overseer whose fingernails were too long.

"Our residents come from a time when the use of such language was common. We regularly caution them about offensive words, but they are old. They forget."

"Thank you so much for everything, Maria."

"No problem. So, see you in a few weeks."

"I'm traveling soon, but once I get back I'll come again."

She led me out to the visitors' car park.

"Safe travels."

15

The Bamana High Commission was close to Trafalgar Square. Tourists swarmed the area, holding maps and asking for directions. There were a few restaurants with maroon awnings and dim interiors. Francis Aggrey would have been barred from such places. To place the national embassy here was to offer an expensive challenge.

The building was grand. A Bamanaian flag—red, white, and blue with a black star in the middle—hung above the entrance. There was a queue winding around the corner, cordoned off by tape. I joined the tail end of the snake. A man in a suit approached and gave me a ticket.

"You are number twenty-five."

"No, I've told you, sir," the woman in front of me said, "my sister and her three children are coming. Four of them in total. So the person behind me is number twenty-nine."

"I've already torn it."

"Then please tear for me twenty-six to thirty."

"I can't tear for people I have not seen."

A newcomer joined the queue. The official ripped out a new ticket.

"You are number twenty-six," he said.

"*Ei*. Did you hear what I told you about my sister? I'm talking to you."

The official returned to the front of the queue.

"Bedlam," the newcomer said to me. His blond hair was cut to fall around his forehead and ears. It was a boyish style for someone going grey.

"Ken. Emerging markets consultant. And you?"

"I'm an architect," I said.

"Here for a visa?"

"Yes."

"My third time at the embassy this year. They only give you a visa for as long as your trip. If you're going for four days, a four-day visa. The place is mad. But wait till you get to the country. What are you heading there for? Part of the new Atlantic City team?"

"No. I'm going to see my father."

I took a step towards the woman in front of me. Her shoulder bag gaped, revealing a bottle of Ribena, crumpled tissues, a wallet, and a phone that was in danger of tumbling out.

"Excuse me, your bag is open," I said.

"*Ei*, thank you, my sister. The zip is faulty. I'm just managing it."

She ran the zip back and forth until the Louis Vuitton bag looked closed.

"This is our third time here. The first time, they said the biometric machine was not working. The second time, they said passport booklets have finished so no more applications till next month. Please God, today we will get it. We have already bought our ticket and these people want to mess us up. What of you? Your passport has expired?"

"No. I'm here for a visa, actually."

"Are you not Bamanaian?"

"My father is."

"*Ehen*. I can see it from your face. I know you're half-caste but that nose, it's a Bamana nose."

I was pleased that there was something evidently Bamanaian about me although annoyed by her use of the term "half-caste." It was archaic at best; offensive at its worst.

"So, you're going home to visit your father?" she asked.

"Yes," I said briefly, ready to end our conversation.

"That's nice. When you get there, you'll just get the passport from Segu. Tell him to do it for you instead of coming here for visa every time. And there, it's even quicker. You just go, if you give them some money, they bring it out for you the next day. Wait, my sister is calling. Francina . . ."

I stepped back from her.

"I'm sorry, I didn't realize you were from Bamana," the man behind me said. "Like every place, it has its problems, like here even, but the people are so friendly. It's a beautiful country. Of course, you don't need me to tell you that."

"It's my first visit."

I slipped my earphones in and listened to nothing until the embassy doors opened. Inside was a waiting area with plastic seats and officials behind glass counters. The ticket man announced, "When you hear your number, go to the counter. If you're absent when they call you, come outside and collect a new ticket number from me."

"What if you're in the toilet?"

"Don't go to toilet when they call you."

He left the room.

"So I should piss myself?" There were chuckles and jeers. I sat on the last empty chair, chair twenty-five. The room smelled of cooking spices, the scents smuggled in clothing and hair. There was also sweat. The heating was almost unbearable and, although it was winter outside, some were fanning themselves.

"No chairs," a man announced once he walked in. "They can't even provide simple chairs. Once you step inside here, you've gone back home to inefficiency. This country is going nowhere."

No one responded.

"Hello, my sister." It was the lady from in front of me in the queue. "My sister Francina has come. She's over there. Please, if you'll just let her go when they call your number, then after that you'll take your turn. Please, I beg. They've come from Leeds."

I looked over at Francina, who was smiling in my direction. She was carrying one child on her hip and there were another two in a double pram. Nobody stood up for her.

"I'd be careful of swapping if I were you. Once you lose your place, you might have to start all over again."

It was Ken, the consultant, leaning against the wall behind me.

"*Obroni*, who asked you?"

She kissed her teeth and walked back to her sister.

"Thank you," I said.

"No problem. So how come it's only your first trip if your father lives there?"

"He used to live in England. He moved back."

"Ah, I see. She was right, you know. You can get a passport easily once you get there. Bamana is trying to get its diaspora back. For a while dual citizenship was banned ... but that was under President Adjei. Things have changed."

"For the better?" I asked.

"Yes, I think so. The country was too isolated under Adjei. I saw him speak once when he was in office. Interesting fellow. Lots of ideas about how to do capitalism the African way and all that. But what were the results? Bamana was still poor. This new guy, Owusu, is really opening the place up."

"No, Adjei was better," the man standing next to Ken said. "Owusu is just selling us to foreigners."

The woman who spoke next was petite and dark-skinned. A cropped wig framed her face. The hair was cut in little triangles that lay flat on her forehead.

"Why are you here living with those same foreigners, then? What Owusu is doing is good. He's bringing jobs to the country, for the young people."

"It's we, the youth, that will pay for these policies," a young man with an eyebrow piercing said. "When we're old, we will wake up and see that Owusu has sold our country."

"At least you will live to be old," the woman replied.

Our conversation spread to the rest of the room—Adjei versus Owusu. My father had his supporters but Owusu was the clear winner.

"Number twenty-five."

When I stood up, I saw Francina and her three children watching me dolefully.

It was a man at the counter, in a grey suit but no tie.

"Morning. What is your application?"

"B-One tourist visa, please," I said.

"Your form."

He flicked through the pages I had filled out.

"Purpose of visit."

"I'm going on holiday."

"You have family there?"

"Yes, my father."

"What does he do?"

"He's retired."

"But your form states you'll be residing in a hotel during your stay. What of your father's house?"

"He remarried. I don't know his new wife."

"Oh. Sorry about that. Your supporting documents?"

I gave him my flight receipt and my bank account statements.

"Three weeks' visa granted. You have the eighty pounds postal order?"

"Pardon?"

"That's how you pay for the visa. It says so on the website."

The embassy website had been a series of broken links and empty pages.

"I didn't see it. I'm sorry."

"No need to be sorry. There's a post office down the road. You can get it from there but, by the time you come back, we may not be able to attend to you today."

"Can I pay by card?"

"We don't have a card machine. You have cash?"

I looked in my wallet.

"I only have fifty pounds," I said.

The man leaned close, until his temple brushed the glass separating us.

"I like you, my sister. Just bring what you have."

He was whispering and I found myself lowering my voice too.

"Thank you so much."

I slid the fifty pounds under the opening. He sat back but left an oil smear. He stamped my form.

"Come next week Tuesday for passport pickup."

"Can I have a receipt? Something I can show at the door?"

He wrote my name and the date of collection and signed a slip of paper.

"Next. Number thirty-two."

Outside, Ken the consultant was waiting on the pavement.

"How did it go? I thought I'd make sure you were all right."

"I'm not sure. I got the visa but I paid fifty pounds instead of eighty. In cash. I didn't know about the postal order."

He laughed. "Congratulations. You just paid your first bribe."

It worried me how easily I'd been duped. If I was no match for the clerk in the embassy, what hope did I have in the actual country? "I thought there was something suspicious," I said.

"Don't feel bad. They probably haven't paid him his wages in months. You've stopped him from freezing this winter."

"So when do you pick up your passport? I have to come back next week," I said.

"Oh, I have my passport already. Express service."

"A bribe?"

"I prefer 'facilitation fee,'" he said. "Walking to the station?"

I met Katherine in the new café on our high street that sold chai-flavored coffee. A sign outside read, BREASTFEEDING MOTHERS GET FREE DRINK. I didn't breastfeed Rose for long. My milk dried up.

"We're the oldest people here," Katherine said when I sat down. "Shall I get us some coffee?"

"Tea for me, please," I said.

In the corner a group of women sat with a fence of prams around them. They looked close to Rose's age, young to have children. They seemed sympathetic to one another. As one spoke, the rest nodded, until everyone had spoken and everyone had nodded.

When Rose was in school, I knew the other mothers. We met at the school gates and sometimes on playdates but friendship always evaded us. They were of a set: striped cardigans, highlighted hair, endless baking—from bread to tiered cakes. Sometimes I felt that Robert should have married a woman like that, a woman who made tea from loose leaves.

I was too quick to judge them. Katherine and I would not have been friends ten years ago. I would have dismissed her as quickly as I dismissed those other women.

She returned with a tray laden with cups and saucers.

"I bought us some pastries too," she said.

"Thank you. How are you?"

"I'm well. Training for a marathon. I haven't run one in two years so I hope I can still do it. Chris, my youngest, has started prepping for his GCSEs. I don't know who's more worried between us. He's gifted but he's not that academic."

I met her son once when I ran into Katherine on the street. He was as I expected Katherine's son to be: tall, delicately handsome, and dressed from a prep-school catalogue.

"Rose thought she was going to fail her GCSEs," I said.

"Did she?"

"No. They never do. They just make you worry."

There were framed quotes on the walls, greeting card profundities. *Be Yourself. Everyone else is taken.* And what if you didn't like yourself?

"You sounded excited on the phone," Katherine said.

"I'm going to Bamana to meet my father. I applied for my visa today."

"Good for you. Are you going on your own?"

"I don't know yet. I might go with a friend. We haven't decided."

"I wish I could come with you. If Chris didn't have his GCSEs I'd be there with you on safari."

"I don't think there are safaris in Bamana."

"Sorry, that sounds so ignorant. I don't know much about Africa."

"Neither do I," I said.

16

The night before my flight, Katherine and Rose came to say good-bye. We sat in my living room with a bottle of wine between us. I ordered Indian food, or the approximation of it that was delivered by our local takeaway. The bottle was half empty when our meal arrived.

"I shouldn't get drunk. My flight is in the morning," I said.

"I've never seen you drunk, Mum."

"We'll stop before she gets there," Katherine said, refilling our glasses.

We ate with our hands, ripping the bread apart and dipping it in the curries. We ate straight from the plastic rectangles, with narrow forks that the rice spilled from, oily grains that I would have to sweep up before I went to bed.

"So how long have you lived on our street?" Rose asked Katherine.

"Twelve years."

"So strange that we never met," Rose said.

"I saw your dad going to work a couple of times."

"Yeah, him." Rose pushed her rice around. She had eaten half a naan but almost no rice.

"How are you feeling about the trip?" Katherine asked me.

"Nervous," I said, then added, "excited."

"It's come out of nowhere," Rose said.

"What do you mean?" I asked.

"You've never spoken about your father before. It just seems a bit sudden."

"I'm glad you're mentioning that, the night before I leave."

"I'm not saying you shouldn't go." Rose's phone buzzed. "Sorry, I have to take this."

She left the room and went to the kitchen.

"Excited is good. Stay on excited," Katherine said.

"Maybe Rose is right."

"No, she's just going to miss you. I'm going to miss you," she said. "The last time I did any serious traveling was in my twenties. Took six months off work and went across South America. Absolute freedom, with which I did some stupid things."

"I can't imagine you being reckless," I said.

"I had sex on a beach without a towel. Sand was crawling out of my vagina for days."

"Was it crabs?" I asked.

We laughed until I felt light-headed.

"I need to lie down." I sank back onto the carpet and closed my eyes.

"I think I might join you," she said. "Do you mind if I pray for you?"

Although she had not made a convert of me, I was grateful for the offer. Prayer was Katherine's sincerest way of wishing me well.

"Of course not," I said.

Her voice was low and earnest when she began.

"Father, please bless Anna and give her safe travels to Bamana. We pray she finds good things when she gets there. In Jesus' name, amen."

"Thank you," I said.

Rose returned. "What happened? Are you guys asleep?"

"We're just old," Katherine said. "You'll get here one day."

Rose lay down and pillowed her head on my stomach. It was a gesture she had not made in years.

"I'm going to miss you," she said.

"I know," I said as I stroked her hair. "I'll miss you, too."

Robert drove me to the airport. He had offered, and his company was preferable to an anonymous driver. I didn't tell Rose. She might make too much of what was a simple favor.

My flight was at 11:00 a.m. but we left at 6:00 to avoid traffic. The road to Heathrow was littered with derelict office blocks. The financial crash had destroyed the hive. The workers had flown. My final year of university, I had a summer job in an office building like that, with a cubicle overlooking a motorway. It was coveted desk space. There were others trapped in the middle of the floor, far from sunlight. It was my first real inkling that life as an architect might not be what I had envisioned.

At university, we thought we were going to be the next big thing in British architecture. We made models that would tumble over if anyone tried to build them, with roofs that curved and swooped and spiraled like orange peels. We were going to alter the skyline of every city in the UK. And then I went to work in a cubicle and then in an open-plan office in the City, drawing WCs on a screen. Marrying Robert and having a child put an end to that life of midnight deadlines. Perhaps I would have designed something notable in the end, after I'd paid my dues in air vents.

"So how are you feeling?" Robert asked.

"Groggy. Rose and Katherine came over to say goodbye last night."

On the radio, two men argued about the Labour Party. Women hardly ever phoned into these shows, and when they did, they seemed surprised they had made it past the throng of male callers. I winced at their voices. Robert turned the dial to classical music.

"I meant how are you feeling about your trip," he asked again.

"I'm looking forward to some sunshine."

I had packed for three weeks. Adrian advised only summer clothes. Shorts were fine but as close to the knee as possible. The UK.gov page on Bamana was not encouraging. "Terrorists are likely to try to carry out attacks in Bamana. Attacks could be indiscriminate, including in places visited by foreigners." When I read this out to Adrian he'd laughed and said, "London had a terror attack last year."

"Your father," Robert said. "How do you feel about meeting him?"

"I won't know until we've met."

In the car park Robert backed into a space in one smooth turn. He was always the better driver. At the check-in desk my bag weighed 18 kilos.

"Well, this is it," he said, when we stood by the security gates.

"This is it," I replied.

"I hope it all goes well."

"Thank you. Thanks for dropping me off."

He reached for an embrace. I stood stiffly in his arms, inhaling the cedarwood cologne that overlaid his raw, unwashed scent. At the last moment, I clung to him. What was I thinking, traveling across the world without my husband?

"I can still come if you need me. I'll buy a ticket tomorrow. Just say it."

His mouth was by my ear. His voice was in my head.

"It's not that simple," I said. "You'd need a visa. And no. Thank you, but I need to do this on my own."

I disentangled myself.

"So you'll let me know when you land in Bamana?"

"I don't think we should talk while I'm there. Just to clear our heads," I said.

"My head is clear. I know what I want, Anna."

"Please," I said.

"All right, then."

"Bye," we said together.

At security, there was a family in front of me, a father and two sons, the same shade of walnut, a set of three. The father wore a suit, the boys wore jeans and hoodies.

I took off my belt and shoes, intimate gestures to make in the open. The floor was cold, finely sanded with grit.

"Laptops, iPads, liquids, keys."

I put my handbag in a plastic tray.

"Laptop?" The official was rushed and unsmiling. There was no one behind me.

"No."

"iPads? Liquids? Gels?"

"No."

I passed through the metal detector and set it off.

"Step aside, please. Stretch out your arms."

She was a head shorter than me, hair pulled back in a ponytail, faint blush on her cheeks. She ran her hands down my back, along the band of my trousers, down my thighs. She poked her fingers into my hair. Last, she waved a wand over me. I was free to go.

In duty-free, they thrust samples in our faces, vials of perfumes and pots of scented lotions. Robert would be halfway to wherever he lived now. For all I knew, there was a woman waiting for him in his pseudo-bachelor flat. I bought a silk scarf and a pair of sunglasses with leopard-print frames. They were dramatic, the opposite of sensible. It was time to stop thinking about Robert.

In the lounge, I saw the walnut family again. The father reclined with an issue of *Time* magazine. The sons wandered around with their Game Boys, grazing on the snacks. Where was the mother who had made this matching family? She would have the same skin, like an expensive walking stick, polished and loved.

"Would you like something to drink?" a waiter asked.

"Champagne, please."

"Celebrating?"

"Yes, I suppose so."

Business class was full, a United Nations of European, Chinese, Arab, and African men. In economy, the passengers sat with empty seats between them and almost everyone was black. I peered through the curtains that divided us. A family in a row, mother and father on either end, two children in the middle. They were formally dressed, the father in a jacket, the children in church clothes, and the mother wearing a smart grey dress.

"Fancy seeing you here."

It was Ken, the man from the embassy. I drew back from the gap I was peeping through.

"Indeed. Are you following me?"

"I follow everyone with an interesting story."

"What's mine?"

"You're going to see your father but you're staying at a hotel."

"You were eavesdropping at the embassy."

"I overheard. I was at the window next to yours. There are no partitions."

"Where are you staying?"

"The Palace Hotel, until I find a service apartment. I'll be in Segu for three months. You're probably staying there as well."

I was. It was very highly rated.

"It has the best ratings," he continued. "Most people in this part of the plane are staying there too. There are rumors it's partly owned by Adjei . . . through a front, of course. But what do I care? The shower pressure is amazing! So how are you getting around when you're not with your father? I could show you some parts of town if you want."

"Thank you. I already have a guide."

"Take my card anyway."

It was the second time he'd given it to me.

"Thanks. I should use the loo."

When I came out, Ken had gone back to his seat. I returned to mine and looked out the window. We were flying over the Sahara, not the golden desert of popular imagination but an area that was craggy and brown. Cracks in the land looked like the courses rivers and streams had once flowed over.

I drew down the blind and turned my chair into a bed. For a six-hour flight it was an extravagance. I brought out the diary and turned to my favorite passage, an entry where Francis guessed at what a child with my mother would have looked like. He guessed at me.

Bronwen and I have had pillow talk tonight. Of children. If Bronwen had a child she would like him to be as close to my color as possible. "Are you pregnant?" I asked. I was horrified. At least here I can be honest. My mother has warned me that if I marry an *obroni* she will cut me off and leave her business to my uncle. I don't know if the old woman is serious. But if I were disowned, how would I look after a family?

"No, I am not pregnant," she said. Caryl has taught her how to the count the days so she knows when to avoid me.

Had she told Caryl about us? No. Caryl thinks her sister's lover works in a shop on her street.

"But if I were pregnant," she said. So we went on to build our phantom child—a son. He must have her eyes. If he has that, he cannot have my skin, or else he will look like an *obanshee*. He must have my size or else he will be bullied. He will speak Fanti and Welsh but no English. By the time he comes of age the Diamond Coast and Wales will be free.

"Cabin crew, prepare for landing."

Segu was not yet in sight. We still flew over the forest. It was a green that perhaps only a painter could capture, with undertones of gold and orange. Patches of red earth appeared, holes in a thick beard. Then the first houses, shacks with rust roofs, straggling on the edge of the forest like crumbs. Dirt roads cut through the landscape like veins. The green receded, torn up by human hands.

It was a low-rise city. Roofs were set close together, like scales on an animal, a fish or an armadillo. The view changed. Asphalt roads appeared, grey and stark. A line of cars moved down a highway, beads on a string. There was a stadium, an open bowl, with an emerald football pitch at its center. Skyscrapers thrust upwards, javelins aimed at the sun. And just before we touched down, a thousand feet above the ground, a glimpse of the ocean.

"Ladies and gentlemen, welcome to Segu. We hope you had a pleasant flight. Please enjoy your onward journey and we hope to see you again soon. Thank you for choosing to fly with us."

There were Bamanaians waiting by the plane door with wheelchairs. They wore a uniform: cream shirts, black waistcoats and trousers. They greeted us as we walked past.

"Welcome."

"Thank you," I said to each one.

The air vents blasted cold air. The escalators were not working. Two young men carried a woman in a wheelchair down the stairs. They carried her backwards, the bearer holding the handles going first. She clutched the armrests and shut her eyes.

My immigration official had a matching scar on each cheek: thin vertical lines, like strokes in a tally bundle. He wore clear aviator glasses, behind which his eyes were bleary and red.

"Hello, good evening. Welcome to Bamana. Purpose of visit?"

"Good evening, sir. Holiday."

"That's good. You're going to see the slave forts?"

"Yes, I plan to."

"How long are you staying for?"

"Three weeks."

"That's a long holiday. Where are you staying?"

"The Palace Hotel."

"That's good. Would you like to show some appreciation for the work we are doing?"

"Yes, thank you. I think you're doing a wonderful job."

We stared at each other until I let my gaze wander away.

"You're a beautiful woman. You can go."

I took my passport and walked the short distance to baggage claims. It was a large hall and voices rose to fill it. In one corner, men and women prayed facing Mecca, rising and falling together.

The luggage carousel was a narrow oval crowded with people. My suitcase circled twice before I struggled to the front and grabbed it.

"Watch it," a passenger said, when my wheels grazed him.

"Sorry."

I followed the exit signs. A languorous man in uniform blocked my path.

"Anything to declare?"

"No, sir."

"What's in there?" He pointed at my suitcase.

"Just clothes."

"No gifts for anyone?"

"No."

"Please step aside for searching."

"She's with me," a now familiar voice said from behind me.

"Mr. Ken, welcome back," the official said. Their handshake ended with a click of the fingers.

"You can go," the official said to me. We stepped out into the evening breeze.

"You don't have to thank me," Ken said.

"I wasn't going to. You seem intent on rescuing me."

It was familiar and unfamiliar. The taxi rank, I recognized, and men holding name signs aloft, but there was a buzz, a current I stood just outside of. People called out, jostled, laughed, spoke in languages that I could not understand. And they were all black.

"How are you getting to the hotel? Shuttle?"

I spotted Adrian and waved.

"Is that your father?"

He was wearing a bright print shirt that was both loose and rigid at the same time. The short cotton sleeves stuck out from his body, stiff with starch. He was tanned from his seven-day head start.

"Anna, you made it."

"Thank you for coming to get me."

"No bothering. That's how the locals say 'no problem.'"

I let Adrian take my suitcase and fell in step behind him.

17

Adrian's friend had lent him a car and driver. It seemed remarkable that an entire human being should be lent along with the vehicle, but there he was, sitting in the front seat waiting for us. He climbed out and took my suitcase from Adrian.

"Welcome, ma," he said.

"Thank you."

The inside of the car was cool. Adrian sat in front.

"So how was your flight?"

"Good. I slept for most of it. How's your week here been?"

"Great. I've taught at the university a few times already. Seen old friends. They're older, richer. Maybe I should have stayed on too."

"Have you spoken to Francis?"

"Not directly, but everything's been fixed with his secretary. He sent a note through her. He seems pleased I'm here. I've told him I'm coming with a friend, but of course I've left the big reveal to you. It seems best to do it in person."

I trembled physically, like a current had passed through me. "Next Monday," I said.

"Yes, but I'd forget about it till then. Enjoy the city. See the sights."

It was easy to convince Adrian to accompany me to Bamana. He had Bamanaian friends he had not seen in years and he was curious to witness how this drama with Kofi's love-child would conclude, a historian's voyeurism perhaps. He'd arranged to guest-lecture on twentieth-century African history at the university in Segu, his academic contacts from decades ago now senior heads of department.

Outside, night had fallen. The streets were well lit. When the car slowed at a junction, people approached with various items to sell. It made no sense to suddenly purchase a hat but perhaps the urge to buy hats came often to Bamanaians.

"Look, a puppy," I said.

"Don't stare. He'll think you want to buy it."

The man thrust the puppy at my window. Its eyes were closed but its back legs twitched in its sleep.

"Who'd buy a pet in traffic?"

"It's for eating," the driver said. "They're not allowed to do it. They only come out in the night."

Most of the buildings were walled, but the walls were low—a man Adrian's height could jump over. The pavements were full of people making their way home, workers in suits boarding crammed buses. They held on to the handrails, hung like meat to dry. Commuting was the same. I sat back in my seat and dozed.

"We're here," Adrian said.

The fountain in the lobby of the Palace Hotel spurted red, white, and blue. The lights changed color underwater. The floors were marble, polished until they reflected blurred images. I walked to the welcome desk.

"Good evening, madam. Checking in?" The receptionist wore a maroon blazer and a striped tie. Wooden beads swung at the ends of her braids. They seemed natural here, not a statement of any sort. I gave her my name and surname, my passport, my home address, Rose's phone number.

"Mr. Moses," she said to a bellboy chatting with the doorman.

"Mr. Moses," she said again, raising her voice and for a moment sliding out of her hospitality training.

"Christina, why are you shouting my name?"

"Please, the guest is waiting."

"Is that why you're shouting? Mind yourself." He wagged a finger at her before turning to me. "Good evening, madam." His uniform was piped with gold braid, a general fallen on hard times.

"Everything's sorted?" Adrian asked.

"Yes."

"I'll see you tomorrow. I'm teaching a class in the morning, but I'm free from noon. I'll come to the lobby and call. What's your room number?"

"Four hundred and seven. Where are you staying?"

"The University of Bamana guesthouse. Not as swanky as our present surroundings but the Wi-Fi is good."

"Thank you for today."

"Thank you for giving me a reason to be here. I've missed this country. Get some rest."

I could have stayed with Adrian in the university guest house, but the online reviews had described it as clean but basic, a plain dwelling on the outskirts of town. I could afford better now. I was left alone with the bellboy.

"Follow me. Your room number?"

"Four hundred and seven."

He led me to the golden elevators. The doors slid open and a couple stepped out. They held hands, an old white man and a young black girl with brass rings in her ears.

"After you, please," the bellboy said.

We rode up to my fourth-floor room. The door unlocked with a plastic card. I entered first and the bellboy followed. I sat on the bed, large enough for three adults. The carpet was olive green, a color that would not show dirt.

"If you need anything, please just ask for me. I'm Mr. Moses."

"Yes, thank you."

A tip. Of course, a tip. This was always Robert's part. I brought out a five-pound note, a fortune here, probably. When he was gone, I put my passport and Francis Aggrey's diary in the safe, and then I connected my phone and laptop to the Wi-Fi. The password was "SeguPalace." I skyped Rose.

"Mum, you're there! How is it?"

Her face was grainy. The image froze when she moved.

"It's too soon to tell," I said.

"How was your flight?"

"Good," I said.

"What did you say?"

"Good!" I shouted.

"You're breaking up," she said.

The screen went blank.

"I'm still here," I said.

"Me too."

We were silent for a moment. There was not much to say. We had just seen each other yesterday.

"What's it like?" she asked.

"I don't know yet. I saw a puppy being sold on the road. The driver said someone was going to eat it."

"That's awful. Is it safe?"

"Of course," I said, as if I had not wondered the same thing until Adrian corrected me. It was an ugly Western bias. The rest of the world was violent and unsafe, while our corner was an oasis of calm.

"When are you meeting him?" Rose asked.

"Next Monday."

"So far away."

"He's a busy man."

"What does he do again?"

"He used to work for the government."

"Well, I hope he's nice. You've traveled so far to see him," she said. "I don't know, Mum. It seems like you're running away from sorting out the divorce."

"Rose, I appreciate your concern, but you don't have to worry about your father and me."

"You've never spoken about meeting your father before. You've never even mentioned him, but suddenly you're on the other side of the world after I book you a meeting with a divorce lawyer."

The connection improved. Rose filled the screen. She was leaning close to the camera and her collarbone jutted out like a spear.

"What did you have for dinner? I think I'll order room service."

"Stop bringing up food when you want to change topic."

"I'm sorry. You're right. What I'm trying to say is I don't want you in the middle of things. You barely speak to your dad anymore."

"I had steak and chips for dinner."

"Now who's deflecting? I've been traveling for hours, Rose. I don't want to fight."

We were silent for a moment. Rose pixelated and reformed. She

was biting her lower lip. When she was younger, she would sometimes bite herself till she bled.

"You should call your dad," I said.

"Why?"

"To speak to him. He misses you."

"Maybe next week. I'll let you go. You must be tired," she said.

"I'll call you soon."

She cut the call without saying goodbye.

Robert and I disagreed on how to raise Rose. He wanted to
teach her resilience and courage and confidence and public speaking, walks in the countryside, camping, swallows and amazons.
This was all well and good, but what about race?

"What about it? he asked.

"Her mother is black."

"She'll be able to see that. And you're half white as well. I don't
want her to grow up having a chip on her shoulder."

"Pardon?"

"I don't know the politically correct way to say it," he said. "I
just want her to be free of adult cares and prejudices."

"I didn't have that choice."

"The world's different now."

I tried anyway. After all, to ignore race was to attempt to be
white, a South African friend at university once told me. I explained
to Rose that race was a social construct with real-life implications,
not to be ignored and brushed over; but to everyone who looked at
her, my daughter was white. No one would ever switch seats in the
tube because of her. No one would wonder where she was really
from. I told her about Martin Luther King and Mary Seacole and
Nefertiti, but I myself knew too little about these icons to make them
convincing heroes for her. How could I fight against the overwhelming white tide of film and television and textbooks and newspapers?

"It doesn't matter anymore, Mum. We're all the same. Nobody cares," she told me when she turned thirteen.

I opened my suitcase and hung my clothes in the wardrobe. The room was scentless, like nothing alive had ever set foot inside it. When I was done, I went to the bathroom. The mirror was large; the lighting strong. The lines around my eyes and lips seemed deeper. I looked tired.

I washed my face and dried it with a fresh towel. I changed into my pajamas and lay under the sheets. Rose was an adult. Rose must take care of herself now. I was in Bamana. I had come to my father's home.

Breakfast was a buffet with rows of warm silver trays. Water condensed when you raised a lid, dripping like sweat. I took what I recognized: sausage, mushrooms, baked beans, left-behind brown balls of *akara*, and a viscous white pap called ogi.

A chef fried eggs on demand. I placed an order and sat at a table. There was something French about the white-gloved waiters, dark-wood booths, and baguettes at the bread station swaddled in red checkered cloth. I wasn't the only solo traveler.

"Good morning."

"Morning," I said to Ken.

"May I join you?"

"Feel free."

His appetite was controlled—one sausage, a boiled egg, and a slice of toast.

"Hotel food will make you fat," he said, gazing at his sparse plate.

"So what brings you to Bamana?" I asked.

"I'm a consultant. My specialty is emerging markets, with a subspecialty in Africa. I started off in oil, but my brief now includes energy. At a push, I can advise on commodities: copper, gold, diamonds."

"Bamana has diamonds. They must keep you busy," I said. I felt mildly hostile to this Englishman who had traveled here to seek profit. It was the effect of Francis Aggrey's diary, perhaps.

"That market has been cornered for over a century. De Witt's and so on. I'm here because there are rumors of oil, just off the coast of Segu. In ten years, twenty years, cars will be running on hydrogen. Some lab rat in Geneva is going to make sure of it. But there's space for one last oil boom and Bamana may be about to get a slice of it."

"Sugar," I said.

"Pardon?"

"Please pass the sugar." He'd moved the bowl to his side of the table.

My omelette arrived, golden and plain, as I liked it.

"That looks good. I'll have that tomorrow. That's another thing with these places. The breakfast menu never changes."

He was capable of silence. We ate without talking.

"Any plans for the day?" he asked when he was done.

"I might go to the beach."

"Be careful. The currents can be quite strong."

"What about you?" I asked.

"I have a meeting at ten, which probably means two, but I'll be there on time. Keep up the side and all that."

"Which side?"

"The punctual side." He smiled at a trap avoided. He was wearing sunscreen. There were white smudges on his chin and cheeks. "Well, I'll leave you to the rest of your morning. I hope I'll see you at breakfast again."

"Perhaps," I said.

I returned to my room. From my balcony I could see the flow of traffic and pedestrians, lives intersecting on the road. The telephone rang. It was Adrian.

"So sorry. There's been a scheduling error. I'm teaching today so I won't be able to come."

"That's fine. I'll just rest. Still a bit tired from the flight. See you tomorrow, then."

"Day after. My lectures are proving surprisingly popular. You could attend one."

The irony escaped him. A white man teaching African history in Africa. It read like an entry from the pages of Francis's journal.

"We'll see," I said.

"All right. Have to run."

I looked out on the road again. The honking traveled upwards. I could go out into the city. I could walk Segu's streets alone as Francis had once walked London on his own. And yet, leaving my hotel without a guide suddenly seemed beyond me. I was used to traveling with Robert, used to his arm steering me through foreign streets, used to him speaking to strangers when we were lost. I had spent all my daring to reach Bamana and now, on this first day, I felt cautious.

Waiting for Adrian was sensible. I switched on the television. It was tuned to BBC News. I recognized the presenter. The events she read about already seemed far away. Flooding in Yorkshire. Tube strikes in London. I dozed off. When I woke up it was past noon. Lunchtime, but I wasn't yet hungry. The hotel had a pool, a gym, a sauna. I put on some sunscreen, picked up a novel, and went downstairs.

I was the only guest by the pool. I lay on a deck chair under a sunshade. It was soon clear that it was too hot to be outside, but I didn't want to go back to my room. The water sparkled, still and lifeless. My book lay unopened by my side.

A figure blocked the sun. It was Ken.

"Did you make it to the beach?" he asked.

"No. How was your meeting?"

"No show. You get used to this kind of thing over here. We've rescheduled for Friday. Any plans for today?"

"Not much," I said.

"We can still go to Bongo Beach. It's only one thirty."

"I'll go upstairs and fetch my things."

Here was the guide I was waiting for. Someone who knew the country well, although a stranger. A beach was an open space. I would be safe.

Ken called a hotel taxi. We pulled out and joined the stream of moving vehicles. It was air-conditioned, sleek, plush seating at the back. He pointed out landmarks: Liberty Square, the Parliament Building, the Central Bank. Segu in daylight felt different. In the evening it had seemed muted and mysterious. Now the sun revealed all its secrets.

The city was brutally concrete. Once in a while a tree would appear in the landscape like an alien ship stranded. Wherever there was a tree there were people in its shade, resting on benches, trading their wares. When the taxi slowed there was always someone selling something.

"Kofi Adjei," I said, pointing to a portrait held aloft by a hawker. It was my father done in oil on canvas, in a lurid, almost cartoonish style.

"Well spotted," Ken said.

We passed a line of European backpackers, walking like ants on a trail, bearing their loads and fleeing from some unknown calamity. How had they come here? They were festooned in tie-dye clothing, pilgrims on their way to where?

The taxi drove right up to the beachfront, stopping just before the gravel turned to sand. At the gate, Ken paid the admission fee of ten cowries and rented a shack with a roof, three walls, and a view. We watched the traffic: families with small children, young men on horses, racing and raising sand.

"I'll go get us something to drink. What would you like?"

"I don't have money. I haven't changed any yet."

"That's fine. It's on me."

"Thanks," I said. "Coke, please."

"I'm afraid Coca-Cola is still banned. Thrown out by Adjei."

"Why?"

"The government said they didn't pay enough taxes, but I think they refused to pay Adjei a bribe. Pepsi?"

"No, thanks. Water is fine."

I watched him walk off. His legs looked thin in the wide mouths of his shorts—camel legs, bearing up a broad chest. Not quite my type. Too reedy. He returned with drinks and food. He spread out the roasted fish and plantains on newspapers.

"This was breathing just a few hours ago."

We ate with our fingers. The fish was covered in a vinegar relish, flaking away from the bone. The plantains were charred on the outside, sweet on the inside.

"They eat like gods here," Ken said. "Even the poorest can eat like this."

As if he had overheard, a beggar approached—a young boy, barefoot, with holes in his clothes. He stood at the mouth of our shack, holding out his hands. Ken gave him some coins. I wrapped the last plantain in newspaper.

"Thanks, boss," the boy said.

"I should have said, *almost* everyone can eat like this," Ken said, when the boy was gone. "I have a son about his age."

"You miss him."

"Yes. He's with his mother. She left me for a man who travels less. A GP. You don't get more earthbound than that," he said. "What of you? Any children?"

"One. A daughter. We should go into the ocean," I said. I didn't want to talk about my family with a stranger.

My swimsuit was under my clothes, a black halter-neck one-piece. The ruching on the torso looked slimming when I bought it, but now it felt frumpy. My middle-aged vanity wanted Ken to think me attractive. I unbuttoned my shirt and slid off my shorts with my back turned.

"Don't leave your bum bag," he said. I strapped it over my shoulder.

The sun's heat was trapped in the sand. It burned underfoot. I ran to the water and waded to my knees.

"Don't go too far. The current is strong."

There were others in the ocean, also staying at its edge, facing the sun. An old woman bathed fully dressed. Her white garments ballooned around her. When the tide pulled in, her dress fell, clinging to her like a winding sheet. A boy held on to his father's leg, the water chest-deep for him. I staggered under a wave.

"Careful," Ken said. He grasped me by the inner elbow and pulled me upright.

"Thanks," I said. He held my arm for a moment longer than necessary.

"Saved your life." He was edging into flirtation.

"I am forever indebted," I said, matching his tone but pulling away.

"Seriously. People get swept out to their deaths all the time. That's why I never swim here."

There were ships on the horizon, large tankers that looked like bath toys from this distance.

"What are they bringing?" I asked.

"Shiny things for rich Bamas. Cars, televisions, sound systems."

"What else?"

"Food. Rice from India, stockfish from Norway, processed food as basic as tomato puree."

"They don't grow tomatoes here?"

"They don't preserve them."

The water got colder. The waves grew stronger. My mouth tasted of salt.

"I'm going back to the shack," I said, and he followed me. We sat facing the ocean, as if we had not just left it. A breeze blew in carrying fine bits of sand.

"Getting chilly. We should go soon. Or huddle for warmth."

He put his arm over my shoulder. I let it rest there. The weight was not unpleasant.

"So what do you think of the country so far?" he asked.

"Still trying to take it all in. I don't want to miss anything."

A seagull flew low and fast, skimming the waves. It circled and repeated the maneuver before flying off.

"What are your plans for the rest of the week?" he said.

"Sightseeing."

"And?"

"Shopping."

It was dusk now. A party had started at the far end of the beach. The boom of a bass reached us, slipped into my bloodstream.

"Let's dance," I said. I got up and pulled him to his feet. His movements were jerky but he laughed at his own inelegance. We swung between dancing apart and dancing together.

"I hope you're having a good time," he said.

"I am."

On one close orbit, he caught me by the waist and kissed me. I was flattered by this interest from a reasonable prospect of a man. I kissed him back, a fumble of lips and tongues. With one sharp tug, he unraveled the knot of my halter neck.

"People will see," I said.

"Not if we're discreet."

We moved farther into the hut. I stood with my back to him, shielding myself from view. His hand fastened to my breast, teased at my nipple, stretched it this way and that like warm toffee. The music sped up, the beat more urgent. I rubbed against his groin. It was a dance from my youth, a night out at university, simulating sex on the dance floor. I could feel the tip of Ken's arousal. He pushed forward and I pressed back, our hips moving in a circle, spinning like a top.

I dragged his hand between my legs. He stroked me with the heel of his palm, up and down the slim triangle of nylon. I felt the distant tremor of a climax.

Muffled footsteps, dulled by the sand. We froze like children in a party game.

"Would I lie to you?" The voice was behind our shack. Only a thin wall separated us. I pulled up my swimsuit.

"I said, would I lie to you? Don't make me drop this phone."

The footsteps faded.

"He's gone," Ken said, reaching for me.

"We should get back to the hotel," I said. "It's dark."

I put on my clothes and gathered my things. The mood was awkward. We didn't know each other well and we were too sober to laugh it off.

In the taxi, Ken tried to hold my hand.

"Not here," I said, tipping my head towards the driver.

Once we drove into the hotel, I opened the car door.

"I'm on the seventh floor," Ken said. "Seven hundred and two. Or I could come to yours?"

"Actually, I'm not feeling too well," I said, "but thank you for a lovely afternoon." I got out and left him with the bill.

In the elevator, I rode up to my floor with a spotless waiter. He glanced at me when I entered, our eyes meeting over silver cloches.

"Good evening, madam."

"Good evening."

In my room I undressed and showered. I was covered in sand from the back of my neck to the crevices of my thighs.

It was not how I imagined my first day in Bamana. It was the kind of thing I warned Rose about when she went traveling on her gap year. Beware of strange men in strange countries. Yet here I was, twenty-four hours into my trip, tits bared to a consultant I didn't even know.

I couldn't imagine sleeping with Ken now, climbing up to his room, clear-eyed and calm-headed, asking if he had a condom before I took off my clothes.

When I was dry and dressed, I brought out Francis Aggrey's diary from the safe to remind myself why I was here. I chose an entry at random.

I have had Sunday lunch with the Bains. I am billed for lodging alone, but Mr. Bain didn't begrudge me a few gratis slices of roast beef and potatoes. They are a close family. There was much discussion as the food was passed around. Bronwen cooked the meal, although Caryl said it was her recipe.

"Older sisters take credit for everything," Bronwen said, looking me in the face and smiling, confident with her family around her. Mr. Bain is fond of his daughters. A Segu man would feel cheated if he had no sons, but the Welsh do not seem to mind.

At breakfast the next morning, I saw Ken sitting on his own. I returned his smile but found an empty table. I remembered the film *How Stella Got Her Groove Back*: a beach holiday, a middle-aged black woman, and a young Jamaican lover who looked nothing like Ken. I snorted into my cup of tea.

After breakfast, I went to the hotel bureau de change and exchanged two hundred pounds for twenty thousand Bamanaian cowries. My father's face was on the fifty- and hundred-cowrie notes. In one image, he faced the artist with a gentle expression. In the other, he was drawn in profile, his nose almost aquiline, more Roman than it looked in real life.

I did not need anyone to show me around. I was in my father's country. I took a taxi to Oxford Street Market, which was listed in all the online tourist guides. This Oxford Street was more alive than the one in London. Stalls lined the road on both sides, stretching as far as the eye could see. Shirts, dresses, and skirts lined racks that rose into the sky, dancing on hangers, moving like flags in the breeze.

"*Obroni!*"

A man approached with a tray of sunglasses.

"*Obroni*, you need sunglass?"

"I'm not an *obroni*," I said, and walked into the market.

I paused to study the prints. I wished I had brought my sketchbook. Some were geometric: hexagons and octagons, intersecting in a dizzying manner. On others, a single motif was repeated: a fan, a lampshade, a crown. What did it mean? And the colors. Four colors on a fabric, or six, or nine. I held a few against my arm. They were made for a richer, darker hue than mine.

Everywhere I turned, I was reminded of my relative paleness. Sellers called out to me, "*Obroni, obroni, obroni,* come and see." I was as conspicuous here as I had been in my childhood.

I bought a dress, a quiet print with only three colors—blue and orange circles on a black background. I wandered until I chanced on an open-air salon.

"*Obroni,* you wan' make your hair?" the hairdresser asked. She was young and heavily pregnant.

"Okay," I said. "But not braids."

"Which style you want?"

"Corn rows."

"Sit down. I'll make it fine for you."

She sat on a high stool while I sat on the lower. Her touch was gentle when she undid my hair from its bun.

"Your hair is very thick. And long. And soft. Me, I like half-caste hair. If my baby can have hair like this, I will be so happy."

There was something in her tone that made "half-caste" almost seem a compliment. She rested my head against her thigh. She was warm, like a pebble left in the sun. She smelled of fish and smoke. Her wooden comb slid down my scalp, dividing my hair into sections. Halfway through each track, she bent forward and I felt her breath on my neck.

My mother was afraid of my hair. When she washed it, it would knot. When she brushed it, it would shed. I bit her once, after a bristle snagged on a knot and she kept pulling. Aunt Caryl read somewhere that oil was good for black hair and so, for a month, my hair was doused with vegetable oil in the mornings. There was no improvement, except that I left smears of oil on every surface I leaned against.

Some hawkers paused with their wares.

"*Obroni*, biscuit?"

"*Obroni*, lipstick?"

"*Obroni*, chewing gum?"

They stared openly at the curious specimen in front of them. I remembered those stares from walking down the street with my grandfather. A neighbor used to say, "There goes the Welshman and his coon." There was no shade for me anywhere. Not here. Not in England. I began to feel faint.

"Are you almost done?" I asked.

A few moments later, she gave me a hand mirror. My face was exposed, every single hair scraped back. My eyes looked larger, my forehead wider. She'd wound gold thread through each corn row, like seams of ore.

"You like it?"

"Yes, thank you."

I stared at my reflection. I didn't recognize myself. I looked foreign.

18

The days passed. Monday grew closer. If Adrian's schedule was free, we went around Segu, sometimes by bus, sometimes with the driver, and always with Adrian's voice providing background, history, context.

"Liberty Square, where Kofi was sworn in, 1978."

It was an Olympic-size stadium with seating on three sides. The fourth was open to the ocean, and the breeze that blew in served as a sort of air-conditioning. The design was clever.

"The euphoria of that night," Adrian said. "The place was packed. The whole country wanted to be here." I imagined the stands full of people waving flags and cheering for my father.

I didn't always mind Adrian's trivia. I liked knowing that Segu taxis were once black, but after independence, in a show of patriotism, drivers repainted them blue and white for the flag.

Other details were more obscure, for example, "Bamana has forty species of sunbird, a close relation of the hummingbird."

It was like traveling with an encyclopedia, novel at first but grating by lunchtime. Adrian had not lost any confidence. He was a white man in Britain and a white man in Bamana.

Sometimes I wanted to shake him off and attempt the city on my own again. After all, half my DNA was from here. If I were a wild animal, I would have some instinct for the place, but each time, I remembered that first trip to the market and the chorus of "*obroni*" that had rung after me with every step. With Adrian, at least, we were a pair of *obroni*.

While Adrian was teaching, I stayed in the hotel and took my meals in the French-themed restaurant. I loitered in the lobby. There was some art for sale: tourist pieces—bright paintings of village scenes, crude wooden replicas of the intricate carving I had seen in the British Museum.

I was reminded of my first exhibition, in a Hampstead gallery just off the high street. It was run by Robert's manager's wife, Martha Reuben, a tall, elegant woman who wore silk scarves to hide the wrinkles on her neck. The Reubens came to dinner. I cooked and Robert carved.

"What do you do?" Martha asked.

"I'm a housewife."

"And an artist," Robert added. I couldn't tell whether he was being supportive or whether he was trying to make me seem more exciting to his boss.

Reluctantly, the canvases were brought out. Martha insisted on buying one. It was her way, I thought, of showing gratitude for the seasoning of the lamb. The next day she called to ask how many canvases I had, could I paint more, did I want a solo exhibition?

The works didn't sell. At the opening, Martha invited a crowd that pressed into the medium space, their backs turned to the canvases, their eyes tracking the flutes of champagne drifting through the room.

Martha said my work was ahead of the market. I painted subjects cut out of newspapers and magazines. I labored over their
hands, their watches, their shoes, but instead of faces, I painted a
storm of color.

The work was too figurative for those who loved abstraction and
too abstract for the figurative crowd, and there was nothing particularly black about it, which confused another type of buyer.

Perhaps I gave up too easily. The paintings were still in my garage. I could have brought one for my father. I should have come
with a gift.

The day before our meeting, my period arrived unexpectedly,
brought on by the stress of anticipation. It was only a matter of
time before it ceased altogether. I had no mother to take me through
this last great change, not that she'd been that adept at taking me
through the first one. There'd been some mumbling about sanitary
napkins and the dangers of sexual relations without a sheath. Aunt
Caryl had filled in the details.

That night, I stayed up to read the diary. A passage from the
beginning of their affair.

> In the evenings Caryl's sister plays the flute. Her room is below
> mine and I hear the low mournful sound that is made in Segu only
> when a chief has died. The music has taken me back to my child-
> hood, the night procession of masquerades with flaming torches,
> dragging their smoke through the town until everywhere smells
> of burning. They have come from the spirit world to escort the
> chief home and the roads are emptied for them. Even the British
> officials respect this law. I used to watch from the window while

my mother lay down with her eyes shut. A woman cannot look on this sight and live.

My room faces the street and I see Bronwen when she leaves for work. Her clothes are beautifully made. I particularly like a red dress with pearl buttons running down the back.

And an entry a few pages later when things had progressed.

What kind of love is this for a girl, never to be seen walking out with her man, to be sneaking to my room at night like ours is a transaction? Yet I lie in my bed each night waiting for the sound of the door opening. I go through my lectures in a daze. I no longer visit Thomas. I saw my results and was neither pleased nor displeased by them. It is only Bronwen I think of.

Feverish as his tone was, Francis Aggrey's affair with my mother was not a grand passion. If he wanted to stay in touch, he could simply have written a letter. He had rejected my mother. There was nothing to suggest he would not reject me tomorrow. Any expectations must be tempered.

Kofi Adjei might demand proof. Adrian had warned me of this. The diary, the photograph given to my mother, even my jawline, might suggest that my story was true. But I should prepare for a DNA test. Men in my father's position were besieged by people like me, people making claims, people asking for something.

"But I don't want his money," I said.

"You're still asking for something. Your very existence demands an explanation."

I dialed Rose. She didn't pick up. I went down to the lobby. The bar was closed. The doormen had gone home.

"Is everything all right, madam?" It was the lone receptionist. She had been slumped against the front desk, but now she smiled and stood up straight.

"Yes. I just wanted to sit here for a minute."

They'd switched off the fountain. Without the water pumping you could see to the bottom of the marble basin. It was streaked with limescale.

"Are you waiting for someone, madam?"

"No."

I chose an armchair made in the Chesterfield style—stuffed leather, sunken navel buttons. The fountain came on. It spurted the colors of the Union Jack, red, white, and blue. I sat back and closed my eyes.

"Good morning, madam." It was the receptionist standing over me. "I think you'll get more rest in your room."

"What time is it?"

"Almost six a.m. Guests will be coming down soon."

"Thank you," I said. "I have an important meeting today. I was restless upstairs. Nervous, a bit."

"It will go well, madam." She beamed at me. The staff here were trained to smile.

"Thank you. Do you have children?" I asked.

"Not yet. But, please God, one day I will have some."

"Can I ask you a question?"

"Yes, madam," she said.

"Anna. That's my name."

"We are not allowed to address guests by their first names." Protocol was never far off in the Palace Hotel.

"I'm sorry. Madam is fine," I said. "I wanted to ask if it's taboo in Bamanaian culture for a man to abandon his child?"

"Are men praised for leaving their children in Europe and America?" I was pleased by the jab of sarcasm. It was the first real note she had sounded.

"No, of course not, but is there some special stigma? Let's say he doesn't want to marry the mother of the child and so he abandons them?"

She considered for a moment. Her unguarded face was serious, almost stern.

"We have a saying: no child is a bastard. Even if the father and mother are fighting, it is not the business of the child. A man must take care of his children. How are things over there?"

"The same. We call it child support."

An elevator pinged. The first guests were descending. The smile returned to the receptionist's face.

"I should go up," I said. "Thank you. I can't remember your name."

"Christina."

In my room I slept for two hours, then woke up and showered. I wore the dress specially chosen: peach cotton with cap sleeves and a fitted waist, smart but not formal. It made me look young, young enough to still need a father.

What did I want from him? What do children want from absent fathers? It was too late for any encounters with Francis Aggrey to be formative. I was too much of an adult for him to erase the confusion of my childhood. And yet, if I truly believed this, why was I here?

At 9:00 the telephone rang. It was Adrian.

"Anna, I'm sorry to disappoint you. Kofi's secretary just called. We're going to have to reschedule to next Monday. He decided, at the last minute, to honor an invitation to the African Union Summit in Addis Ababa."

"I suppose I could have followed him to Ethiopia."

Adrian and I were outside the slave fort in Cove Coast. We had driven an hour over roads crowded by dense forest. The forests were not empty, Adrian assured me. In their depths lived the Bonoma people, whose lives had not changed significantly in the past five hundred years. They were protected by UNESCO, along with Stonehenge and the Great Barrier Reef. In other words, they were doomed.

The slave fort overlooked the beach. It was a looming, solid structure, built from stone. The walls were white, the steps were decorated with balustrades, and the roof was a pleasing shade of terra-cotta. With lower walls and a garden, it could be a summer palace in Europe. There were a few cars in the car park and a bus from which tourists disembarked, clutching cameras and water bottles. They were from America, black America. Only a few were dressed in Western clothing, but all appeared to be *obroni* like me.

"The fort was built by the Portuguese," Adrian said.

"I can tell."

It cost fifteen cowries to enter and another ten to take a guided tour. Adrian bought a third for our driver, Kwesi, who had never been inside, although he knew it was popular with *obroni*. The guide was an old man. He wore a jerkin made from coarse fabric. Around his neck, an amulet hung from a leather strap.

"Welcome to Elsantos Castle. I am Bonsu, and I will be your guide for today. The castle was built in 1490 by the Portuguese. Before that, there was a village here, which was demolished to build the castle. It started off as a trading post for gold and ivory, but the Europeans soon began another trade in a priceless commodity: human beings. More than three hundred thousand Africans passed through this slave market. They were transported to the Caribbean and to the Americas."

"A few ended up in England. Olaudah Equiano, for example," Adrian whispered to me. I went to stand with the Americans. Bonsu led us up a flight of stairs. The woman climbing beside me asked, "So did you get your DNA done?"

"Sorry?"

"To trace your ancestry here."

"Oh, I already know it. My father is Bamanaian."

"Well, I traced mine. I'm only seven percent from Bamana. I'm fifteen percent from Senegal and twenty percent Nigerian, but Bamana has the best tour packages. I came with my friend Rita. She's fifty percent from here, which is really high. Oh wait, he's starting."

"These were the governor's and senior officers' quarters. As you can see, there's a nice view of the ocean, fresh breeze, nice holiday. Back then, these rooms would have been furnished luxuriously. They could come here and relax with their wives."

"There were European women here too?" an American tourist asked.

"No. They married African women."

"African women are the best. They have the best shape." It was our driver Kwesi, a patriot.

Cameras clicked around us. A Bamanaian couple dressed in matching denim took a selfie.

"Would you like me to take a picture for you?" I asked.

"Yes, please. It's my birthday today," the woman said.

"And you came to the slave fort?"

"Yeah. We thought we'd try something different."

They posed with their arms around each other. Robert and I used to pose like that, one organism with two heads.

"It's time to go to the dungeons," Bonsu said.

They were the only part of the fort that felt untouched, although this itself was an illusion. The walls and ceiling were dirty, as they would have been when the dungeons were in use, but the floors were clear of blood and there was no smell of shit. It was cool. The walls were thick stone, soundproof.

"How many people do you think were put in here?" Bonsu asked.

"Two hundred."

"Three hundred."

"Five hundred."

"Sounds like an auction."

"One thousand human beings," Bonsu said. "They were pressed close like cargo, like bales of cotton. People could stay here for months before they were transported."

"How did they get here?"

"The tribes farther inland, when they went to war against each other, they brought their captives here and sold them for guns, or beads, or Manchester cotton."

"So Africans sold other Africans."

Bonsu cleared his throat. "They weren't Africans then. They were Fanti, Ashanti, Bambara, Mandingo, foreigners to one another. Let's go to the church."

It had been deconsecrated now. The cross was gone but not the empty pews. Bonsu let us wander around the courtyard where bodies were haggled over. How much would I have cost? I was flat-footed and not very fertile, but I still had all my teeth. Finally, Bonsu gathered us at a door carved out of the perimeter wall. It led to the beach.

"We will end by walking through the door of no return. Slaves linked in chains passed in single file through this door to where boats were waiting on the beach to take them to the ships that would carry them away from Africa forever. After you crossed this point, there was no going back."

He walked through and we followed in single file. When it was my turn, scenes from *Roots* and *Amistad* filled my mind. The Bamanaian couple were the last to pass. They took pictures and struck goofy, inappropriate poses.

On the beach, the Americans grew quiet. A man with a sonorous voice announced, "We would like to sing a few songs for our ancestors whose spirits are here with us today. We thank them for their courage and their will to survive so we could one day come back home. You are all welcome to join us."

They sang "Swing Low, Sweet Chariot," "By and By," and Boney M.'s "Rivers of Babylon" slowed down to a dirge. Some of them began to cry. I left then and walked towards the ocean. The couple were running in the shallows. Our ancestors had not been sold.

I sat on the sand and brought out my sketchbook. I drew across a double page, the slave fort on the left leaf, the beach on the right. The cluster of Americans, singing and crying. The couple wading in the water and laughing. A lone figure with a sketchbook, drawn in the crevice where the pages met, so she would disappear into the binding.

I was too working-class for art school. Ms. Rendell encouraged me to go. I had a talent, she said, for the human figure, an eye for color, a skill with draftsmanship, but what were these when leveled against the need to support myself? "Try architecture, then," she said. "It's a second choice for artists."

The ocean was calming. I felt settled, the most at ease I had been in Bamana. The heat, the smells, the jostling of Segu, and the waiting to meet Francis Aggrey had produced an agitation that dissipated on this shore, dispelled maybe by the suffering that had occurred here, much greater than mine.

The outcome of my journey was uncertain. My father might postpone our meeting again. I might come this far and never meet him. I would be disappointed, but the trip would not be a waste. I had seen other things: the markets of Segu, the slave fort of El Santos, and the overconfidence of white men in an African country.

"That's good." It was Adrian standing over me. I closed my sketchbook.

"I'm ready to go," I said, standing up and dusting the sand from my clothes.

"What did you think of it?" I asked Kwesi, our driver, when we got back to the car park.

"What I thought?"

"Yes."

"It's a very strong building. Good place for military defense."

"But what of the slaves?"

"That's in the past. It's bad, but it's in the past."

19

My father lived in a bungalow on a street with many mansions. The area was called the Peak, a gently sloping neighborhood from which you could see the city spread out like a map. Some portions of Segu were laid out in straight lines. Others defied the imposition of a grid and grew to some more complex, organic pattern. There was a checkpoint on his road, manned by an officer with a rifle and no shade from the sun.

"Good morning. We're here to see Citizen. My name is Professor Adrian Bennett."

The officer ticked a name on his clipboard and waved us through. The perimeter walls were low, low enough to see the one-story house and the garden that surrounded it. It was a prize garden, landscaped with care. Unlike the mansions on either side, no barbed wire garlanded the walls. Adrian pressed the buzzer. A voice spoke out of the intercom.

"Good morning. Your name, please."

"Adrian Bennett."

"Please push the side gate and walk to the house. President Adjei will welcome you himself."

We paused when we entered the compound. The gardener sprinkling the grass looked up and raised a hand in greeting.

"I suppose we just go to the house like she said," Adrian said.

It was a bungalow built in the colonial style, with low eaves and long windows. The entire house stood on stilts, a whole foot above the ground, enough space for a body to crawl under. A man dressed in white was waiting on the veranda. White trousers, white shirt, and thick silver hair that grew close to his scalp. He was tall and upright, but something in his posture was beginning to bend.

"My old friend, welcome."

He embraced Adrian.

"And who is this? Your beautiful wife?"

"A good friend of mine. I mentioned to your assistant."

"Of course. And what is your name?"

"Anna Bain."

"Pleasure to meet you, Anna Bain."

The surname meant nothing to him. We shook hands. I touched my father for the first time.

"This is for you," I said. I handed him the bottle of wine I bought in the hotel gift shop.

"Thank you. Very kind. Come. Our breakfast is getting cold. And we have many years to catch up on."

His accent was upper-class English, a BBC announcer from a certain era. He walked like a soldier, with his hands clasped behind his back. He led us down a corridor, past photographs of famous men: Muhammad Ali, Bob Marley, a U.S. president, Jimmy Carter perhaps, all pictured with my father. In the dining room there were three places. He sat at the head of the table, and Adrian and I sat on either side.

"Welcome to this humble repast. Anna, I hope you don't have any food allergies. They're in vogue these days. My grandson tells me he cannot eat wheat or dairy."

He clapped, and two servants appeared bearing covered dishes. They were the only extravagance. The dining table was simple, unvarnished wood, and the dishes and cutlery were plain.

"Adrian, forgive me. I didn't ask if you have any allergies because I know you eat anything. Do you remember when I served intestines at a state banquet?"

"Yes, the French ambassador was quite upset."

"I wrote him a letter apologizing that while he had no taste for intestines, I also had no taste for frogs. Don't worry," he said, turning to me, "there will be no intestines served at breakfast this morning . . . although they are a national delicacy. You must try them before you leave."

I let a boiled egg and a slice of toast be put on my plate, and listened while Adrian and my father spoke. Under the table, my hands smoothed my dress over my knees until my palms grew warm with friction.

"So how was the African Union Summit?" Adrian asked.

"Same as always. No one is really willing to unite. The Nigerians were throwing their weight around, of course. Oil prices are high this year and so their delegates were feeling particularly buoyant. There's one fellow I had my eye on, president of Rwanda—I forget his name, but he'll make something of that country yet."

"I hear he's a dictator," Adrian said.

"Perspective is everything. I didn't get too involved. One only goes to these things as an elder now, to play the Mandela as it were, may he rest in peace. It's the greatest of secular miracles how that man was transformed from a terrorist to a Messiah. And you? Why has it taken you so long to return to Bamana? You should have written another book about us. What was the first one called again?"

"*Bamana: One Hundred Days*," Adrian said.

"Yes, of course. It was very popular here when it came out. It did a wonderful job of recording our achievements for the world. You're too old to go around on a motorcycle, but maybe you could hire a car. I might even come with you this time."

"You'd be recognized," Adrian said.

"I suppose you're right. Even in the rural areas my image is well known. It can be a burden sometimes. How is the family? I have six grandchildren. It's hard to believe. It seems like it was only yesterday I was fighting for Bamana's independence."

There was no opening for me in their conversation. My father posed questions and then answered them. He asked for an opinion and then gave it. He did not eat much. Sometimes he would lift his spoon and return it to his bowl of porridge without it touching his lips.

"So what brings you to Bamana?" he said, turning to me. I felt the brunt of his attention bearing down on me. I clasped my hands to still them.

"I came to see you."

"I'm flattered. What do you do?"

"I studied architecture."

"A noble profession. This area, the Peak, was once white men's quarters. This very bungalow was the home of the chief secretary to the governor. He left his guns behind. In fact, this whole neighborhood used to be full of houses like this one, but most of them have been torn down. They're too small for a certain kind of Bamanaian taste. So how may I help you?"

I glanced at Adrian. He nodded.

"There is a family connection between us. You knew my mother when you were a student in London," I said.

"Is that so? And what was her name?"

"Bronwen Bain. Is it familiar to you?"

I watched closely for a reaction. My father gave none. His face remained as still as a wooden carving.

"Go on with your story," he said.

"My mother died earlier this year and I found your journal when I went through her things. You left it in her keeping. The entries are mostly about your life as a student, but you also wrote about your relationship with her. She fell pregnant after you'd gone."

"After?"

"I mean she found out she was pregnant after you'd gone. She was already pregnant when you were there, because the child was yours. The child was me."

"What is this, Adrian?"

"It seems an unlikely story, Francis—"

"Kofi."

"I'm sorry. It seems an unlikely story, but Anna contacted me in Edinburgh saying she had a family connection to you. She brought the diary to me, I read it, and the facts are authentic. She is Bronwen Bain's daughter."

"Where is this diary that I allegedly wrote?"

"It's here."

I gave it to him. The servants returned to clear away our dishes. They walked with their backs bent. They did not straighten, even after they had lifted the plates from in front of us. When my father finally spoke, he addressed Adrian.

"I don't know how this fell into her hands. It has obviously helped her concoct this ridiculous story. I want the two of you out of my house. I'm disappointed in you, Adrian."

"What did you want me to say? 'Hi, Kofi's secretary. I'd like to see him. I'm coming with his daughter he's never met.'"

"I know all my children."

"If you'll just let me explain," I said. "My mother never spoke about you or else I would have found you sooner. All she said was that you'd gone back to Bamana and the two of you had lost touch. The only thing I had was your name: Francis Aggrey. I don't want anything from you. I'm comfortable in England, but I am your daughter."

"I am almost sorry to see her in distress over what is a complete fabrication. I cannot help her. Only a psychiatrist can do that. This meeting is at an end."

He stood up with the diary.

"This is my property."

"That's not fair, Kofi. You gave it to her mother."

"Not to let it fall into the hands of some lunatic. I have entertained this long enough. Get out of my house. Either you go willingly or I will have someone escort you."

My mother knew when she hid his diary that there would be no father waiting for me in Bamana. We walked down the corridor on our own this time, past the famous faces, past a playful Muhammad Ali with his fist clenched.

Outside, the gardener was pruning. He raised a hand again in salute.

"You mustn't take it personally. I told you Francis has changed completely from the man in that diary."

"I can take it any way I like," I said, but he was not listening.

"I wish I had photographs. Such a historical find. Now he's got his hands on that diary, he'll probably burn it and erase all evidence that he was ever a human being. Did you manage to—"

"Don't. Please."

Adrian had tried to warn me, had tried to shield me from disappointment, but here it was anyway, crouched like a small, dense animal on my chest.

Meanwhile, Segu continued, immune to my own personal dramas. A young man whizzed past on roller skates, dodging traffic, skimming through the gaps between cars. I had had an hour with my father, perhaps all the time I would ever have, and I had squandered it.

When I got back to my room I went to the bathroom and stood over the toilet. The egg from Kofi's house rushed into the bowl followed by clear, thick spit. When I was done, I brushed my teeth and confronted my reflection. My hair had grown out of its corn rows. I was a disheveled middle-aged woman, too old to be Kofi's child. I undid the weaving and pulled out the gold threads. I splashed cold water on my face. I cried.

20

I ordered my meals to my room and piled the plates by the door. I watched television, Bamanaian television. The films were poor quality, rich drama. Sons duping fathers. Wives poisoning rivals. When room service knocked to clean, I went downstairs to the gym. It was empty most of the time. There were mirrors on the walls and posters of bodies to aspire to. I rode a stationary bike until my face was wet.

My anger arrived two days after our meeting, like thunder lagging behind lightening. How dare Kofi dismiss me without even asking for proof? I should have demanded a DNA test. It was the least he owed my family, the Bains who housed him in London when no one else would.

I chanced on a wedding reception in the hotel's banqueting suite. I stood by the doors and watched the guests come and go. The women were dressed like celebrities—feathers stitched to bodices, headdresses that added a foot to their height, fabric trains that dragged behind them, sweeping up dust. Far away, so far away that there were screens to help you see them, were the bride and groom on a dais, two small figures on a cake. The bride's dress overflowed the bounds of her throne, like foam rising out of a glass. On the throne next to her, the groom sat with his legs crossed. They held hands across the armrests and looked out into the crowd.

They were young and in love, but how long before the tinsel faded? I felt like the wicked fairy godmother, arrived to cast gloom. An usher approached with a clipboard.

"Bride side or groom side?" she asked.

"Neither. I'm a guest at the hotel."

"Please, ma, this is a private event."

I ignored Adrian's calls. I preferred to be alone. Rose phoned to ask about the meeting. I did not want to admit what a failure it had been. I had come to Bamana despite her misgivings, and now she was proved right.

"It went well," I said.

"It did? I was worried he didn't want to meet you after he postponed. Did you tell him about me?"

"Didn't get the chance."

"What did you talk about?"

"He talked about himself mostly. He's old."

There was no need to tell her who Kofi really was. I would never be a part of his life and he would never be part of mine. Once I returned to England the incident would be forgotten.

"Did you get a picture at least?" she asked.

"Not even that."

"That sucks. I'll be glad to have you back, though. Should I book another meeting with Anna?"

I was beginning to understand that the divorce was more for

Rose's closure than mine. Her single-mindedness verged on mania. At first, I interpreted her refusal to speak to Robert as her taking my side, but it was only her way of punishing him. She was like an ex-believer. She might turn on her old faith, but she was in no search of a replacement.

"Thanks," I said. "But not yet."

On my last afternoon in Segu I left the hotel for a walk. Kofi was not the only thing to see in Bamana. The Palace Hotel was on a road lined with glass buildings. If you kept your eye above street level, you could be in any financial capital in the world.

"*Obroni!*"

It was a coconut seller, late in the day, and his wagon was full. I bought a coconut for two cowries and he split it open with one knife blow. The water was cool, a balance of sweet and salt. I bought a second and a third.

I took a left turn and declined the wares of a mango seller. I remembered the empty streets in Kofi's neighborhood—no hawkers, no market stalls. That whole area had been cleared as thoroughly as his garden. I did not fit into the story of his life and he did not fit into mine.

As I moved farther away from my hotel, businesses grew more modest and glass was used more sparingly, for windows, not walls. There was no pavement and the other pedestrians walked close. They brushed against me. Their skin touched mine.

I walked until I reached a church. There was no cross, no dome, but a billboard advertised its name: TABERNACLE OF LIGHT. Like the shops, it had a logo, a flaming torch in a green circle. Music reached the street through the open windows, a soprano on a microphone, cymbals.

"Jesus is Lord, my sister," said a stranger, trying to enter the building.

"Pardon me," I said. "I'm in your way."

"You're not going inside? We have a prayer meeting." His gripped his Bible by the spine, holding it like a clutch bag.

"Sorry. I have other plans."

"There is no plan more important than salvation."

I turned from the evangelist and walked back to the hotel. The lobby was full of suits. Adrian was distinct in that crowd, the only one whose elbows were visible. His limbs were tanned. His neck and face were closer to their Edinburgh hue.

"Anna! You've ignored my phone calls." It was the tone perhaps he used with erring students, confronting them with their wrongdoing.

"I'm sorry," I said.

"I hope you don't feel the whole trip was wasted."

"No. Of course not." I didn't need one last lecture.

"Excuse me, Ms. Graham." It was the receptionist. Her face was familiar.

"Claire?"

"Christina. Please, there is a man here to see you. He said I should tell you that he's from your father and the message is urgent."

"Let him come."

The man was looking in our direction, but he made a show of waiting for Christina to walk back to him.

"How does he know where I'm staying?" I asked Adrian.

"He has the resources. He might ask us to sign something. A nondisclosure contract saying we won't repeat the contents of the diary, for example," he said.

"And if we won't sign?"

"We're in his country."

Christina returned with the stranger, who was wearing an expensive suit. In another set of clothes, he would have been found out as being fat. His silk tie was cut large. It glistened like a cow's tongue. He bowed to Adrian and then me.

"Good evening, ma. I'm Sule, and Sir Kofi sent me to meet you. He would like to speak to you."

"Where is he?"

"I'll call him now," he said. "Please, can we go somewhere quiet?"

I took them to the gym. There was a lone runner going uphill on the treadmill. He did not look up when we entered. I filled a paper cup with water. Sule dialed my father.

"Anna, I would like you to meet with you again." Kofi's voice was deeper on the phone.

"I'm leaving tomorrow."

"I would like you to stay."

"Even if I wanted to, my visa expires tomorrow."

"I can take care of that."

"What about Adrian?"

"The invitation is for you," Kofi said. "I am not good at speaking over the phone. If you choose to stay, my aide will make the necessary arrangements. If not, thank you for traveling to see me. Let me talk to Sule."

Sule left the gym. The man on the treadmill had reached the end of his run. When he got off the machine, his first steps were unsure. His feet faltered on steady ground. I sat down on a pink exercise ball. I had been standing for almost an hour. A flush of heat rose through me. I was perspiring under my clothes.

"What did he say?" Adrian asked.

"He wants me to stay."

"I wouldn't advise it. Not after your last meeting."

"It was a shock to spring on an old man," I said. "We could have arranged things better."

"Are you considering this?"

"Yes."

I hadn't come this far to meet Kofi only once.

"You will be putting yourself completely in his power. Kofi is no longer president, but so much in this country still rises and falls on his whims."

"I can leave anytime I want. I have a British passport."

"You don't understand this place, Anna. You think things operate by the rules you're used to, but they don't."

"I want to try and understand things for myself," I said. "Terrible as our first meeting was, Kofi is my father. It may be my only chance to know him. He's old and I live so far away. Wouldn't you stay?"

He hesitated. "Yes, but I've always been too curious for my own good."

I walked Adrian to the hotel entrance. He had been my guide these past weeks, both knowledgeable and pedantic, enthusiastic and grating. It was time for us to part.

"You won't reconsider?" he said.

"No. You're not going to change my mind. Have a safe flight. I'll see you in Edinburgh."

Sule was waiting by the front desk.

"I've extended your stay by two weeks," he said.

"That's too long."

"Those were Sir Kofi's instructions."

"Well, you can tell him I'm only staying four more nights and that's what I'll pay for now."

"It's been taken care of already," he said. "I'll help with your bags."

"What for?"

"Your room is not available after tomorrow. I had you moved."

"No, thank you. I like my room," I said.

"Please, ma," Christina interrupted, "You will like this one better."

It was a suite on the eighth floor, partitioned by double doors into bedroom and living areas. There was a Jacuzzi on the balcony, freshly cut flowers in a vase, and an ocean view.

"Please, you are a guest of Sir Kofi. Anything you want in the hotel is on his tab."

"Does he own it?" I asked.

"I do not know what Sir owns or doesn't own." It was like talking to a wall painted in neutral colors, cream or dull white. "I will need your passport for the visa extension."

"Sorry, I can't give you that," I said.

Downstairs, he had seemed a man in his thirties. Now I noticed the grey at his temples.

"How long have you worked for my father?"

"I do not count the years, but it is a long time," he said. "I will come tomorrow morning after breakfast. Good night, ma."

He bowed and left me with the minibar. I ate some peanuts and opened a bottle of wine. I sent Rose an e-mail about the change in plans, something about giving my father a second chance, then turned on the 60-inch TV and watched an episode of a Bamanaian talk show. The host had a gap in her teeth and a way of leaning forward when she asked a question. The topic was domestic violence. One after the other the guests trooped on: victim, perpetrator, psychologist, and at the end, all three on the couch, all issues resolved.

21

I did not see Kofi for another three days, by which time I had
become a Bamanaian citizen. To extend my Bamanaian visa, I
would have needed to submit my British passport for processing,
a risk I was not comfortable with. What if it got lost in a maze of
Bamanaian bureaucracy? Or what if Kofi just refused to give it back
to me? I remembered Adrian's vague warnings. I had to be careful.

Sule made all the arrangements. He drove me to an office where
I filled out a form, and my photograph and fingerprints were taken.
The next day he returned with the blue booklet. My new passport
was one of the weakest in the world. There were only forty countries
I could visit without a visa.

I took to walking in an ever-widening radius around the hotel. I no longer noticed the calls of "*obroni.*" Sometimes strangers
touched me deliberately, often men but not always in a sexual manner. There was an innocent curiosity to the hands that sought mine,
that brushed against my elbows and arms. I was curious about them,
too—what they ate, how they ate, eschewing cutlery, sampling the

food first with their fingers, licking their nails clean. At the hotel, our meals were soiled by the taste of metal.

On Sunday I joined the stream of people flowing into the Tabernacle of Light. I wanted to see what a church in Bamana was like. The older women wore blouses that sparkled with sequins. Their head ties stood straight like sails full of wind, volumes of fabric wound around their waists, a double knot the only thing standing between them and nakedness. The younger women wore Western dress and looked vulnerable in their polyester and flimsy cotton. No ballast. No bulk. You could trace the lines of their forms. Ushers handed us envelopes by the door. The envelopes were worn and the glue underneath the flap had dried up.

The focus of the hall was the glass pulpit on the stage. The choir began singing soon after I arrived and went on for almost an hour. The music was percussion-heavy, simple tunes, lyrics that repeated themselves in an endless chanting loop.

The dancing spilled out into the aisles until the building seemed to be swaying. At some secret command, everyone raised their chairs above their heads. The white plastic chairs became part of the dance. The experts twirled them. The daring flung and caught them. From the air, it would look like the foam of a great cresting wave. What did it mean?

When the singing stopped, they put down their chairs and the prayers began. They prayed out loud. The feeling was that of a stadium, of roaring voices desperate for a goal. The woman on my right wanted a child. The man on my left needed a promotion.

"Promotion! Promotion! Father, God, promotion!" The leather on his shoes was cracked.

For all their volume, the prayers seemed to depress the congregation. When they sat down they seemed spent, their manner subdued. The sermon buoyed them up again until they were whooping, clapping, waving their hands at the man behind the pulpit. Then the worn envelopes were brought out for the offering. Cane baskets were passed around. More dancing. I left at this point. It was different from Katherine's church in England but also the same. They all believed in miracles. Outside, the busy road seemed quiet.

My wanderings were clichéd. I was the traveler desperate for an authentic experience, an event that would turn me from an outsider to an insider, a door that I could step through and become Bamanaian. And even as I roamed the streets of Segu, I knew no such doors existed.

On the evening Kofi and I are scheduled to meet, I wear my dress from the market. My skin is brown and the bright pattern is flattering. Sule drives me to his house.

"This is not the place," I say. "He lives in a bungalow."

"That was one of Sir Kofi's houses. This is another."

This house is a more fitting mansion, square and obvious, with small windows on the ground floor, all barred with security grilles. A Bamanaian flag hangs limply from the roof.

Kofi is waiting in the library. He is conscious of setting, of how he contrasts with his background. At the bungalow, he seemed relatively frugal and humble. Now, in this library, he has chosen to appear wealthy and venerable. The shelves are dark wood and the light fittings are bronze, polished to reflect the glow. A mural of Adam and Eve adorns one wall, the couple drawn life-size and nude, the vines from Eden winding up their jet-black legs and through their halo afros. Kofi is sitting with his back to the door. He waits a moment before he rises to greet us. He is dressed in navy today.

"Leave us, Sule. *Akwaaba*, Anna. Shall I pour you some red wine?"

"Water is fine, thank you," I say.

"Are you teetotal?"

"No, I just don't feel like drinking tonight." I feel bold. I have decided to bypass Kofi and speak directly to Francis. Kofi is a former president and a stranger, but Francis I have studied. Francis, I know well.

"Of course," he says, and puts down the uncorked bottle. "Please have a seat." He seems wrong-footed by my directness.

I sit opposite him in an armchair with my hands crossed on my lap. There is a low table between us on which he sets my glass of water.

"Well, here we are. For a man my age to discover a daughter is a big shock. You were born the year after I left London, which would have made me twenty-six. A father at twenty-six and I didn't know."

His tone is affable, generous, like our last disastrous meeting never occurred.

"Why have you chosen to believe me?" I ask.

"I have certain means of discovering the truth."

"What means?"

He weighs whether to speak.

"You drank from a glass when we last met. You used cutlery," he says.

I am not surprised, even though I did not expect such subterfuge.

"You could just have told me you wanted a paternity test," I say.

"It is done. What does it matter? I am your father, you are my child. We are reunited."

Reunited: a pleasant gloss on this situation.

"My mother thought you would write," I say. There are things I must know before I return to London. I will not miss my chance a second time.

"Come now. A postal service was not readily available to guerrilla fighters."

180

"You saw Thomas Phiri in London after you became prime minister."

He smiles at the mention of his old friend.

"You know my good friend Thomas? How is he?"

"He died. I met his wife, Blessing," I say.

"I remember her. She did not like me much. A woman does not like anyone to be too close to her husband. That is a shame about Thomas's death. He was a good friend to me. You should have seen us in those days, two fine men about town."

He is sliding into more comfortable memories.

"My mother waited for you," I say, pulling him back.

"I didn't know she was pregnant."

"What would you have done differently?"

It is a childish question, but I am not grown up, only older. Little Anna is the kernel; big Anna is mere flesh, easily bruised, easily pared away.

"I would not have let any child of mine be raised in that savage country where black men were treated like animals. I mean, I was spat at in public. On more than one occasion."

"You told her you would come back," I say, refusing to understand or absolve him.

"I loved your mother very dearly. She made me feel like a man, simply because she looked up to me. You can't know what it was for a white woman to admire a black man in that time, not lust after him, nor treat him as a pet."

"You make her sound like a salve for your ego."

"Not that. She was a balm to my heart."

I suddenly feel sorry for Kofi Adjei. He is an old man. He has his own stone, Francis Aggrey, who would not recognize the strange fruit that has grown around him. Kofi does not fill up his armchair as Francis once would have. He is not yet frail, but he will soon be.

"I could not return to that country as an ordinary black man," he says, finally. "When I visited England as a prime minister, on the surface it appeared a different country from my student days. But, of course, it was the same, only that my new status shielded me. I would have liked for you to have that shield, Anna. Believe me."

He is a politician, trained to convince. Yet, despite myself, I am moved by his words.

"Come," he says. "Let us go outside."

Sliding doors open into a well-lit garden. Flowering bushes line the gravel path. The air is lush with fragrance. A bird startles, rising out of a tree in a rustle of wings and leaves.

"We didn't meet here the first time," I say.

"The bungalow is where I conduct my business affairs. When I first became prime minister, it was my home, but my family outgrew it. I have four children, five including you. The architects of those houses did not expect colonial officials to keep families. Wives, perhaps, but not children."

We stop to let a peacock strut past, cawing for its mate.

"I was sorry to hear of the death of your mother," he says. "When we were in the bush fighting, I often thought back to those London days. They were like a dream. She was very important to me."

Kofi's steps make no sound on the grass. He walks like a creature hunting.

"There was a man in my first cabinet—Jim Hastings. He married a white wife, met her in London and brought her back after his studies. The other African wives never took to her. They were like chimpanzees, ostracizing the stranger. Once, at a dinner party, she spoke sharply to a servant. Of course, all the cabinet wives did the same in their own homes, but it became a racial incident. We all had fathers and uncles who had been boy to some white madam."

"My mother wasn't like that."

"I was three years working and fighting and another five in a jail cell. I couldn't expect a young woman like her to wait."

"She never married. It's not so easy with a black child."

He ignores this. "What of you? Do you have a family?"

"I have a daughter," I say.

"Which means I also have another grandchild. May I see a photograph?"

I show him a picture of Rose on my phone.

"She is white?"

"Her father is white."

"She has your mother's eyes."

"Yes."

"Tell me about your childhood."

We walk in slow laps around the garden, Kofi's stride matching mine.

"I grew up in Grandpa Owen's house. The same one you lodged in. There was always a 'paying guest,' as he called it, in that top room—to help with bills. But we only took on women. No men."

"Because of me?"

"I don't know. Perhaps. Aunt Caryl would visit often. My mother worked as a sales assistant. Grandpa Owen was retired and could watch me after school, teach me a few Welsh phrases. Things were fine until he died when I was eight. We couldn't keep up with the rent without his pension. We moved into council housing," I say, passing over the year we lived with Aunt Caryl when she and my mother argued over her "unsuitable callers."

"And what was that like?" Kofi asks.

"It wasn't terrible. I had enough to eat. The heating worked most of the time. There were a few African families on our block. They showed me how to manage my hair. And then I got into grammar school. That's when the great drift began."

"What do you mean?"

"From my mother. I traveled out of her life, went on to university, went to places she'd never dreamed of, and I saw a different way of being. I joined the Afro-Caribbean Society at university."

"Sounds like the African Student Union of my days."

"Yes, but less politics. We did some marches around Free Mandela, but we really were there for a good time, potluck parties and so on. They used to make fun of me. Anna White. That's what they called me."

"But you are not white."

"Yes, but they said I talked like a white person, thought like one, and, worst of all, I danced white." Ostracize the stranger. The memory still stings.

Whenever the path narrows Kofi gestures for me to go first. Perhaps these were the manners my mother had fallen in love with.

"What did you study?" he asks

"Architecture. I worked for a year, met my husband in that time, and then never really finished. I didn't do the masters. Tried to be an artist for a while. That didn't work either."

"One of my daughters is an artist. Benita. Her work is popular in Sweden."

"Well, one of us succeeded," I say. "You don't need to tell me about your childhood. I've read about it."

His face is a study in neutrality.

"You must have read other things, other less-flattering things."

"I have."

"Then you must remember that there are two sides to every story," he says. "Thank you for returning the diary. It has been interesting to be reacquainted with my young self. Much has changed. Much has remained the same."

"I didn't think I'd ever get the chance to meet you when I read it. I didn't even know you were alive," I say.

"Would you have abstained, if you knew? To respect my privacy?"

I think for a moment. "No," I say.

"Neither would I."

We pause outside the sliding doors that lead into the living room. We have spoken with frankness, a frankness I never had with my mother, my daughter, not even with Robert. Kofi knows what it is like to be an ordinary black person in England. We are akin in that regard.

"It's time for you to be getting back to your hotel. I trust the suite is to your comfort," he says.

"Yes, thank you. Could I have the diary back, please? It was your gift to my mother."

"I meant the gift to be temporary. But soon, perhaps, when I finish reading it."

The drive back to the Palace Hotel was short. In my room I ordered a meal of rice, chicken, salad, and chocolate cake. When it arrived I had a small feast.

22

My phone rang at five o'clock the next morning.

"Good morning, Anna. I'm visiting my country home for a few days. Would you care to join me?"

"Kofi?"

"Yes. Your father. I will be leaving in two hours. Will you join me?"

"I don't know," I said. "Where is it?"

"Gbadolite."

"Is that far?"

"It depends how you travel."

"How would we be traveling?" I asked.

"By plane. Fastest way to get to Gbadolite. Nine hours by road otherwise."

"You have a plane?"

"Bamana has a plane. Come now, make a decision."

This was why I was here. To spend time with Kofi. "I'll come," I said.

"Excellent. Sule will pick you up at seven thirty. Goodbye."

The airstrip was twenty minutes outside Segu. Kofi was waiting on the tarmac beside a plane with a pointed snout and a tail that branched off into two metal fins. The tips of the wings curved upwards. The twin engines were humming.

"Welcome, Anna." He grasped my shoulders and pressed his cheek to mine.

Inside was spacious. Even Kofi could stand upright. On one side was a row of armchairs. On the other was a single leather sofa. An air hostess in a red-and-blue uniform welcomed us with a platter of cut fruit. The air was misted with lavender.

"Good morning, Sir Kofi." She bobbed a curtsy.

"Good morning." She curtsied to me, too.

No one knew where I was. No one needed to know, except Rose, and even then, she depended on me for nothing. My decisions were mine. Reckless or not, only I would bear the consequences. My British passport was zipped into a side compartment in my bag. It was my talisman. In the Name of Her Majesty, allow the bearer to pass freely.

"Would you like something to drink, madam?" The air hostess's lipstick matched her skirt.

"Yes, please. Some water."

Sule took the armchair at the back of the plane, while I sat behind the pilot's closed door. Kofi lay on the sofa. If I looked back, I could see the soles of his feet. I was curious about him, as scientists are curious about new species they discover. I wanted to observe him in detail, to take notes on my findings. Once I had buckled my seat belt, the plane sped down the runway and rose into the sky. It was a cloudy day and the city was obscured.

I'd bought a magazine from the hotel shop. The woman on the front was larger and darker than your average European cover girl.

She was not a model or, if she was, she was modeling to a standard I had never seen. Her pose was sassy, obvious almost, with the hand on the hip and the bold stare. I couldn't tell her age, but she was older than Rose when she went for her first casting.

At fifteen a modeling agent had spotted her outside a McDonald's, a hunter drawn to prey. She was almost as tall as Robert by then, with an erect, striding gait from lacrosse and netball. She wanted to do it. I was skeptical of a profession that depended solely on looks but Robert didn't see the harm. Professional head shots were arranged, with her hair ironed flat and her eyes surly for the camera.

I went with her on castings and waited outside with other mothers of minors. She got to the final round for a big fashion house and came out of the casting in tears. One of the girls, a pale English rose who would eventually be booked and feature in *Vogue* three months later, had pointed out the muscles in Rose's calves. "Her legs are nigger big," she said. Rose quit modeling after that. Then a year later she quit food.

Were Robert and I to blame? All the advice we received said no. It was the culture and its harsh focus on female bodies, not parents who dieted or didn't diet, not mothers who were strict or lax with food.

"But we let her go on that casting," I said to Robert on one night of tearful recrimination. He replied that there were other girls in her year who had never been on a casting, yet they had also stopped eating. It was scant consolation.

The plane juddered and swung to the left. My glass rattled in its cup holder.

"Don't be afraid. The winds are strong this time of year," Kofi said.

"I thought you were asleep."

"The flight is short. We'll be landing soon."

Our descent was rapid, and I felt the pressure in my ears. When we broke through the clouds, Kofi pointed out Gbadolite. It was cut out of the forest in the shape of a key. There were buildings scattered along the long central road. The plane circled twice before we landed.

"Welcome to Gbadolite," the air hostess said over the PA system.

Kofi and I sat in a golf cart. He was driving. There were no cars in Gbadolite, or if there were, they were tucked away in an underground garage. Ours was not the only golf cart. There were families, couples, even some solo travelers who had come to see the theme park that Kofi had built in the middle of the forest. They could choose from museums, a television studio, a cinema, a zoo, a water park, and a cable car ride. We were driving to the zoo.

"Our collection of animals is one of the biggest in Africa. We have the only tiger in West Africa."

"Is he happy?"

"A she. We're trying to get her a mate from a zoo in Beijing. Of course, we could just mate her with one of the lions and create something called a liger."

When passengers in the other golf carts spotted Kofi, they beeped and waved, a few bowed in their seats. There were camera flashes. He lifted one hand in acknowledgment; the other remained steady on the wheel. We did not stop until we reached the zoo. It was empty of visitors and the keepers were standing by the entrance in their overalls. The females curtsied. The males bowed.

Kofi was still a powerful man, that much was obvious, but he did not seem dangerous, as Adrian had warned. Kofi seemed like these animals in their cages: once wild, now domesticated.

We went to the giraffes first. Their necks rose into the air like industrial cranes. Fresh leaves were brought but they showed no interest in our offerings. A keeper ran a stick along the bars but they ignored the noise. Finally, the keeper jumped over the bars and herded them to us with stamping and clapping. Their tongues when they emerged were thick and black, a shock buried in their pretty heads.

"They're beautiful," I said.

The tiger sat alone under a tree, marooned in her sunken pen. She looked up briefly and then looked away. The hippos remained submerged. The flamingos had a pond to wade in, their legs sticking out of the water like pink straws.

"Do you want to watch the feeding of the crocodiles?" Kofi asked.

"What do they eat?"

"Chickens, mostly."

"Alive?"

"Yes. They prefer a kill."

"I don't think I can watch."

"It happens very fast."

A water habitat had been built for them. They sunned themselves on the bank, merging into the brown of their background like curious rock formations. The chickens were lowered in a cage. A few feet from the ground, the cage floor slid open and the birds tumbled out, battery chickens, uniform white feathers, plump from animal feed. They strutted in a loose circle, flapping and pecking the ground. They seemed unaware of the predators close by. Their instincts had been deadened.

When the crocodiles charged, the carnage was quick and complete. Flesh was crushed between teeth as sharp and even as the teeth of a saw. Blood drizzled the earth and feathers littered the ground, like a pillow burst on a crime scene.

"They are the totem of my clan. In my village, there are many men who bear the nickname Crocodile," he said. "Come, you must be tired. I will take you back to your room. You can see the rest tomorrow."

The roads were laid out at right angles with a stop sign at every junction. Kofi rolled to a halt each time, even though the streets were now empty of other golf carts. Signposts identified the large buildings on either side: National Art Museum, Bamana Museum of Natural History, Bamana National Archive. We were dwarfed by the scale of the place as ants are dwarfed by their anthills.

"Do you recognize the shape?" Kofi asked as we approached the main building.

"An hourglass?"

"A talking drum."

I had seen the drum in the marketplace, rounded at both ends, narrow at the waist, like a woman in a corset. As an instrument, it could be held comfortably under the arm. As a building, it would not easily fit into a photo frame. The drum was tightly bound by ropes. The middle section of the building was circled with thin lines of bronze, like rings around a planet. It was too literal an interpretation but the effect was striking. Sule was waiting outside.

"Welcome to the People's Palace," Kofi said. "Sule will show you to your room."

Sule and I entered through a side door and stepped into a corridor that extended on either side of us. A car could drive comfortably down what felt like kilometers of marble highway. Our path was lit by chandeliers, every few feet another cluster of crystal and bulbs. Labor gangs of builders, painters, and plasterers must have worked for years to realize Kofi's vision of an African palace. The architects had achieved their objective. I felt awed. What would Rose and Robert make of it? Or my in-laws, so proud of their Royal Enclosure membership at Ascot?

Sule led me to my door, which was unlocked. The first thing I looked for was my overnight case. Someone had placed it by the imitation Louis XV wardrobe. There was a four-poster bed in the room complete with damask curtains and carved wooden poles. The windows looked out onto a garden and a silent fountain.

"Is there Wi-Fi?" I asked.

"It's down at the moment. I will alert you once it's functioning. Do you need anything else?"

"Dinner?"

"Dial one on the intercom to get the kitchen. They will prepare any meal of your choice."

"Thai curry?"

"Our chefs are internationally trained. If you need me, dial nine."

After he left, I lay on the bed with my shoes on. The sheets were freshly laundered, high thread count, cool to the touch. I studied the canopy over the bed, the frame that held the curtains up. I would have given anything to have slept here as a child, a princess in a fairy tale, tossing and turning for a pea.

It was dark outside when I woke up and dialed the kitchen.

"Good evening. I hope it's not too late to place an order."

"We're here whenever you need us." The voice was male and accented. I would guess French.

"I'd like a Thai green curry, please."

"Chicken, beef, or prawn?"

"Beef, please," I said.

"And will you have jasmine or basmati rice?"

"Jasmine."

"And wine? There is a selection in our cellars."

"Water is fine."

"Still or sparkling?"

"Still."

"And for dessert?"

"Not tonight, thank you."

I put down the phone and went to the bathroom. It had both a tub and a shower. There were white towels on the railings and lapis tiles on the floor. The sink was marble; the taps were golden, or at least gold-plated. I twisted one. The water gurgled from afar, moisture traveling up a dry throat, waiting for a cough to expel it. When the water finally arrived, it ran brown.

How many rooms like this? How many golden taps? It was opulence modeled on Versailles, joining Kofi to a long line of tacky despots and oligarchs. Francis Aggrey would never have erected such a folly. This was Kofi grasping at all the things his earlier incarnation had rejected: Western dominance, European modes of thought. The ideology of the place was writ large in gilt and mortar. My awe swung to distaste.

I returned to the bedroom and pulled back the heavy brocade curtains. Floodlights illuminated my view of the garden. Flying insects streamed to the hot bulbs in an exodus of wings and antennae. In the distance, they looked like rain.

My dinner was brought by a young woman. She spread a white tablecloth, tucked me into my chair, poured my water, and was gone. Apart from her greeting of "good evening," she worked silently. One tap might pay her annual wages. Why had they not all been stolen?

The curry was prepared with more chilies than I was accustomed to. The rice was fragrant. The beef was tough. When I was done, I changed into my nightclothes. There was no key in the lock. I slept knowing anyone could walk in.

23

I woke up with no sense of dislocation. I was in Gbadolite, brought here by my father, Kofi Adjei, once known as Francis Aggrey. I was here to know him, to understand where I had come from, not to pass judgment, I reminded myself.

The plates from last night's meal had been cleared. Someone had come while I was sleeping. I dialed Sule.

"Good morning. How was your night?"

"Fine, thank you," I said. "I'd like the key to my room, please."

"Of course."

"What is Kofi doing today?"

"Sir Kofi is sitting in congress this morning."

"What's that?"

"He holds congress in the village of Gbadolite. The villagers come with their disputes and he settles them. It is an old African way of doing things."

"I'd like to see it," I said. "Please. If that's not too much trouble," I added. He was Kofi's manservant, not mine.

"I can arrange a car for you. It is open to the public, but we are leaving soon. Have you taken breakfast?"

"I don't need to. I'll be ready in fifteen minutes. Please can you send someone to fetch me? I'm not used to the building."

We sped out of Gbadolite in a convoy of black Mercedes, police escorts at the head and rear. The other drivers pulled over to let us pass, smaller beasts scattering from a charging bull. We slowed when we turned onto a narrow side road. It was lined with people fluttering handkerchiefs and palm fronds. I wound down the window.

"Madam, please wind up for your security," my driver said. We were alone in the car. His glasses and the windows were tinted the same shade. The faces outside seemed benign but I obeyed his order.

The congress was held in a large earthen square. The villagers were already waiting. They were dressed in a homespun fabric I recognized from the markets of Segu, a coarse cotton called *kafa*, dyed in primary colors, sewn into smocks, loose trousers, stiff blouses and wrappers. Their clothes contrasted sharply with their skin. Music played from a loudspeaker while hawkers drifted through the crowd with food. It had the feel of a fête. Kofi emerged from his car, a kente robe draped over his shoulder. His chest was bare, one nipple exposed. Sule walked behind him, shading him with a fringed umbrella. The villagers began to cheer.

"*Daasebre!*"

He responded with a clenched fist. A woman with a bundle broke past the cordon. Guards moved to restrain her, but Kofi waved them away. The bundle was a baby. She knelt. Kofi blessed the child, or at least touched it, his palm covering the face. She was overcome with emotion. She could not stand. She was lifted to her feet, supported by two guards.

"*Daasebre!*"

They would not stop until he had taken his place on the raised wooden throne, until his feet had been covered with a leopard skin, until he lifted his hands for them to be quiet.

I had never seen a black man presented in public like my father, regal, beloved. I was suspicious of populism, cynical of emotional display in politics, and yet I felt pride rising in me.

I stood in the crowd. For once, I was not the spectacle. There was no time to ogle at an *obroni* when a troupe of acrobats performed. They wore bells on their ankles, their feet tinkling like courtesans. At the end of their routine they stacked themselves in a pyramid, holding the pose for a few seconds before collapsing into individual human units.

If I were to paint this scene, what would my subject be? Kofi on his wooden throne was an obvious choice but I did not want to paint him as a king. In time, perhaps, I might make a more intimate, vulnerable portrait, but today, if I had an easel and canvas and paints, I would choose the crowd in their primary colors. I would use quick, sharp brushstrokes to give the piece movement. Perhaps Sule might be able to find some art supplies for me. He seemed the person to ask.

When the formal proceedings began, I grew restless. Few claimants spoke English, or spoke an English that was recognizable to me. I could pick out only a few words: for land, property, in-law. The ground was littered with fruit peelings and sweet wrappers dropped from careless fingers. Flies were drawn to the food remains. I felt like an animal trapped in the warm center of a herd. I struggled to the edge of the square.

"Hello. What brings you to Gbadolite?" The woman who spoke to me wore trousers in contrast with the other women present. Her weave was dyed auburn and pixie-cut. The frames of her glasses slanted into cat eyes and her fingernails were painted green. I could not blend in, and she did not want to.

"I am a guest of Sir Kofi."

"Yes, he flies in foreign journalists to write about his white elephant. I know all about that. Have you seen the zoo? Did you feed the giraffes?" she asked. Her tone was mocking but with good humor. "You *obroni* like that. A newspaper in New York called it an African center of culture. What culture? I tell you, it's a curse when a former president thinks he's an intellectual."

"What do you do?" I asked. She seemed close to Rose's age and I wanted her to keep talking. She was the first young person I had spoken to in Bamana.

"I work with an NGO, Bright Futures. We support children's rights in the region and advocate against child abuse. We say no to their oppression."

The words were practiced, said by rote, but her zeal felt fresh, unwrapped today. I had not felt strongly about anything in years.

"Did you see the crocodiles?" she asked.

"Pardon?"

"The crocodiles, at the palace?"

"Yes, I did."

"They say he fed his enemies to them in the nineties. Maybe you can put that in your article. What paper did you say you write for again?"

"I didn't say." I couldn't confess I was a mere housewife to this bright young thing. In the distance, Kofi was processing to the motorcade.

"I have to go," I said.

"Wait. Your name?"

"Anna."

"Marcellina Kote. Take my card. Maybe I can show you some of the village."

"Yes, please." She would be my guide into a part of Bamana that neither Ken nor Adrian, nor even Kofi, could show me. "I would like that very much," I said.

I made my way back to the convoy. The crowd surged around Kofi. Sule and a few men in suits formed a ring around him, shoving people back. The devotees seemed ready to trample their *Daasebre* with love.

My car was at the tail end of the convoy, ignored by most. When the driver opened the back door, he saluted. I returned with a limp half-wave. I was glad no one was watching.

Marcellina picked me up from the Gbadolite gatehouse at 7:00 p.m. Her car was a white Datsun with a broken rear light. The back seat was piled with clothes and boxes of leaflets and flyers with titles like "Supporting the Girl-Child," and "Primary Education for All."

"Pardon the mess," she said. "I live and work out of here sometimes. So what's it like in there?"

"It's open to the public," I said. I was Kofi's guest. There was a certain discretion I owed him.

"Not the tourist attractions. The palace itself. I've heard the bathtubs are made of gold."

There was no air-conditioning in her car. We rolled down the windows and the sound of crickets calling for their mates poured in.

"Where are we going?" I asked.

"To the village first, then a bar. Gbadolite didn't have much happening here before Sir Adjei built that monstrosity. Now there are a few hotels just outside the village for tourists, and some small bars and things."

"You don't like the palace?"

"The money could have been better spent. Don't print my name if you use my quote."

It was too late to explain I was not a journalist. Marcellina would think me foolish for pretending in the first place. I let the misinterpretation stand.

The streetlights did not stretch far beyond the village entrance. We passed the square, silent now after the congress. The deeper we drove into the village, the worse the road became, until the asphalt dissolved into the earth.

"We have to walk from here. Otherwise my car will get stuck."

I was wearing the wrong shoes. The flimsy pumps sank into the mud.

"The trick is to walk like you're swimming," Marcellina said.

"I don't know how to swim."

There was no moon. It was a pre-industrial night, of a type long vanished from Europe. The slaves shipped from Cove Coast would have come from a village like this, would have been force-marched from here to the ocean. I wasn't very athletic. I would have died on the way, been buried by the wayside or not buried, left on the surface to rot, to return to the soil. I took off one shoe and let my foot drag in the earth.

The air was heavy against my face, like a thin film or a strip of gauze. Was this the authentic Bamanaian experience? More real than my life in Segu, than at Kofi's palace?

"We're turning right," Marcellina said.

I did not see the house until we were almost touching it. It was built in the traditional style with thatch roofing that hung down like matted hair. I put out my hands and felt the mud walls. They were cool and surprisingly firm.

"Why are we here?" I asked.

"Inside, please."

There was an opening in the wall, the size of a slim person. She passed through and I stood outside in the dark. I did not know Marcellina, yet I was not afraid. Nothing in Bamana had harmed me. I followed.

Inside it was warm and claustrophobic. We were not alone. The creature, the person, had a smell of meat just gone off, sweet and rank.

"Abena, it's me. Marcellina."

"Yes."

I started at the voice, which came from the ground. "What's going on?" I said.

Marcellina switched on her phone torch and I squinted at the light. A girl lay on the floor, a *kafa* cloth drawn like a blanket around her. I did not see the chain until she sat up. It ran from her ankle to a stake in the ground, a thin, iron snake. There were bones piled in the corner in a small pyramid.

"Abena," Marcellina said, "I brought someone to meet you."

"Ma, when can I go?"

"Soon."

Marcellina turned to me.

"This is Abena. Her uncle accused her of being a witch. She has been here for four days now. I'm working to rescue her. The police are not responsive. I've spoken to an orphanage in the next town. They will take her, but only if they know that nobody will attack them for it. You can ask her your questions."

I shook my head.

"Your questions for your article," she said. "Are you not a journalist?"

"There's been a misunderstanding."

I was at her mercy. I could not get back to the main road, let alone return to Kofi's fortress without her.

"Even if you're not a journalist, you have access to Sir Adjei," she said. "Talk to her."

I was an *obroni*. That was all Marcellina saw. *Obroni* were always looking for Africans to rescue. We were no use beyond that. But what could I do for this chained girl?

"Good evening, ma," Abena said.

There was a gash above her eye. A scab had not yet formed. The wound glowed red. I was too far above her, too tall. I crouched. The smell was stronger around her person.

"Good evening," I said. "How are you?"

"I'm fine, ma."

She was not fine. Be of use, Anna. Be a useful *obroni*. I calmed my breathing, steadied my thoughts. Marcellina was right. I did know Kofi, and if he was still powerful enough to pack a village square, he would surely be able to free this girl.

"Who put you here?" I asked.

"My uncle."

"Why?" It was a foolish question. There was no answer that could justify her present state.

"He said I am the reason why his business is failing. He said I should change what I have done, then he will release me."

What else could I ask? I looked to Marcellina but she was sending a text.

"How have you been eating?" I said.

"He brings food for me in the mornings. He just says I should fix his business, then he will let me go."

"How old are you?"

"Nine."

I stood up and backed away to the entrance.

"What's the matter?" Marcellina said.

"I'm sorry. I can't."

"Can't what?" She knelt by the girl and checked where the chain gripped her ankle. They spoke in their language softly and under their breath. She stood up.

"Okay, let's go." She was brusque, businesslike. The *obroni* had proved a disappointment.

"We can't leave her here," I said.

"I can't take her tonight. Let's go."

One foot was still bare. I tapped at the ground with my heel. It was soft, would shift easily. I bent and began to dig around the stake.

"We've tried that already. It's cemented to the ground. Stop. The uncle will know someone has been here."

"We can't leave her."

Abena's hand on my arm was light, like a butterfly perching.

"It's okay, ma. Sister Marcellina will help me."

Marcellina stamped the soil I had dislodged back into place.

"Let's go."

I wore my shoe outside. We did not speak until we returned to her car.

"I just assumed. Most of the foreigners we get here are either journalists or aid workers. You didn't seem like an aid worker," she said. "Mama Christie's next?"

I remembered why I was always suspicious of people with causes. Their self-righteousness could justify almost any behavior. I was angry and still a little frightened.

"No, please take me back to the palace."

"Look, I'm sorry I didn't tell you where we were going. Let's go to Mama Christie's. I've shown you the worst of the village. You must see something else."

Mama Christie's was close to the main road. Meat roasted on an open brazier, skewered over hot coals. There was indoor and outdoor seating. Indoors, patrons huddled around a television, watching a football match. Outdoors, colored bulbs wound around poles like Christmas lights. We sat outside on plastic chairs. There was an ashtray on the table, half-full.

"Your face is still long," Marcellina said. Her eyes had taken on the mood of the bar, twinkly like a garden gnome.

"Sorry, I can't stop thinking about her."

"Don't worry. She'll be okay. I'll get her out by tomorrow."

"Everyone is so cheerful, and just a few miles away there's a little girl chained in a hut."

"Don't people do bad things to each other in your country?"

"Yes, but—"

"And don't people still get on with life?"

"Yes, but—"

"It's no different."

She was right, of course. I felt I had witnessed the depths of darkness tonight, but I had never thought of the cases of abuse I read about in London, of babies found in quiet suburbs with cigarette burns on their skin, as the "depths of darkness." My *obroni* prejudice was revealed, and by a woman not yet thirty.

There was shouting indoors. A ball tumbled into a net in Europe and, in West Africa, people rejoiced. Mama Christie herself brought us two beers and meat on sticks. The meat was spicy, the beer was strong.

"How do you find living here?" I asked.

"In Gbadolite? I was born close by. I'm a government scholarship kid. That's one thing Sir Adjei did for my generation. Gave with one hand, took with the other."

"What do you think of him? Sir Adjei."

"I thought you are not a journalist?" Her tone was teasing. I relaxed into the bar ambience, pulled away from the horror of Abena.

"I'm curious about the country," I said. "I'm half Bamanaian."

"Which side? Your mum or your dad?"

"Dad. I never knew him. My mother was a single parent. I came back to try to reconnect to the country."

"Have you seen your dad?"

"Yes. We met for the first time this year."

"Wow. So how did you end up in Sir Adjei's palace?"

"I came as a tourist."

"I didn't know tourists were allowed to sleep there. Anyway, I suppose for *obroni* tourists it's different. Me, if I tried to spend the night, they'd kick my black ass out. You were asking what I thought about him?" she said.

"Yes."

"He did some good things. My parents' generation love him. *Daasebre*. It's a title that means 'we can't thank you enough.' He freed them from colonial rule, gave their children free education, all of that. But I can't think of him without remembering the Kinnakro Five. I wasn't born when it happened but I'm into history."

"I read about them," I said.

"So you know. Found dead in the dorm room of Patrick, their leader. Police said it was armed robbers or cultists. A few of their parents are still seeking justice, but they're old. It was a big scandal back then. People even thought the international pressure would make Sir Adjei step down, but it didn't happen. Bamanaians moved on and forgot."

"Why was there no trial?"

"Which judge would try the president that appointed him? And even if they did, how to link him directly to the murders? It would not have been his hand that killed them."

"So you were glad when he stepped down?"

"Yes, I was fourteen in 2008 and he was the only president I'd ever known. It was time for him to go. But I'm no longer sure that Owusu is any better. Inflation is crazy. Two years ago a loaf of bread was five cowries. Now it's ten. Most of my classmates are in Canada now."

"And you?" I asked.

"Canada is cold," she said. "Are you married?" The swerve in the conversation made me laugh.

"No," I said, erasing Robert from my life. I wanted to keep Rose, though. "But I have a daughter. You?"

"I have a fiancé. He's a doctor. We've been engaged for one year. He wants me to move back to the city. Maybe emigrate after we marry. Bamana is not a place to raise children, he says."

"What do you think?"

"We were raised here. Are we not normal?" she said. "What do you do over there?"

"I studied architecture."

"What have you built?"

"Not much. I couldn't even build a fake journalism career," I said, matching her banter.

"You're funny. My parents want me to emigrate too. They don't understand what I'm doing only twenty kilometers from where I started. I have a university degree. I should be earning more."

The match was over. A few couples opened the dance floor. I was too old to learn how they moved, leading with the waist and hips, not the arms and feet. The energy they expended seemed reckless.

"Care to dance?" He was younger than Rose. He wore a metal chain around his neck, silver links looped in a tight circle. I could see the yellow of his eyes, jaundiced and bright. When he smiled, his teeth were even and small, like niblets on corn.

"No, thank you," I said.

"Why not? I like my women mature."

"I like my men the same," I replied.

He wandered off to try his luck elsewhere.

"You know, it used to be just the young girls who went after the foreigners, but now the young boys are doing it too. I hear in the bars in Segu you'll see a seventy-year-old white woman and a nineteen-year-old Bama boy."

"Gender equality," I said. "Isn't that what you're fighting for?"

"Better life for girls, not worse life for boys."

I had never felt as rich as I did sitting at that plastic table opposite Marcellina. At the Palace Hotel in Segu and in Kofi's Gbadolite castle I was dwarfed by the wealth on display, a middling tourist who could only gawp, but here in this dirt bar, only a few miles away from a young girl chained in a hut, I realized that perhaps to many Bamanaians, the money from the sale of my mother's flat made me as rich as Croesus. I could build my own manor, pick vassals from the natives, turn them into serfs. Why was Bamana so poor when the country had diamonds? It was a question Menelik had asked Francis Aggrey, a question Kofi Adjei still could not answer.

"I should go. Thank you for your hospitality."

On the journey back we listened to country music. Marcellina was a Dolly Parton fan. Down the flat road, from more than a mile away, we could see Kofi's folly blazing. The closer we got, the stronger its light became until, as we parked by the walls, it was as bright as noon.

"Thank you," I said.

"You're welcome. Please remember Abena. Do what you can."

She drove off with her broken taillight. Sule was waiting for me in the guardhouse.

"You did not inform me that you were going out," he said.

"I didn't know I had to."

"Please. For your safety. Who did you go with?"

"A friend. How long have you been waiting?"

"Never mind. Please follow me."

Sule drove us in a golf cart back to the palace. I sat at the back like a teenage truant. When I got to my room, I washed my feet in the bathtub. The soil ran off, staining the marble black.

24

It was raining and I had exhausted Gbadolite's attractions. I had not seen Kofi since the congress three days ago. He was no longer president, but he was still sought out, still busy, Sule assured me when I asked to see him. I did not bother asking him for canvas or paints. The mood had left me. How long Kofi intended to stay in his fiefdom I could not tell, but it was time for me to return to England.

I was no longer at ease in Kofi's wonderland. During the day I drove in a golf cart, joining the traffic of tourists and holiday-makers that came to visit the zoo, the water park, and the different museums.

A cable car circled the entire property. I went up with a family of four. The mother would not open her eyes, even when our glass egg cut through a flock of birds and scattered their formation.

At night I slept fitfully. I woke up drenched in sweat, the air-conditioning blasting cold air. I locked the door and heard noises in the dark. The young men of Kinnakro. Five ghosts to haunt the corridors of Gbadolite, see-through specters passing through walls, seeking revenge.

Marcellina texted me. She had rescued Abena. I felt relieved, and then ashamed of my relief. I should have found Kofi, wherever he was holed up in this palace, and demanded that Abena be freed. I should have done more.

Or perhaps it was better in the end that Marcellina engineered her rescue and not me, with my clumsy attempt of playing the *obroni* savior. I remembered with embarrassment trying to dig the stake out of the ground, a mistake that would have endangered Abena even further.

I thought of calling Rose but I did not really feel like speaking to my daughter. Her voice did not belong here. My life in England was one world, and my life here was another, two planets that must not collide.

I watched the rain from the library. It drummed on the roof and windowpanes. The water ran into concealed drains and did not settle in pools. Kofi had achieved here what he could not achieve in Segu. Gbadolite was the dream of urban planners, a city built from scratch, humans added after the fact, sidestepping the warrens and hovels they erected spontaneously.

"So, this is where you are hiding."

The woman who walked in was tall and dark-skinned like Kofi. Gold earrings dangled from her ears, brushing her shoulders. I rose to greet her.

"I think you've mistaken me for someone else," I said.

"I know who you are."

"Kofi told you about me?"

"Kofi? He's your age mate."

You could tell she was Bamanaian but her accent was glossed

with something British, something clipped and slightly braying. It was strange to hear that voice here.

"What is your name?" she asked.

"Anna Bain."

"Very good. Anna Bain, you will pack your things and leave Gbadolite this afternoon. I don't know what sort of adventurer you are. I can see from your looks that you are foreign. Wherever you came from, you must go back there and never come within a hundred miles of my father. Have I made myself clear?"

"I am Kofi's guest," I said. I would not be intimidated by her bluster. I had learned from dealing with Kofi.

"A guest? The latest whore is wagging her mouth."

"Is that what you think this is?"

"A woman your age with my father. What else can it be?"

"I see," I said. "It's best for you to speak to him in private."

"The only thing I'm going to do is personally escort you to your room so you can pack your belongings. Your bags will be searched before you leave."

"I think you should speak to him first."

My half sister had not expected to find me reasonable. I was pleased by my calm. I was becoming used to the unexpected in Bamana. I dialed Sule.

"I'm in the library with Kofi's daughter," I said. "Please tell him we're waiting. Thank you."

"How long have you been here?"

"He'll explain everything."

The rain had stopped, and the room was quiet except for our breathing. My half sister was breathing like air had been trapped in her lungs for hours, like a whale surfacing. I turned my back to her and took a book down from a shelf, a hardback copy of *Great Expectations*. Its pages sprang open, swollen with moisture, like ticks with blood. Mold grew over the frontispiece, mottling the "i" and "n" in Dickens. I put it back in its place.

Kofi arrived at a stroll. I imagined him pausing at the door, willing himself to appear relaxed. Over his career, he had mastered entrances and exits.

"Afua, I see you and Anna have met," he said.

"Who is she?"

"No greeting for your father?"

"I will not greet you. This is a disgrace. How can you bring her here at this crucial moment?"

"You are forgetting yourself, Afua," he said, lowering his voice. The effect on my half sister was immediate. She hung her head.

"I'm sorry, Papa, but you are here with this . . . this woman who is young enough to be your daughter."

"She is my daughter," he said.

Afua's eyes twitched between Kofi and me.

"What are you saying?"

"Afua, this is your sister Anna. Your older sister."

"Papa, what are you saying?" She looked ready to charge but I was not sure who she would rather trample first.

"I know. It came as a shock for me, too," he said. There was mockery in his voice. He was enjoying her discomfort. "Sit down if you need to."

"But she is a half-caste," Afua said.

"What a keen eye you have. Her mother was white. We met when I was a student in London."

"How long have you known? How long?"

Kofi drew himself up. "Since when do you demand explanations from me?" His voice boomed and Afua flinched.

"I'm sorry, Papa." She curtsied. "I'm sorry," she said again.

I should have left the room and given them their privacy.

"I don't see the problem," Kofi said. "A new sister. There should be rejoicing, not recrimination. Go and lie down until your mind has grasped the good news. Then join us for dinner. Come, Anna. There is something I want to show you."

Afua gathered her kaftan robes and swept out of the room. She would never like me. She was proud like our father, and I had witnessed her shaming. Her anger would turn on me first, instead of finding its more obvious object: Kofi.

"She is most like me in temperament," he said.

"How did she find out?"

"A blog. We shut it down, but a photograph is circulating on the Internet. A picture of us in the golf cart. Innocent enough, but people these days have such filthy minds."

Panic welled at the thought of my face multiplied across a million screens, mistaken for a mistress. That was the only explanation for an anonymous woman being beside a powerful man.

"Don't worry. It will blow over. A real scandal will emerge and you'll be forgotten."

"But who did you say I was?" I asked.

"It's not necessary to put out a statement over online gossip but, of course, if I were asked a direct question by a reputable journalist, I would say you are my daughter. Which is what you are. Come," he said. "Let me show you the lake."

"I need to get back to London."

"The matter is over, Anna. Forget it. Please come with me."

After days of neglect time had suddenly appeared in his schedule. He would have been an inconsistent father, appearing between rallies and speeches, a father only when it was convenient. I had been better off with the quiet, steady presence of my mother.

Outside, the sun was back and the rain was making its reverse journey to the sky. Sweat streamed from my face, pooled in my clavicles, gathered in the folds of my knees. My father owned a palace, a zoo, a plane, and now a lake. We walked through a part of Gbadolite that was wilder than the rest. Damp grass tickled my bare ankles. Wet plants slapped my arms.

It was a large lake, so large that figures on the opposite bank would appear small. Trees hung over the water, their reflections broken by the ripples of small fish swimming beneath the surface. The air was fresh. The world was cleansed after the rain.

"Lake Makgadi. It used to be sacred for the villagers. We enclosed it in the compound because of some practices."

"Practices?"

"Relating to the supernatural. Some were harmless. Women believe if you drink from here, you will be cured of infertility. The same as the waters at Lourdes."

There were pleasure boats painted in primary colors stacked under a shed, the colors of boiled sweets. Kofi took off his shoes, rolled up his trousers, and began to drag one to the water. I left my shoes on the shore and joined him, pushing from behind, wading knee-deep into the lake. The water was cold and clear. I could see my feet distort as light passed from air to water. My toes looked like bleached slugs.

Kofi held the boat steady while I climbed in. The bottom was littered with dead leaves and shriveled insects. The oars were old and starting to splinter. We sat facing each other, our knees a few inches apart. He took the first turn with clean strokes. The blades dipped and rose with almost no splash.

"So is our modest city of Gbadolite to your liking?"

"It's unusual. Very different from the village," I said.

"The villagers wouldn't want to live in a place like this. They have a very separate conception of the world. One must respect that."

"What are your other children like?"

"Afua, who you have met, is a judge. Kwabena is in the UN—peaceful, diplomatic, as befits his job. Benita, named for my wife's mother, is the youngest, an artist of some sort. I don't understand the work myself but her art is popular in Sweden. Kweku works in an oil company."

"What would you have named me?"

"If I had been there at your birth?"

"Yes."

"I would have called you Nana. It means 'Queen.'"

The air over the lake was still. The noise of our rowing was the only sound. Two crescents of sweat darkened the armpits of his shirt.

"Would you like a turn?"

"Yes, please."

The oars were heavy. My strokes fell at an angle that met the most resistance. The boat moved off course, away from the line Kofi had set. I had never been so close to Kofi's face. I had his nose. I had the strong jaw that was too wide for a woman, an artist once told me. Kofi had shaved that morning but his chin was already sprouting silver.

"Don't fight the water, Anna. Relax your shoulders. Use your arms. That's better."

I could feel the drag of the oars in my stomach and thighs. I drew in air through my mouth, in audible breaths.

"I have been thinking about what we spoke of in Segu," Kofi said. "I want you to know that immediately after my mother's funeral I did consider returning to England to complete my degree and, of course, marry your mother. What stopped me was the thought of our children. If I raised them in England they would be completely lost. Like you described."

"I wasn't completely lost."

I was suddenly protective of my mother. There had been no one to teach her how to raise a black child. She had done her best. She had dared to keep me where others gave up.

"Well, I wanted all my children to be raised here," he said.

"She could have moved."

"How could I bring a European woman to my family home in 1969? To an outdoor kitchen. Food bought from an open-air market."

"You could have done the cooking."

"Well, yes. I didn't think of that. I was quite a conventional young man."

He laughed and showed the open cave of his mouth, his pink tongue scraped clean.

"Yes," he said. "I suppose I could have gone to the market and done the cooking, and everyone would say a white woman had bewitched me."

"She was very beautiful."

"Yes, she was. Eyes like the Atlantic at noon."

He had read Francis Aggrey's diary as closely as I had. Like me, he had gone through its pages and picked out favorite phrases.

"What would I have known if I had been born here?"

"That the world was made in four days, not seven. Abbana made land on the first day. Animals on the second. Birds on the third. When he saw the beauty of his creation, he wept on the fourth day and his tears made the ocean. Abbana means Father. We had a revelation of a loving God long before the missionaries came. In fact, their version was rather harsh."

His voice had a soothing cadence, modulated for storytelling. He would have been good at bedtime.

"What else would I have known?" I asked.

"There are initiation ceremonies for girls. At thirteen you would have been inducted into womanhood."

"That seems young."

"People lived shorter life spans in the old days. My daughters took part in the ceremonies. As a man, I am not privy to the exact details, but it is mostly symbolic. They went back to school at the end, not to a husband's house."

He dabbed his forehead with a fresh handkerchief. He was careful of his person, still in some ways the dandy Francis Aggrey had been. I was ragged next to him with my crumpled cotton dress, stained with sweat.

"You asked me some questions in Segu, and now I would like to ask you a few also," he said. "Why did you come to find me?"

"It was the diary. I recognized the voice and I felt like that man, Francis Aggrey, would recognize me, too. He was an outsider, wasn't he?"

"And Kofi Adjei, how does he compare to Francis Aggrey?"

"He is different."

"How so?"

I considered my answer. I did not want to offend but I did not want to lie.

"He is in the center of things now," I said. "He is used to being worshipped."

"The villagers do not worship me."

"What of the congress? *Daasebre*?"

"The pronunciation is poor. But, yes, I am that to them. It is a title to show their appreciation. Almost every road in Bamana, I built. Almost every school. Do not be deceived by colonial propaganda. The British left almost no infrastructure. I have brought wealth to this country."

"But they are poor."

"Is that what you see? They are not poor. They are just not flooded with cheap foreign goods. They make their own clothes. They eat the food they have grown. They are healthy. Their children are literate. Where is the poverty?"

"Bamana has diamonds," I said. "It should look like Sweden."

"We do not own the diamonds. They are in the hands of European companies. When you are outside government it is easy to say, 'I will nationalize everything,' but once you get into power, you realize the whites stick together. Nationalize one of their companies and none of the rest will do business with you."

His Rolex gleamed on his wrist, its diamond-studded face catching the sun.

"But Marcellina said . . ."

"Who is Marcellina?"

"No one," I said. "I heard about a girl in the village. She was chained in a hut because her uncle thought she was a witch."

"Who told you this?"

"Just someone I spoke to at the congress. She's been rescued now, but I was shocked by the story."

"Yes. That is regrettable. The villagers still hold on to some of the old harmful beliefs. I do not approve, of course, but it is hard to stamp them out. Even with legislation."

"Why not just arrest people for tying children up?"

"We have prosecuted some of these cases, but how many can you arrest? I believe in education, changing minds then changing actions, which is why I led one of the widest education programs in Africa. In a generation or so, those beliefs will be gone. They are already on their way out."

"Not fast enough for this girl," I said.

"Perhaps not. But fast enough for her daughter. You must understand, I cannot force change. Only guide it. It is part of why the people respect me. I recognize the limits of my power. Like your British queen."

It always came back to the mighty *Daasebre*. We were at the center of the lake now and I could see to the opposite bank. A man looked out to us, naked except for a loincloth. His skin was covered in white chalk.

"That is a *woyo*," Kofi said. "The whites would have called him a witch doctor, but he is a powerful healer. His knowledge of herbs is as extensive as any pharmaceutical company's. He also understands the deeper psychological and spiritual roots of ailments."

"Why is he here?"

"To gather plants, or perhaps just to pray. There is a gate to the lake on the other side. A security risk, but we cannot completely stop the use of the lake. We can only regulate it."

The *woyo* scooped water in his hand and then let it trickle through his fingers.

"What is he doing?" I said.

"Pouring the sacred waters over our lives."

Kofi put his hand in the lake and repeated the gesture.

"Give him your blessing too."

I blessed the *woyo* and then I blessed Rose. The water ran through my fingers twice, flashing in the air before returning to the lake. We let the boat drift after that. There was nothing to bump into for miles.

At dinner, Afua and I sat facing each other in an empty banquet hall. Afua wore a black sequin blouse and white silk trousers. I looked shabby in comparison. She dabbed at her mouth after each bite. Lipstick bruises formed on her napkin. She was too prim, too proper. I imagined growing up in a household with the *Daasebre*, marked by the force of that character, perhaps bent by it.

"How is the fish, Anna?" Kofi asked.

"Very good, thank you."

"It was caught in the lake this morning. You know, the two of you, your grandmother was a fisherwoman. It was catching and drying fish like these that paid for my expensive education. Afua, you are not asking your sister any questions."

She speared a morsel of fish with her fork. "What do you do in London?" Her voice was flat with disinterest.

"I studied architecture."

"When will you be returning to work?" she asked.

"I don't practice anymore."

"She has a daughter, my oldest grandchild. Twenty-five years old," Kofi said.

"Maybe Papa will update the family tree that hangs in the house in Segu."

"What a wonderful idea. Will you oversee it?" he asked Afua.

"There is no need for that," I said. I did not want to become a pawn in their struggle.

The table was set with enough silver to back a currency. Gloved servants watched the levels in our glasses, refilling them once they dipped. The wine was a good vintage, a fragrant accompaniment to the fish. I could feel myself lifting off from sobriety.

"I must return to London soon. I haven't spoken to my daughter in almost a week. She'll be worried."

"Let her come," Kofi said. "She, too, must know her roots."

"And where is the father of the child?" Afua asked.

"My husband? He's in England." I reinstated Robert into my narrative. I suddenly wanted to look respectable in front of these Adjeis.

"You haven't spoken of him much," Kofi said. "He needs to come to Bamana to pay your bride price. That is the way we do things here."

"We do things a little differently in London, thankfully. I might not have survived over here."

"What do you mean?" Afua asked.

"Someone might have accused me of being a witch," I said.

"Where did you get that idea from? A Western liberal news-paper? They're always looking for some barbarism to campaign against in Africa, isn't that so, Papa?"

"There was a girl chained in a hut for witchcraft, just a few miles from here."

"An isolated incident. Such things are obviously illegal. Tell her, Papa."

"We have discussed this," Kofi said. "I will look into the matter as and when I see fit. Do not speak of things you do not understand."

"What is so difficult? It's barbaric. It must be stopped."

"Barbaric? So the villagers are savages?" Kofi said.

"The man who wrote that diary, what would he have made of such a thing?"

"What diary, Papa?"

"Never mind," he said.

"A diary he wrote as a young man, when he wanted to change this country for the better."

"But Papa has changed things for the better. You should have seen the state of Bamana at independence. Bama people are more literate, have a higher life expectancy, are wealthier even."

"Don't you see?" I said.

"See what?" Afua asked.

"That he is too rich."

"You want me to be poor," Kofi said. "Is your queen poor?"

"Did Francis Aggrey want to be this rich?"

"The people wanted him to be. You do not understand our ways. You are my daughter, but at the end of the day you are still an *obroni*."

"What's difficult to understand? That killing people is wrong?" I asked.

"What are you talking about?" Kofi said.

"The Kinnakro Five."

"You have been speaking to my enemies."

"What happened to those boys?"

"Who made you judge over me?"

He stood up before a servant could pull back his chair. Afua rose more gracefully. Kofi's hand was raised. Would he strike me? I gripped my table knife. But his hand was merely raised in farewell.

"Good night," he said.

I did not leave with them. I was not an Adjei. I finished my fish, avoiding the bones, each one a choking hazard.

25

My room phone rang early the next morning. It was Sule.

"Sir Kofi has been called away on urgent political business. The plane will take you to Segu today."

"When will he be back in the city?"

"It is not certain."

"Then I must return to England."

"He foresaw that and asked me to make the necessary arrangements."

"Will I see him before I go?"

"I cannot tell. His schedule is difficult to predict."

So that was the end of that. Perhaps Kofi was right. What did I understand of this place? I had no ties here, no commitment. What could I do about the Kinnakro Five? They were dead, their bodies long returned to the soil. If it were Rose that a president had killed, I would not rest until I had justice, and if justice were not possible, I would not rest until I died. But there were only so many grievances one could carry in this way. How much evil had I overlooked in my lifetime so I could drink coffee from the Amazon and wear clothes sewn in Bangladesh?

I ordered breakfast for the last time in Gbadolite: eggs Benedict with salmon and toast. I packed my things into my small suitcase. I counted my Bamanaian cowries. There were enough to buy a few presents.

It was time to go home to my own problems, to my own divorce. My time here was my way of avoiding reality. What was missing in my life was still missing. What was present was present. Rose and Robert would be waiting in London.

I left the palace through a side door. Sule was waiting in a golf cart. The engine was running.

The Annual Global Sustainability Summit was being held at the Palace Hotel in Segu. There was a banner in the lobby, a table with the names and nationalities of delegates printed on paper squares. A hostess waved me over to find my name tag. I was not dressed for a conference but I was an *obroni*.

In my suite I found a basket of fruit on my bed. I was still at the mercy of Kofi's hospitality. I skyped Rose. She answered after one ring.

"Mum, you shouldn't have disappeared like that."

"I'm sorry."

"Dad and I were so worried. We even thought about going to the Bamanaian embassy."

"I was in a rural area and there wasn't any Wi-Fi. Poor reception too."

"We called your hotel. They didn't know where you'd gone."

"I should have found a way to get in touch. I went to see my father's village home."

Her frown relaxed on screen. She was still angry but willing to move on at this new piece of information.

"Was it nice? Did you take pictures?"

"I'll describe it when I come back."

"Have you met his wife? His children?"

"He has four children. I've met one, a daughter. She didn't like me very much. She thought I was his mistress or an imposter."

"Why would you go to the trouble? It's not like he's rich."

"He's quite rich," I said.

"Quite rich in Africa. That's like average in Europe, isn't it? What's his house like?"

"A bungalow."

"Exactly," Rose said. "I have to get back to my desk. When are you coming back?"

"My flight is tomorrow evening."

"I can't wait to hear all about it. I miss you."

Her face looked gaunt.

"I miss you, too," I said, and dropped the call.

I sometimes grew tired of worrying about whether or not Rose was eating. I resented the stopping and starting, triggered by what you could never tell. It kept our emotions dancing, manipulated by her daily calorie intake.

Robert was the better parent. I was sure he never had such terrible thoughts. He grew up in a conventional family, close to his parents and to a sister who neither cut her hair nor wore deodorant. They were mildly inbred, suspicious of outsiders, and yet I envied the flow of the Grahams, the picking up of conversations that were months or sometimes years old. Robert had that ease with Rose, which was why he would have to be the one to talk to her.

I went downstairs for lunch. The conference delegates had been let out and almost every table was full of suits with name tags hanging from their necks. The sound of cutlery striking plates cut through their conversation. I found a table in the corner and signaled for the menu.

"Can I join you?"

It was Ken.

"Sorry, in a bit of a rush," I said.

"I noticed you hadn't been at breakfast for a few days."

A waiter arrived and took my order. Ken set his plate down. There wasn't much on it. A few leaves, some potato salad, and a piece of chicken.

"I saw the photograph," he said. "They took it down fast, but it's my business to keep abreast of these things. I was the only one in the country who knew the name of the mystery woman. So, what was his Gbadolite palace like?"

"It's open to the public," I said.

"I've heard so many rumors. My favorite is the one about the golden toilet that he pees in. I was hired to consult for a project a few years ago. A Dutch company wanted to build a textile factory close to the village. They grow good cotton in the region. Adjei blocked it."

"The villagers don't need a textile factory. They make their own clothes."

"That's what he said. So, he's contesting?"

"Contesting for what?"

"All right, keep your cards close. Good to see you again."

His delegate name tag hung out of his pocket, the blue cord trailing down his trouser leg. I was still not sure what exactly he did in Bamana. At least he had reassured me that I was still anonymous in this country. If I stayed any longer, my face would become famous and my person obscure. I would eventually become known as Kofi Adjei's illegitimate daughter. Anna Bain would disappear for a second time. There was no better time to leave.

When I got back to the room, I checked my in-box. There was an e-mail from Campbell and Henshaw Family Law asking if I would like to keep my file open. There was also an e-mail from Adrian.

Dear Anna,

As I haven't heard from you in over a week, I must hope that all is well. Perhaps I overstated your danger in staying in Bamana. Kofi may be a crocodile but he's an old one.

There are rumors that he's running for the next election. You don't have to take my advice. In fact, you probably won't, but if he does contest, I'd leave before things get hot.

I'm sitting at my desk as I type this and it's raining in Edinburgh. I'm sure your view is far superior.

With affection,
Adrian

It was obvious once pointed out. The congress was a political rally. Kofi was gathering support. Warnings everywhere. Portents. And outside the bustle of Segu continued. What did it matter? I was leaving tomorrow. I went back to Skype. Robert was online. I called him with my camera off.

"Anna, thank God. We were worried about you."

His camera was too close to his face. I could see the fine wrinkles that had grown around his mouth.

"Rose is looking thin," I said.

"I know. I saw her last week. We finally had a proper conversation. She says it's stress."

"Last time she said it was because work was too quiet," I said.

"Don't worry. I'll take care of it. How's your father? Rose told me you found him on the Internet. I can't believe you traveled so far on your own."

"I'm perfectly capable."

"Can you turn on your camera?"

"I don't know how."

"It's a little button in the top corner of the screen. It has a camera sign on it."

"I have to go soon. I need to pack."

"Just listen. Please. I have a therapist now." He paused, waiting for a response to his revelation. When I gave none, he continued. "I was drinking too much and my GP advised I speak to someone. It's strange. You sit in a room, talk about your childhood, and suddenly you're in tears. It's a bit embarrassing."

I'd never seen Robert cry. He got teary, perhaps, when Rose was born or when his mother was diagnosed with breast cancer, but never shed any actual tears.

"How often do you go?" I asked.

"Once a week."

"Good luck with it," I said.

"I want us to try again. I know we said we wouldn't talk until you got back, but you called and I just had to say it."

He was even closer to the camera now. His face filled the screen. It felt intimate, almost claustrophobic. I leaned back.

"Hello? Anna? Are you there?"

"Yes."

"I miss you," he said.

"No. I've become a challenge you want to win."

"Is that what you think of me? I've never been sure, all these years. You hide yourself, Anna, and the irony is, the more you hide, the more people are drawn to you. They think, gosh, she's mysterious, and if you're foolish or foolhardy like me, you decide, I'll be the one to charm her."

His speech was rushed, overly excited.

"You don't sound like yourself," I said.

His mood inverted. He smiled, the serene smile of the mildly drugged. "I know. I've been having these sorts of conversations with my family. My parents think I've gone a little crazy. Camilla says I've had a religious experience like the one she had in Nepal."

"When she stopped wearing deodorant?"

"Yes. What about you? What have you discovered in Bamana?"

"I'm white," I said.

"Pardon?"

"*Obroni.* That's what they call me here. It means 'white person.'"

I glanced at the wall clock.

"I have to pack," I said.

"Of course. Can we talk when you get back?"

"Okay."

"Everything at a pace you're comfortable with."

"Yes. Please call Rose. Thanks."

Be married to Robert again, even a Robert after therapy? If I went back surely it would be trying to force my new shape into an old mold. I had become a woman who traveled alone, who confronted ex-dictators, who could make her way in the world.

Perhaps if I'd forgiven him his affair, he would have gone off with that other woman who could walk confidently on a beach in a string bikini, but I asked him to move out. First, he lived with the mistress, then he left to live on his own. Rejection was a sort of goad to Robert. He'd never met a "no" he wasn't bent on turning into a "yes." I wonder how many sessions of therapy it would take for him to make this discovery.

I unzipped my suitcase and gathered my things. I was going

home with dirty clothes and no story, just a few episodes with Kofi that added up to little. Perhaps Rose was right: this trip was born out of cowardice. I had wanted to flee to Bamana instead of deciding where things stood with Robert. The intercom. I let it ring until it was almost too late.

"Yes," I said.

"Good afternoon. Sule speaking."

"Hi, Sule."

"Sir Kofi's son is holding a small gathering this evening and he has asked me to invite you."

"Which of his sons?"

"Kweku. Kwabena lives abroad."

"Am I allowed to meet his children? After what happened with Afua?"

"They are your brothers and sisters."

"Half."

"There is no such thing in Africa. What shall I tell him?"

"Why not. How will I get there?"

"I'll pick you up at seven."

Kweku's house was on the beach. The ground floor had floor-to-ceiling windows and you could see the guests from the road, like exotic fish in an aquarium. I was wearing my market dress. I walked close to Sule. I brushed against strangers, against fabric, not skin. Waiters circulated with canapés and flutes of champagne. Jazz poured out of hidden speakers. The women wore heels. The men wore jackets. There were a few non-black faces sprinkled through the room, frosting on a brownie.

"Kweku, allow me to introduce you to Ms. Anna Graham."

He turned to face us.

"Afua didn't say you were beautiful." He studied me openly but with no malice in his gaze. "I see why they thought you were Papa's mistress. I didn't get to see the picture myself. They took it down so fast. Welcome to my small gathering."

Kweku was the center of the party, a roving sun. I felt the eye of the room shift to me.

"Thank you for inviting me to your lovely home," I said.

"Pardon? Let's go outside. It's noisy here."

Even with the ocean only a few feet away, Kweku had a pool in his backyard. He was extravagant like our father. There were smokers flicking ash into the water.

"Use an ashtray," Kweku said. He did not have Kofi's authority. No one moved. We sat away from the smokers on cane chairs with armrests that curled like vines.

"Let us begin again. Welcome to Bamana. I hope the country is to your liking."

"It is."

"So, we are siblings."

"Half," I said.

"We don't have that in Africa." He leaned back in his chair. His manner was relaxed, almost slothful, in contrast to Kofi's rigidity. "How did my father meet your mother?"

"As a student in London," I said. "He was my grandfather's lodger."

"He doesn't speak much about those days. Who would have guessed he left behind a love child?"

"I don't want to cause any trouble. I just wanted to meet him. I'm returning to England tomorrow."

"If you'd been a boy there would have been trouble. You would be the oldest son instead of me, an heir who can't control his appetite."

Kweku was the fattest Bamanaian I had seen. When he was not

speaking, his lips remained parted so he could breathe. He wore rings on four fingers. Apart from that, he was simply dressed in black.

"What was he like as a father?" I asked.

"Kofi Adjei. The great *Daasebre* of Bamana. He had very high standards. Me, I dropped out of trying to meet them once I turned about thirteen, but Afua, she's still competing for his approval. I understand her reception was not very warm."

"She was shocked," I said.

"She was jealous. Papa hasn't taken her for a golf cart ride in years. What did you think of Gbadolite?"

"I liked the giraffes."

"Yes, of course. The zoo. Did you see the tiger? He's very proud of that. Only tiger in West Africa. Needs a mate. He should start a matchmaking service."

I liked him. He was the first Adjei I'd met with a sense of humor.

"What about your mother? What's she like?"

"Very quiet . . . calm, but also brave. She smuggled medical supplies to the liberation struggle at great personal risk. Essentially, though, she's happy to stay in the background. You'd have to be, married to a man like my father."

It appeared Kofi had a type. Kweku's mother sounded, in some ways, like mine.

"How come I haven't met her?"

"They live apart," he said. "Neither wants a divorce. None of my business. Araba!" he shouted across the pool. "Araba, come and meet someone."

The sequins on her jumpsuit shimmered like scales. She was nearly as large as Kweku. Her skin was seamless, almost too smooth to be entirely natural.

"So, you're Pa Kofi's new daughter. They said you're almost fifty. You don't look your age. Is that your real hair?"

"Araba, show some manners, please," Kweku said.

"Sorry. Good evening, my name is Araba. I'm your second half cousin. That's what we decided, *abi*, Kweku?"

"Araba."

"What? We've all been talking about her since Afua's phone call yesterday. You bought that dress from Oxford Street market."

"Yes. I did," I said. "How can you tell?"

"It's for tourists. I'll take you where you can buy proper Bama clothes."

"You can't take her anywhere. She's leaving tomorrow," Kweku said.

"Oh, so soon. You must visit us again. You are the best-looking of Uncle Kofi's children."

"Araba, you are drunk. Go away, please, before she thinks there is madness in our family."

He waved her away and she returned to the other smokers.

"Do you ever come to London? Maybe we could have a meal together," I said.

"I visit. My daughter is there."

"How old is she? I have a daughter too."

"Eighteen. A youthful indiscretion that Papa almost killed me for. I'm only thirty-seven, you see. If only I'd known about you."

"Was he strict?" I asked.

"Very. I'm not sure you missed out on much."

"I think I offended him in Gbadolite."

"How?"

"I told him Francis Aggrey would be disappointed in the man Kofi Adjei has become."

"You're braver than you look," he said.

"I was a little drunk."

"Papa doesn't like to be criticized. In fact, for a long time, you couldn't criticize him in this country. He will get over it or he won't. What does it matter? You're leaving, unlike the rest of us."

"Kweku," a woman called from indoors.

"I'd better return to my guests."

"Yes, before someone thinks I'm your mistress."

"A wit. I thought I was the only Adjei wit. It's been lonely."

He got up with difficulty.

"It was a pleasure to meet you, Anna. Sule will keep us in touch. He runs everything in our family."

I sat alone by the pool for a few moments. Ash drifted on its surface like the scattering from a cremation. A breeze blew in from the ocean, setting off hidden wind chimes. I should have gone to the beach more often. I should have seen more of Bamana. Except for my brief evening with Marcellina I had viewed the country through too narrow a lens. Perhaps I might come back with Rose.

"I thought it was you."

I looked up and saw Ken. His face was so familiar in this crowd of strangers that I felt a brief flutter of relief. We were almost friends.

"You again," I said.

"How do you know Kweku?"

"It's a small country. You?"

"Kweku always throws a good party."

It seemed true.

"So, who's here?" I asked.

"The bright young things of Bamana: artists, entrepreneurs. That's one of the biggest film stars, Julia Hammond. Next to her is the vice president's son. Drug addict, apparently. A few diplomats, embassy staff, some expats from Kweku's company."

"His company?"

"He's the CEO of Shore Petroleum," he said. "You didn't know. How do you know the Adjeis? They're an interesting family."

"I met them in passing. You ask a lot of questions."

"I'm a spy."

"You're too chatty to be a spy," I said. "I'm leaving tomorrow."

"You'll be missed. Look, some people are going down to the beach. We should join them."

He was a man who would always try his luck.

"I'm married," I said. It was still true.

"We're just walking on the beach. No vows. How's your father? He's the one you came to visit."

"He's fine. We're not close."

"Wasn't close to mine either."

The sand was cold without the sun. A bonfire was lit and Kweku's guests streamed towards the flames. Someone had brought a guitar. People began to dance, in pairs and groups. They moved near the fire, close enough for their sequins and silks to be singed. I stepped away from Ken and swayed to the music on my own.

26

The departure hall was full of people who were not traveling. They drifted around offering unwanted services, swarming anyone who looked indecisive. Sule cut through the crowd, wheeling my suitcase behind him. When we were alone, he seemed mild, almost vacant. Now he moved fiercely, purposefully. I followed him like the fish that trail behind sharks, gaining their protection, eating their parasites.

At the check-in desk we walked to the front of the Priority queue.

"*Oga*, Sule, welcome."

"Checking in. One bag."

"Traveling to London?"

"Yes," Sule answered for me. He walked me to the security gate.

"This is where we part," he said.

"Thank you. You've been so helpful."

"I hope you enjoyed your stay in Bamana."

"Please thank my father."

"I will pass on your greetings to Sir Kofi. You have my e-mail address and phone number, should you require anything."

"Yes."

We shook hands and then I embraced him. It embarrassed us both but I did not regret the gesture.

I kept one cowry note back when I went shopping in duty-free, one with an image of Kofi. It was my only likeness of him. I spent the rest of my money buying a wooden statue for Katherine and a bead necklace for Rose, three times what I would have paid in the market. I thought briefly about a gift for Robert, but the only thing he really wanted from me was our marriage back. There were a few restaurants, a bookstall, a charging station with passengers tethered to their phones. I roamed around, settling nowhere until a woman announced over the PA system: "Passengers on Flight 232 to London Heathrow should go to Gate Seventeen, where boarding has begun."

I could see the plane from the gate, a sleek Boeing model with the hump of an upper level. A queue shuffled forward for one last check. At the desk I handed over my ticket and passport. The attendant was well groomed, hair styled in a slick cut that looked held in place by spit or gel.

"Madam, it says here that you will be traveling under a Bamanaian passport."

"It's a mistake. I'm British."

"But do you have a Bamanaian passport?"

"Yes, I do."

"May I see it?"

I had almost packed it away in my suitcase. It was as much a souvenir of my time here as my market dress. I gave her the navy passport embossed with the Bamanaian coat of arms, a lion rearing under a palm tree.

"Madam, please step to the side."

"Why?"

"A routine check. Don't be alarmed. Please take a seat."

The other passengers filed past. Business types dressed for meetings in London, families with children dashing ahead, the elderly in wheelchairs, pushed to the front of the queue like VIPs. I returned to the desk.

"I don't want to miss my flight. What's this about?"

"Please exercise patience. You will be attended to shortly."

Two security agents approached with a gun and a dog between them, wafting menace into the sleepy terminal. The dog, a gaunt German shepherd, was hunting for drugs or explosives or its next meal. When they stopped in front of me, I lowered my bag. The dog sniffed and lost interest.

"Please come with us."

"Pardon?" I said.

"You are on a no-fly list of Bamanaians."

"There has been a mistake."

"You are Anna Graham?"

"Yes."

"Then you must come with us."

"Not without an explanation. I am a British citizen."

"As long as you are on Bamanaian soil your Bamanaian citizenship takes precedence over all others."

"I need to make a phone call."

"That will not be possible."

I walked sandwiched between them, the dog brushing against my legs like a pet. A toddler strayed into our path and was dragged away. They led me behind a door marked *no entry*. We walked in single file down a narrow corridor lined with unmarked doors. We stopped in front of one.

"Your phone."

"I don't have one."

"You wanted to make a phone call."

"I was hoping to use yours."

"Search her bag."

I gave it up before it was taken by force. They left me in a room with a low ceiling and no windows. There was another woman, asleep despite the heat. Her chair had no armrests and her arms hung slack by her side, dangling like rag limbs. Ten minutes passed. I tried the door handle. It opened.

"I wouldn't go out." My companion was awake.

"I'm going to miss my flight if someone doesn't attend to me."

I waited another ten minutes. Final boarding calls would be announced; stragglers' names read out. I knocked on the door. The official I summoned had two brass buttons missing from his shirt. When he pointed in my face, his hand smelled of eggs. I stepped back.

"My flight is leaving soon."

"And so? Don't knock on this door again."

He left, and I went to sit by the woman.

"Do you have anyone you can call?" she asked.

"They took my phone."

"You should have hidden it."

The gate would close. My flight would leave. No one would know at which point I had gone missing.

"You sound foreign. British, right? My boyfriend is white."

I looked at my companion. She had a row of piercings down the curve of her ear. In each hole was a small diamond stud. Her skin was clammy, like the surface of a frog.

"Are you all right?" I asked.

"They're waiting for me to shit."

"Pardon?"

"Expensive shit. What about you? Why are you here?"

"I don't know."

"Start thinking."

She closed her eyes again. She was breathing through her mouth, short, shallow breaths. Her hair was blond and tufted in spikes, like dry grass. The uniformed man returned.

"Come with me," he said.

"She's not feeling well. She needs a doctor."

"You better mind your business."

The room was interrogation kitsch, copied verbatim from a Hollywood set. Bare walls, low-hanging naked bulb, no furniture except a table and two chairs, one occupied by an officer. He was dressed in plain clothes. His badge was pinned to a T-shirt that was too tight at the sleeves, pressing into his biceps in a way that would leave a mark. His permanent wave dated him precisely. I sat in the empty chair. The orderly saluted and left. I decided to be direct, the Bamanaian way.

"Look, I have money. I can pay you," I said.

"No introductions?"

"You must know who I am."

"Yes, I do, Anna Graham, but you do not know me. I am Inspector Appiah."

"I have money," I said again.

"Trying to bribe an officer. We can add that to your charges. Do you know why you are here?"

"No."

"I have one question. Answer me honestly and you may go. How did you obtain your Bamanaian passport?"

"My father is a Bamanaian citizen."

"Who is your father?"

"Kofi Adjei."

"Interesting. A namesake of our former president," he said. "Now please explain to me how you obtained a genuine Bamanaian passport when there is no trace of you on any database."

"My father is a Bamanaian citizen. Kofi Adjei, the former president, is my father."

"And I am the nephew of the queen of England. I have another explanation for you. You are a spy."

I laughed. The idea of it was so ridiculous. Anna Graham, housewife and 007.

"It's funny?"

"I'm not very observant. I'm not even sure what day of the week it is."

"This is a joke to you?"

"Of course not. There's obviously been a mistake."

"Obtaining a passport under false pretenses is a very serious offense, Ms. Graham."

"I've told you. My father is Bamanaian."

"Sing the anthem."

"I don't know it," I said.

"How many provinces are there in Bamana?"

"I don't know."

"You didn't do the citizenship test?"

"I didn't have to."

"Who said?"

"It was all arranged for me. I had a Bamanaian visa that was about to run out. I decided to get the passport instead of paying for a renewal."

"Walk me through the arrangement?"

"I was taken to an office. I filled out a form, took a passport photograph, did my fingerprints on a machine."

"Who took you?"

"Sule."

"Sule? No surname?"

"I don't know. I have his number on my phone. One of your men has it. Call him and he'll explain everything to you. Hurry, please. My flight."

"You are telling me if I call this Sule person he will explain how you obtained this passport."

"Yes."

"Felix!" he shouted. An officer returned and saluted.

"Sir?"

"Bring this woman's phone."

My phone returned. Its leather case had been removed, baring its fragile screen. The inspector put the phone on speaker when he called Sule.

"Call him again," I said, when there was no answer. He called a second time. The result was the same.

"So, what next, Ms. Graham?"

"I don't know why he's not picking up."

"You don't seem to know anything. You'll have to go to the station to be charged."

"I'll miss my flight."

"You haven't grasped the gravity of the situation. You're facing a sentence of up to four years."

"I demand to speak to a lawyer."

"After you've been charged."

"Call my father. Call Sir Adjei. He will not be pleased if you detain me."

"I don't have his number. His daughter should have it."

"I don't. I haven't known him for very long."

"You haven't known your own father for very long? I think we should obtain a psychiatric evaluation as well."

He stood up. He had the stoop of a tall man. The table was too low for him. It stopped below his knees.

"I've heard enough of this story. Follow me, please."

What would become of my luggage, checked in and decanted into the hold of the plane? It would be culled from the other approved baggage, destroyed along with my market dress. Inspector Appiah led me through corridors that looped like intestines. Outside, a van was waiting.

"I need to speak to my family in England. Tell them I won't be arriving tomorrow."

"The time for phone calls has passed, Ms. Graham. Get in, please."

The back of the van was a cage. The gaps between the bars were wide enough to slip a small package through. There was a bench and an empty bucket that smelled faintly of shit. I sat down.

"Ms. Graham, how did you get that passport?" Inspector Appiah asked.

"My father, Sir Kofi Adjei, is a Bamanaian citizen."

He rapped the side of the van. We jerked forward. The smell of the city rushed in through the bars, cooking on open fires, charcoal and soot. Drivers stopped to stare at the *obroni* woman in a cage. I stared back. I was not yet afraid. I was too stunned to be afraid.

The police station was quiet. We drove into the courtyard and stopped. The driver unlocked the cage.

"Come down," he said.

"No."

"I said you should come down."

"Take me to the British Embassy."

He entered the cage, advancing slowly like I might strike. He tried to pull me upright but my body resisted, inert and heavy like a stone.

"Wait, first."

He left. I wished I was as fat as Kweku, then I could be moved only with a harness and a crane. The driver returned with reinforcement, a much taller, stronger-looking man. When he entered the cage, the bars rattled from his weight.

"Come with me, please."

"Take me to the British Embassy."

He held my arm but I slid from his grip to the floor. I had no plan, except to stay in the van. He hooked me by the armpits and dragged me outside. Some loose metal scraped my leg as my body left the van, drawing blood. I screamed.

"Stop screaming."

He hit my face, first with the flat of his palm and then his fist. I lay on my back with my legs splayed, a specimen pinned to the ground. A red dot flashed in the sky, like a star hanging too low. It was a plane, perhaps my flight to London.

"You no suppose slap her," the driver said.

"Wetin I suppose do? She no gree comot."

The station was on a busy road. The swish of passing cars reached us. Were they going to kill me?

"Get up."

The second man's foot was by my head. With one kick he could damage my brain permanently. I had not spoken loudly enough for Abena and now there was no one to speak for me. In a country where a child could be chained, a woman could be killed before she reached her jail cell. I stood and dusted my skirt, like I had lain on the ground by choice instead of being dragged there.

Inside, my handbag and duty-free shopping were taken from me.

It was too late to charge me. They gave me a cell of my own, perhaps my last vestige of *obroni* privilege. Around me, other prisoners were sleeping, breathing evenly. There was rustling in one corner of the cell, another creature trapped here with me. I held on to the bars and waited for morning.

27

am kneeling with my head against the bars when I wake up. My cheek stings where it touches the iron. There are prisoners in the opposite cell, all men. I can smell them. The windows are small and close to the ceiling. I feel faint, on the verge of passing out. I am sweating, even behind my ears is damp. I stand up slowly.

"Hello," I say.

"*Obroni*, you're awake," a prisoner calls out. In the low light I can't see his face clearly. I look at him and look away.

"*Obroni*, are you deaf? I'm talking to you."

I recoil from the force of his voice and then remember we are both caged. He rattles the bars and grabs his crotch but he cannot bend metal. It is the men outside I must be wary of.

"Hello! I need to speak to someone. I need water!" A door creaks open. Fresh air gusts into the cells.

"Who is making noise?"

The officer looks like he has also slept in a cell. His hair is disheveled, and the top buttons of his shirt are undone.

"Good morning, sir. I need some water. I have not drunk anything since yesterday. I also need to make a phone call. Please."

"Who are you?"

My hands tremble and I clench them.

"It is my right to have water and it is my right to make a phone call."

We stare at each other, and then he turns and leaves. There is laughter in the opposite cell.

"*Obroni*, you think this is a hotel?"

I put my hands to my temples. My skin is warm and clammy. I am breathless, even though all I have done is stand up. The door creaks open again. It is the officer, returning with water, a large plastic bottle dusted with frost. It catches the light, sparkling. The prisoners are drawn to it. Their hands stretch out between the bars.

"No cold water for us."

"Only water for *obroni*?"

"Second-class citizens in our own country."

The officer passes the bottle through the bars. It is burning cold.

"Thank you. And my phone call, please."

"One at a time," he says, and leaves.

I rest the bottle against my forehead. I am under arrest but I have not been charged, which means I may be released soon. Or I may never be released. I steady my breathing. Someone outside must be working on my behalf. Sule will have seen my missed calls. Or if the worst happens and I am not released soon, I will call Rose in England, and she and Robert will devise a plan to rescue me.

I break the seal and drink. The other prisoners watch me.

"I can't finish it all," I say, when I am full.

"Give us, please." It is my taunter. His voice is wheedling now.

I throw the bottle and it lands in the space between our cells.

"Skeleton. Come and do your work."

A thin man pushes his way to the front and slips a leg through the bars. It extends like a retractable pole, longer and longer until his foot touches the bottle. The prisoners cheer as he guides it to them. They all drink, a secular communion. The first sip goes to the oldest, a grizzled man, then the bottle is passed around until it is empty.

"Thank you," the old man says to me. "My name is Samuel."

Samuel wears his hair in thick, silver locks.

"I'm Anna."

"You have grass?"

"No."

"You're not from here. Where from?"

"Actually, my father is Bamanaian."

"Me, I'm a foreigner. Nigerian."

"Don't they give you water?" I asked.

"They do, but not till the afternoon. We eat twice a day, zero one one."

"What does that mean?"

"Zero breakfast, one lunch, one dinner. It could be worse. In Nigeria, it's zero zero one. Or sometimes zero zero zero."

The other prisoners laugh.

"*Oga*, Samuel. You've been in prison in every country in West Africa."

"You can call me a prison tourist."

There is a bench in my cell and I sit.

"How long have you been here?"

"Two weeks," Samuel says. "I'll be out soon. My wife will see to it or maybe one of my sons. What about you? Why are you here?"

"I'm not sure. I think there's been a mistake."

"So do we all."

My cell is roughly the same size as theirs. I count seven men.

Most of them are shirtless, some without trousers. There is a bucket in the corner. A man crouches over it and shits. The smell fills the air and we avert our gazes. Outside, a fly dashes itself against the window, desperate to get in. It will exhaust itself soon and drop dead. The door to the outer world opens.

"Anna Graham."

"Yes."

"You're free to go."

The guard unlocks my cell. The prisoners begin to stir.

"*Obroni* is leaving already."

"*Obroni*, I need a lawyer."

"Remember me to my wife, Bunmi! Sixty-seven Peterson Road," I hear Samuel shout as the door clangs shut behind me. I am led to the reception where Sule is waiting by the front desk in a suit. I squint in the daylight.

"You're bleeding," he says.

They return my handbag, and my gifts for Rose and Katherine. Sule carries both. Outside, the courtyard is full of policemen on parade, raising dust as they march. There are women selling food, ladling stew and rice on to the plates of off-duty officers. There are always women selling food in Bamana. I sit in front.

"You need a tetanus shot," Sule says.

"I've been vaccinated. I called you yesterday. Twice."

"I'm sorry," he says, and bows his head. "I didn't see it on time."

"There's no record of my passport on the Bamanaian database. That's why I was detained. They said I'm on a no-fly list."

"I'm still trying to get to the bottom of this," he says.

"You made the passport arrangements." It is his fault and he does not argue.

"I know," he says. "It will all be taken care of." His deference deflates my anger.

"When can I go to England?"

"Soon."

We drive to Kofi's mansion in the Peak. He is waiting outside, standing under the flag, hands crossed behind his back. It is the same pose as the first time we met.

"Your face," he says, when I get down from the car. He puts his hand on my cheek. It is an intimate gesture, fitting for a father to a child. I step back from his touch.

"Who did this to you?" he asks.

"I don't know. It was dark."

"Owusu must be behind this. It will all be taken care of. Don't worry. As long as you're in this house, you're safe. Come with me. You must be tired. Sule will bring your bag."

"I don't have it. It's still at the airport."

"Of course. Don't worry. Sule will arrange everything. Come."

I follow him through the entrance of double doors, up a wide staircase, down a corridor, and into a place that has been prepared for me. The curtains are closed and the interior is dim, as if the room is in mourning. I sit on the bed, where a fresh towel and dressing gown are laid out. When he is gone, I take off my clothes and lie down. Kofi's enemies have become mine. This is what it means perhaps to be family.

I sleep till late in the afternoon. I wake up thinking about my mother. We hardly spoke when she was dying. She could lie for hours in her thoughts.

"Are you in pain?" I would come in and ask.

"Yes," she would answer, or "No," sometimes, but she never said any more. Was she thinking about Francis Aggrey? Had he faded completely from her mind by then?

I get out of bed and feel unsteady. The room is too big for one person. There are shadows in the far corners, areas of darkness. I have left marks on the white sheets. I wear the dressing robe and go to the bathroom. The mirror shows my eye is bruised black. My cheekbone a more delicate purple. I shower longer than is necessary. The water rushes out in a strong jet, the highest pressure I have felt in Bamana.

When I am done, I put on the dressing gown and return to my bed. I am ready to call Rose. Her phone rings just once before she picks up.

"I took a half day so I could meet you at the airport. I waited two hours. Two hours, Mum!"

"I'm sorry. Something unexpected came up." The excuse is flimsy, even to my ears, but how I can tell her I spent last night in jail?

"What is going on with you? Are you on drugs?"

"Rose! Of course not."

"Then why are you acting so unstable? Is this because of Dad? The separation? You guys need to get back together. He told me he's trying."

"I thought you wanted us to get a divorce," I said, trying to make light of things.

"Not if it's going to make you crazy."

"I'm not crazy."

"You're acting like it."

"That's enough, Rose."

"I don't care anymore. Stay in Africa. Come back. Whatever. I'm at work. I'm shouting in the corridor and people are starting to stare. I have to go."

"I'll call you when—"

"Bye."

All it took was a missed flight and she was back on Robert's side. They'd convened to assess how unhinged I had become. Behind this pose of concern was mere selfishness. I had found a life outside Robert and Rose. They refused to adjust.

There is a knock on the door.

"Come in."

It is Kofi.

"You are awake," he says.

"Yes."

"What will you eat?"

"I'm not hungry."

"You must eat something."

I have turned the *Daasebre* into a nursemaid. He sits by the foot of my bed in an armchair, his hands worrying his knees. It is the first time he has shown me concern. It is the first time I have felt I might matter to him.

"What was my mother like?" I ask. I am suddenly curious to see her through his eyes. She is the missing piece to the puzzle of this trip. I wish she were here to explain my father to me.

"You know better than I do."

"I don't."

"She had a certain quality, a lightness about her spirit. Seeing her could make me smile. And she was a good dancer. Very quick on her feet."

"I never saw her like that."

"We'll talk about that later," he says briskly, shoving aside memories of my mother. "Now you must recover. I'll ask the maid to bring you something."

"I forgot to ask you about Aunt Caryl," I say.

"What about her?"

"You courted two sisters."

"I did no such thing. Caryl courted me. Your aunt was a woman who knew her mind."

"When I was a child, I ran after a black man in the streets once because I heard someone call him Francis. I was so sure it was you."

"Well, here I am at last. Somewhat of a disappointment if I remember our last conversation correctly. You must be tired."

I overslept on the morning of my wedding. I woke up with a sense of loss, although I could not immediately remember what I was grieving for. I feel that loss now. I may never again feel safe in Bamana.

"Anna," he says.

"Yes?"

"I'm going now, but we will talk again soon."

"Off to your campaign?"

"Who told you about that?"

"I have eyes and ears, *Daasebre*."

"Don't be flippant."

"I am not your daughter in the way Afua is your daughter."

"You need to rest," he said.

"I need to go back to London."

"Soon. Rest now."

My wedding dress was white even though I was already pregnant with Rose. The sleeves tore when I put it on. My arms had grown plumper. I stood in my underwear while my mother mended the tear. It was the first time I truly realized how fast and how neatly she could sew.

28

There are two trays by my bed the next morning. Supper from last night and now breakfast. I am still not hungry. When Rose stopped eating, the muscles in her legs were the last things to waste away. Even after the rest of her had broken down into glucose, her thick West African calves continued to bulge stubbornly.

I phone Sule. He picks up after one ring.

"Good morning, Anna."

"I need to go home."

"We're working on it."

"I need to go home this evening. If you can't fix things, take me to the British Embassy."

"Your Bamanaian citizenship takes precedence here. If you try to leave the country, by any border, what happened two days ago will only happen again."

"I'll give it up, then. I didn't ask for citizenship. It was Kofi who offered."

"It's not so simple in a case like this."

"My daughter is waiting for me. My husband is waiting for me."

"I understand, Anna. I'm doing my best."

My urgency drains away once I end the call. I want to go back to London but only when it's safe. I remember the prison cell like a dream. The smell of sweat and shit, the indistinct features of the other prisoners, like faces in a nightmare.

For the first time in six weeks I think about my neighbor Katherine. Our quiet life on Hanover Road seems far removed from where I am now. I miss her sensible, practical manner. I call her.

"Hello. It's Anna."

"Anna! You've been on my mind. Are you still in Africa? Did you meet your father? Was it a success?"

"I'm staying with him for now. How's the street?"

"Much the same."

"And church?" I ask.

"Good. I'm setting up a food bank. Simon thinks I just want to be in charge of a bank. But enough of me. How is it?"

"Things haven't gone to plan."

I blink back tears. My face is swollen. Rose is angry with me and I still can't go home. Katherine makes a sympathetic sound.

"Do you want to talk about it?"

"I only call you when I'm upset."

"Don't be silly. I'm glad you called."

I haven't spoken freely about Kofi to anyone. The words, when they come, are rushed.

"I've been here longer than expected and I still don't really know my father. Sometimes he's kind to me. Sometimes he ignores me. I don't see any part of myself in him. The man from his old diary is gone."

"He did write it a long time ago. My twenty-year-old self wouldn't recognize me, either. She'd be quite disappointed I haven't ended up a CEO."

This is the common sense I called Katherine for. She is right. Francis Aggrey is a man in the past, a man I can never meet. Why go on pining for him?

"Does he have a wife? Other children?" she asks.

"I've met one of his daughters. We didn't get on. I fared a bit better with my half brother."

"So what are you going to do?"

"Come back. Once I can."

"Is there anything stopping you?"

I don't want to worry her. I am safe in Kofi's house now.

"Some paperwork. It'll be sorted soon," I say.

"You know, you're so brave. Traveling all that way and staying so long. I couldn't do it."

"You could," I say.

"Just to let you know I've been keeping an eye on your house. Everything looks fine."

"Thank you."

There is a moment of dead air. The call has come to its natural end.

"It's been so good to hear from you. Let me know when you get back," she says.

"I will."

"Bye now."

I feel better. My house is in order and I have a place to return to. With the time I have left in Bamana I must know Kofi for who he is now, or not know him at all.

I shower. Yesterday's towel is damp and so I pace around the room naked, like a tethered animal. The room is a store for curious things: a large vase in the Ming style, fired in a man-sized kiln, white and faintly luminous; a set of sofas upholstered in *kafa*, patriotic and homegrown; masks on the walls, and one abstract painting of grey, blue, and green swirls. I put on my dressing gown and stand close to the canvas, studying the thickly piled pigment.

"Knock, knock."

My brother is in my room. I don't know how long he has been here. Despite his size, he moves as silently as our father. I knot my robe a second time.

"Kweku."

"Your face."

"What about it?"

"Is more beautiful than ever."

He joins me in front of the painting.

"A gift from the prime minister of Canada. They say it's of a woman's body. You have to stand upside down to see her. How are you?"

"A little shaken but I'm fine."

"What reason did they give?"

"They thought I was a spy."

"You? How?"

"They said there are no official records of my Bamanaian passport. Kofi thinks President Owusu was behind it."

"I see. Do you call Papa 'Kofi' to his face?"

"Yes." He is not my *Daasebre*.

"Come, let's sit down. You shouldn't be standing for too long."

We sit on one of the *kafa* sofas. They are overstuffed and hard.

"Do you want to talk about what happened?"

"I'd rather not."

"I've been arrested before," he says.

"Why?"

"I crashed one car too many the year I turned eighteen. Papa had me put in jail for a week. To cool my heels, he said." Kweku smiles at the memory.

"What did your mother do?"

"She tried to stop him, of course. That's the problem when your husband is head of the house and head of the country. You don't know who's punishing your son. The president or the father of your child. It wasn't so bad. I had the cell to myself."

"So did I."

"Yes. Papa's name still carries enough weight to get you a good jail cell."

He jokes often about our father, but the humor is black. It is not easy being Kofi Adjei's eldest son.

"I heard he's running in the next election," I say.

"Is he? Who knows with Papa? I told Benita and Kwabena about you. Your other siblings."

"What did they say?"

"We've always thought it couldn't just be the four of us. It's unusual for a man of Papa's status to have only one wife . . . but we didn't expect it to be an older sibling."

"What are they like?"

"Benita, I think you would get on with. She speaks her mind. She's an artist. I have a few of her pieces—twisted wire and paint splattered on canvas. I don't understand it myself but it's very popular in Sweden. Kwabena is our human rights UN advocate. Too self-righteous for us all, even Benita. Papa's children that can stand him live in Bamana, and those that can't live abroad."

He leans back into the chair. He is the right size for the room, built to the same scale as some of the other objects.

"So did you apologize to him?" he asked.

"To who?"

"Papa."

"For what?" I said.

"Telling him Francis Aggrey would be disappointed in him."

257

"Should I?"

"It's up to you. Me, if I offend Papa, I apologize. I live off him. Can't afford to be proud."

"The oil company belongs to him," I said.

"So you do know something about our affairs. It's his. It's Bamana's. Whatever. I wouldn't have my job if I wasn't Kofi Adjei's son."

"Do you feel guilty about it?"

"What? His stupendous wealth? Kwabena does. And Benita, too, sometimes. Maybe that explains the twisted metal. Afua is in denial. She believes all that Gbadolite-belongs-to-Bamana crap. Me, I am pragmatic. Papa is better than most of the African leaders of his generation. He did more for the people. They still love him till now. Remember, he was not ousted. He stepped down."

He is not as willfully blind as Afua but he still views Kofi through a falsely flattering lens. I am tired of the Adjeis and their gilding.

"I just want to go back to England," I say.

"You will. Papa will arrange it. He takes care of his children."

Kweku begins to stand up. It is like watching a turtle flip itself off its back. It will not be long before his weight prevents him from walking.

"Pathetic, aren't I?"

Finally, he is on his feet.

"I have to go. I have meetings. I just came to see that you were all right after Sule told me what happened. Do you need anything?"

"Clothes . . . and a toothbrush."

"I'll make sure it's sorted."

"And canvases."

"Pardon?"

"Canvases for painting. I want to paint."

"You're an artist."

"I used to be. And brushes. I need brushes and oil paints."

"It can be arranged."

"Thank you."

"Don't mention. What are siblings for?"

"Half siblings."

"We don't have that in Africa."

Afua was my next guest. She came two days later.

"Kweku said you were here."

She was not as tall as I remembered. I checked the wall clock. It had just gone past noon.

"Good afternoon."

I was sitting in a dress that Kweku had sent me, a bright print with short sleeves and a sequin-embellished neckline. I had gone out that morning, walked through the front gate and made it to the end of the street before turning back. I flinched when a pedestrian brushed against me. I cowered at every passing car. I felt safest in my room and so I returned there. The canvases and oil paints had still not arrived. When Afua knocked, I thought it might be their delivery.

"May I?" she asked, gesturing to the opposite sofa.

"Feel free."

"How are you? How's your stay with Papa been?"

"Good," I said.

"I hope our weather is not too hot for you?"

"No."

"And how's your family in England?"

"Fine, thank you."

She fiddled with the clasp of her gold bracelet. She wore a matching necklace and a gold watch on her other wrist. Her lips were painted, her eyebrows were drawn, and every finger, except her thumbs, was ringed. There was a knock on the door. It was the maid with my lunch tray.

"Aunty Afua." She curtsied and set down the tray. "I didn't know you were around. What will you eat, ma?"

"Actually, I was hoping to take you out for lunch," Afua said to me.

"That's kind."

"I should remove this?" the maid asked, looking at Afua, the recognized authority.

"Yes, please, Angela. If that's fine with you, Anna?"

"Sure."

Angela left with my tray. I had never thought to ask her name and she had never thought to curtsy to me.

"Shall we?" Afua said, rising.

Afua's car was a black Mercedes with tinted windows and a siren on the roof. TV screens were buried in the leather headrests and a glazed panel separated us from the driver. He was dressed in police uniform, navy shirt and trousers with one silver star sewn to each epaulette.

"Bagatelle," Afua said over the intercom.

The engine started and the car moved off, sealed from outside. Her perfume clogged the air, floral with bitter undertones. When the car slowed, hawkers swarmed. At a red light, a child flattened his face against the glass. Afua slid down the window, startling him.

"Don't dirty my car," she said.

"Sorry, mama. Please give me something."

She brought out a two-hundred-cowry note.

"Mama the mama."

It was a lot of money, a performative amount. We drove off.

"The thing about Papa is he doesn't keep secrets from us," she said, picking up a conversation that had never begun, "which is why it was such a surprise to find out about you. I'm not that good with surprises so you must excuse my initial reaction, but we'll talk more in Bagatelle." She gestured at the driver.

Bagatelle was set back from the street, with a large fountain in its front garden. A plaster cherub spouted water from pursed lips, like a projectile of spit. The interior was more modern: plants growing up an exposed brick wall, sleek dark-wood tables, black leather booths. There was no lunch crowd—only a few solitary diners, eating with their phones and laptops.

"Your Excellency."

A man approached. The top buttons of his white shirt were open and his chest hairs sprouted black and silver.

"Amir."

They clasped shoulders and pressed cheeks.

"Amir, this is my friend Anna."

He turned and shook my hand. He was short. The crown of his head would slide neatly under my chin.

"Welcome to Bagatelle, Anna. The oldest first-rate restaurant in Bamana."

"Hello," I said.

"I detect a British accent."

"We came here to eat," Afua said.

I slipped my hand out of Amir's grip.

"Where would you like to sit, Your Excellency? Anywhere you want, even in my office."

"I've told you. It's 'my lord' for a judge."

"'My lady,' surely," Amir said.

"I prefer to think of myself as a man when I administer justice. Your private booth. Don't seat anyone near it."

I followed in Afua's wake and she led us to a booth screened off by wooden panels. Inside, it was faintly claustrophobic. There was a half-melted candle in the center of the table: a space perhaps reserved for romantic assignments.

"I went to school with Amir. He's from an old Lebanese family. Very wealthy. They've been in Bamana for almost a century, but the Khourys still ship their brides from Lebanon—to keep the blood pure."

"I'm your friend?" I asked.

"I would like us to be despite our not-so-promising start. It's we Adjeis against the world. What you must first explain is why you left your life in London to find Papa if it wasn't for money?"

"I have some."

"Then what?"

"I wanted to meet my father."

"Couldn't you at least telephone, give us some warning?"

"Kofi is a difficult man to get hold of."

"You still call Papa by his first name."

Amir brought us flatbread and hummus. He unfolded our napkins and spread them on our laps. He wasn't wearing cologne and he smelled of bread and sweat.

"What would you like, ladies?" he asked.

"Really, Amir, you can get one of your waiters to do this."

"And miss the chance to serve two beautiful women? What will you have to drink?"

"Diet Pepsi," Afua said.

"Water, please," I said.

"And to eat?"

"A sharing selection. You decide."

Amir left us.

"So, you grew up in England," Afua said.

"Yes."

"What was it like?"

"Racist."

"Papa told us some stories but we didn't really experience that over there. We went to boarding school and everyone knew our father was a president."

"Lucky you."

"No, you mustn't think of it that way. It wasn't always easy being Papa's child."

"I grew up on a council estate," I said. I sounded bitter. Perhaps I was, knowing what my life could have been.

"All right. You suffered more. Were you loved?"

"I was. And you?" I asked.

"Sometimes. Not enough."

The dishes arrived balanced on Amir's hands and forearms. Hair grew from his wrists to his elbows. He fanned the food around us—small platters of meat and bread, and ceramic dipping bowls filled with sauces. We did not speak until he was gone.

"Try the meatballs. It's their specialty," Afua said.

"Kofi mentioned you were a judge."

"Yes, I am. I have a first-class law degree from Oxford. A judge at thirty, a high court judge by thirty-five, and always, you wonder, is it because of Papa? Look at you. You're not bad-looking, you have some money, a husband and daughter in London, you've made a life without Papa. Why are you here?"

"My husband and I are separated."

"May I ask why?"

"Adultery," I said.

"Is that all? He didn't beat you?"

"Yes, that was all. It was enough."

"I don't know. I'm not one of those women who keeps track of a man's penis."

"What about your husband?"

"I've had two. The first was physically abusive. He liked being the president's son-in-law more than he liked being my husband. I have what Bama men call a strong face, and I'm too tall and outspoken. Not like you. The boys would have been wild about you over here. Half-caste girls were very popular."

"Well, I wasn't always the rage in London. And I'm sorry to hear that—about your husband."

"No. It was a long time ago. I told Papa. He took care of things."

"Is he dead?"

She laughed with her mouth open, revealing falafel, ground grey. It was her first slip in decorum.

"Mensah is alive and well in Australia. Our son visits him once a year. Don't believe all those rumors about Papa. They're spread by his enemies. He was a tough man when Bamana needed toughness, but he has never been evil. Let's just say Papa made divorce the easiest option for Mensah."

She was a judge but she was also in Kofi's debt, as was almost everyone in this country. How could you condemn your savior?

"You must have some questions for me," she said.

"I do. When the photograph of Kofi and me went viral, you said it came at a crucial moment."

"That was when I still thought you were his mistress. Papa is considering contesting the next election. Nothing official yet, still unannounced. But you can see how such a young mistress might make him look unserious."

"And a daughter?"

"Oh, Bamas don't mind illegitimate children. Precolonial Africa was a polygamous society. Maybe one or two journalists might ask about you after the announcement."

"Announcement?"

"Well, people would want to know who this new woman always seen with the Adjei family was. I'm sure somebody recognized you when we walked in. We could even do a television interview, answer all the questions once and for all. Me, personally, I find the holiday romance between Papa and your mother charming."

"It wasn't a holiday," I said.

"Of course. Anyway, it's not as if you have to come on the campaign trail. This is not America, where sons and daughters mount the podium and make speeches before an election. I go along with Papa because I'm a public figure, but Kweku doesn't. He can't even stand for long periods."

"It won't be necessary. I'm returning to England soon."

"Really? I thought you might stay. Papa has grown fond of you."

Fond of. I was a trinket for the Adjeis to hold on to, a new creature for their zoo.

"You're all so entitled," I said.

She narrowed her eyes. It was a look she used in court, perhaps, to quell anyone who threatened the Adjei rule of law.

"We don't notice. It comes as naturally as our skin color."

Yes, that was it. If I had been raised here, I would never notice standing at the front of the queue.

"Was he a good father?" I asked.

"Absent and strict but loving."

"Kweku said he put him in jail."

"Yes, I remember that. He was very stubborn. Papa doesn't like his children to cross him. It wasn't a bad cell. I visited him."

She smiled and Amir came to clear our plates.

"The bill, please," Afua said.

"On the house," Amir replied.

"Really. That's unnecessary."

"Thank you," I said.

"Perhaps I can show your friend around town, if she's here for a while longer. If that's all right with you, my lord?"

He gave me a card with a phone number written on it.

"You don't need Afua's permission," I said.

"Of course. Anytime you're available, I'm free. Just call me."

Outside, the driver was waiting in the car with the engine off and windows down, slowly baking in the sun.

"Amir has a child," Afua said, once we were in the backseat.

"So do I."

On the drive back, she answered a phone call and left me to my thoughts. I did not care for the future Afua had mapped out for me in Bamana, an appendage to the Adjei machine, but what future did I have in London if I refused Robert's offer? My house suddenly seemed a distant, grey memory on a silent, graveyard street. I had already attempted life on my own there without much success.

Afua walked me to the front door and pressed her cheeks to mine.

"Thank you for lunch," I said.

"The pleasure was mine, *me nua*."

"Pardon?"

"It means 'my sister.'"

"*Me nua*," I said.

When she was gone, I lingered in the hallway entrance. The sun shone through the stained-glass windows and cast colored lights on the floor. It was fine workmanship, worthy of a cathedral, worthy of the Adjeis.

Kofi had not asked me to stay but he was fond of me, Afua said, and I was drawn to him by some strong homing instinct. Staying would be casting my lot with the powerful and standing against the

Kinnakro Five, against Marcellina and Abena chained to a stake in the ground. There was no space in Bamana for neutral Adjeis.

Kofi does not come that day or the next. Sule is still trying to get me out of the country. I save Amir's number but I do not call him. Robert's declaration has left me once again feeling bound by fidelity. There is no one to ask for advice. I know Rose's opinion, and I can guess at Katherine's because of her faith. And what of Anna?

I would never have come to Bamana if Robert and I were still a couple, but then I also wouldn't be stuck in Bamana. My marriage did lend a certain stability. And what of love? Robert no longer loomed so large in my mind. Coming to Bamana had put him in perspective.

I wear the dressing gown, which is starting to take on my musk. My canvases do not arrive. I lie on the floor several times and try to see the woman in the painting. The artist must have been a man to obscure her so completely, to pile her with paint until she disappeared.

On the opening night of my exhibition at Martha Reuben's gallery, she invited me to answer questions. It was the point in the evening where all the guests were tipsy and thus supposedly full of goodwill.

"I noticed none of the figures have faces. Can you tell us why?" The question was obvious and I was grateful for it. My answer was practiced.

"The mind is more important than the face but sadly, in our society, the face has become more important than the mind. I wanted to distance myself from our obsessive beauty culture and try to paint thoughts instead."

I sounded like a cheap guru but I was pleased with my answer. Next question.

"There are so few depictions of black bodies in Western art, so why are all your figures Caucasian? Especially as you're painting as a black female artist."

The woman who asked was wearing an orange print dress, large gold hoop earrings, and a headscarf that added a foot to her height. She was the darkest person in the room.

"My mother is white."

It was the first answer that came to mind. A foolish one, I saw, from the scorn on her pretty face. I glanced at my mother. She was shrinking from my public reference to her but Aunt Caryl lowered her champagne flute and spoke up.

"My niece can paint whatever the fuck she likes."

I'd never been so proud of and embarrassed by a person.

I was still lying on the floor when Kofi finally arrived.

"Did you lose something?"

"I'm trying to see the woman in the painting."

"She's a myth."

He drew the curtains. When the light hit the canvas, her foot was suddenly obvious, arched playfully, a ballerina's foot. It was almost worse. She was now dismembered, a woman with a foot but no body.

"Come. You've stayed in this room for too long."

"When can I go back to England?"

"Soon, but first I have some things to show you."

"Like what?"

"Get dressed. Pack some overnight things."

"Where are we going?"

"You'll find out. Meet me outside."

I could not resist Kofi. He understood this, perhaps: that a child can long for a parent in a way that a parent can never long for a child. He was fully formed when I was born, while I have always been missing a father.

I didn't have any overnight things except the clothes that were brought for me. Kweku had guessed my size correctly but not my taste. Everything was excessively embroidered or, in some instances, studded with rhinestones. I chose the plainest outfit, a black *boubou* with gold threads on the neckline. I looked in the bathroom mirror. My bruises had faded to the color of a tea stain.

I had not left the house since my lunch with Afua two days ago. I lingered. This mansion was more straightforward than the one in Gbadolite. The east and west wings met at a central staircase that led to the front door. It felt like a museum. There were evenly spaced paintings on the walls and Roman busts on columns, faces sculpted in black stone or cast in bronze. Kofi's taste in art was literal. The paintings were mostly portraits: famous Bama historical figures, perhaps, sitting and standing, dressed in Victorian garb, dressed in traditional Bama kente. At the bottom of the stairs, I paused on the threshold. When I stepped outside, I felt exposed in the sun's glare, like an animal in an open field.

Kofi was waiting in the driver's seat of an SUV. Sule was by the window speaking to him.

"Sir, I don't think this is a good idea," Sule said.

"Come now, I did not employ you to be my nanny."

"Forgive me. I am just concerned for your safety."

"Who will recognize me? I am in disguise."

He wore a hat and sunglasses. Apart from that, he was in his trademark monochrome, an olive-green set today.

"Anna. Wonderful. Put your things in the back seat. The boot is full. Sule, open the gate."

"But, Sir—"

"Enough."

Sule, like me, did as he was told.

"Where are we going?"

"I want to show you your country."

We drove for three hours and seemed no closer to our destination. The highway stretched to the horizon, a point where the sky met asphalt. Water mirages sprung up in the distance. I had forgotten my sunglasses and I squinted to see.

Lorries dominated the road. The cabs were open and their goods were on view, pyramids of logs held together by rope, baskets of tomatoes, live cows packed so close that their horns locked and formed branches.

On either side of us, the forest thinned into grassland. We passed a few settlements, too sparse to be called towns, too dense to be villages. We ate lunch in one of these places, in an open-air canteen that faced the road. The other diners looked up at our entrance, but it was me, not Kofi, they stared at.

Kofi ordered two plates of *banku* and palm-nut stew. The *banku* was smooth and white, rising from the stew like a chalk hill. Kofi ate with his hands, cutting off a morsel of *banku* with his fingers, dipping it in the red stew before putting it in his mouth. It was elegant when he did it. When I tried, the *banku* burned my fingers and the stew ran down my wrist.

"It takes practice. Try again."

The *banku* on its own was sour but it was balanced by the thick, rich stew. It was a taste I might acquire with a few attempts. The other diners were mostly men, roughly hewn, with worn clothes and broad shoulders. They ate with their mouths close to their food, their eyes alert. Every time a lorry thundered past, we felt the quake in our plastic chairs.

"Do you know how much this meal cost for two of us?" he asked.
"No."

"Ten cowries. A man can eat a hearty meal in this country for five cowries, less than two dollars, with fresh, pure ingredients, no genetically modified junk. What do you think about that?

His question had a note of challenge, although I couldn't see why. I'd never complained to him about the cost, or for that matter the freshness, of Bamanaian food.

"It's good," I said.

"Are you finished?"

"Yes."

He signaled to the waitress. She brought us fresh water in metal bowls and a sliver of soap on a dish. We washed our hands and turned the clear water red.

On the road, Kofi did not play music. The car was sealed off from noise by thick, perhaps bulletproof, windows.

"Tell me about my grandmother," I said.

"What would you like to know?"

"What was she like?"

"She loved me too much. The Europeans, they'd call it transference. She took the love she had for my father when he died and gave it to me. Of course, as a child I didn't want it. Nor did I want it when I became a man. It weakens you. I couldn't have led the resistance if she hadn't died."

"What made you take that step?"

"I was young with nothing to lose and I loved my country. The conditions in the diamond mines were so terrible. They were killing our people."

I remembered the Kinnakro Five but I did not mention them. I didn't want to anger Kofi. I wanted to know him. There was evil I must overlook if I was ever to become Kofi's daughter.

"You don't speak much about your family," he said.

"My daughter is grown. She works in a large company, travels often. She doesn't have much need for a mother now."

"And your husband?"

"We're separated. Getting a divorce. Maybe."

"Tell me about your wedding," he said.

"It was a shotgun wedding."

"I'm not familiar with the term."

"I was pregnant."

"I see."

"I didn't marry him because I was pregnant. We just got married sooner than I'd planned. I had to walk down the aisle by myself. My mother didn't want to do it. She thought it'd make a spectacle."

I'd made the same choice as my mother, had a child too young and altered the course of my life. I was convinced of our difference and yet our fate was the same. When Rose turned twenty-five, I was relieved that her womb remained peacefully empty.

Outside, the afternoon was fading. Headlamps were switched on. A few drove without illumination, ghost cars on the highway.

"This road runs from the coast to the northern border. My government built it in 1987 and it is still standing. I once had dreams of a trans-African highway stretching from Cairo to Cape Town, but the other African presidents thought I was too ambitious. Who was I, president of tiny Bamana, to dream up a plan for the whole of Africa?"

He was campaigning to me. He wanted my good opinion. We turned off onto a side road and drove for a few miles before veering into the bush. There was no path but the SUV trampled the shrubs and plants that stood in our way. I bounced against my seat belt.

"Where are we going?"

"Almost there now."

He stopped and switched off the engine.

"Where are we?"

"A good place to make camp."

"What?"

"Come. We must set up quickly. It will be dark soon."

He opened the door and got down. It was a natural clearing, perhaps recently razed by fire.

"I'm not dressed for camping."

There was a tent rolled up in the boot, along with other supplies.

"Is it safe to camp here?"

"As long as we don't run into any crocodiles. Help me with these poles."

He was good with his hands. The tent rose quickly. It was lightweight and waterproof. He handed me a small mallet.

"Drive the stakes into the ground. I'm going to gather some brush."

The soil was firm but not hard. The metal stakes sank into the earth with a few blows from the mallet. A half-moon hung in the sky, casting light and shadows. It was the mystical African bush that *obroni* went into raptures over.

Kofi came back with dry leaves and twigs.

"Bring me the wood."

There were logs in the boot, chopped into even pieces and bound with string. He arranged them on the ground and lit a match. It was elemental, the need for fire. Even though the night was warm, I drew closer to the flames.

"Of course, we didn't have all these shortcuts back then. We mostly caught our own food, or villagers who supported the cause would hide supplies in marked places. It was dangerous for them. Some were killed—unarmed civilians shot by British forces. I am sure you did not learn about this in school."

There was raw meat in a cooler bag, still chilled from the fridge. He showed me how to prepare a skewer, piercing each lump of beef in the middle so it would cook evenly. I felt the grit of spices rubbed over the meat like sand. We squatted on our haunches and held the skewers over the flames.

"We could cook only when it rained and the rain would hide the smoke. But, of course, if it rained, it was almost impossible to light a fire. Most of the time we were on the run from the British forces. They would have wiped us out if they could, but they did not have enough men."

When the meat dripped clear juice, it was done. We ate on paper plates and drank from plastic bottles. We wiped our fingers on the grass and burned our plates. From these simple tasks, a mist of camaraderie rose between us, fine as spray.

"I'm sorry about your experience in prison," Kofi said.

"It wasn't your fault, and I survived. Like you."

"Hardly comparable. I was in prison for years, and I didn't have a cell to myself."

His lips and cheeks were shiny from the fat in the meat. He glistened in the firelight like an idol.

"Who told you?" I asked.

"What?"

"Who told you that I had a cell to myself?"

"Oh, Sule."

"I didn't mention it to Sule."

"Someone else, then. I can't remember."

Kweku was the only person I'd told. Kofi could not forget his own son, a son that he had also imprisoned. It was suddenly obvious and clear.

"It was you. You're the reason I can't leave the country."

"What are you talking about?"

"You had me put in prison, just like you put Kweku in prison when he crossed you."

"I didn't know you and Kweku were so close already."

"You admit it?"

"Well, you wanted a taste of the real Bamana, running around and finding stories about child witches. I thought you might enjoy a night in jail."

"They were right. You are the crocodile."

I was close enough to strike him. If he thought he was vulnerable, he did not show it.

"Spare me the sanctimony. Flying in my private plane, eating at my table, sleeping in my hotel, everything paid for by me and you want to play the human rights activist."

"Adrian warned me about you."

"What do you know about him? That traitor. He betrayed Menelik. He betrayed us all. It was only decades after the fact that we discovered it."

"He said he wasn't a spy."

"And you believed him? His intelligence days are over, but in the seventies he was instrumental in destroying the radical black left."

"But you agreed to see him."

"Because I know how to leave matters in the past, where they belong. I was going to give you this, but clearly you cannot handle the weight of history."

He had carried Francis Aggrey's diary all the way from Segu, perhaps in the glove compartment or even on his person, slipped into his trousers and held in place by his waistband. He held it now, its sudden appearance a sleight of hand.

He ripped a page out and dropped it into the fire.

"Don't," I said.

"Why not?"

"The man who wrote that diary would spit on you."

"I am the man who wrote this diary. I am the man who grew up and discovered you cannot make an omelette without breaking eggs."

He ripped out another page and another. It was violence against the past, against Francis Aggrey, my real father.

"Stop."

"It is my image. It is my right."

The pages glowed brighter than the rest of the flames, like thin sheets of gold. I emptied what was left of my water on the fire. It shrank but did not die. I stamped on the tiny flames, the heat rising through my rubber soles. I kicked at the ash, scattering it, but the pages were gone. My father's words had disappeared. Kofi was staring at me.

"You looked like a phoenix. Take it. Take the rest. I'm done."

I took the diary from him. It felt lighter. I was about to speak when something crashed in the bush. We were still for a moment.

"You shouldn't have put out the fire completely. The embers scare off wild animals. Come, Anna. Enough of quarrels. It was wrong for me to have you arrested."

"It seems a rite of passage for your children."

"At least your sense of humor was not damaged. All right, strike me."

"Pardon?"

"Strike me in return. For the blow that was dealt in the course of your arrest. An eye for an eye. You were not meant to be harmed in any way."

He stood with his arms on either side of him, palms upwards like a figure of Christ. It was melodramatic and ridiculous.

"I'm not going to hit you."

"Well, then, it's time to sleep. I will sleep outside. We often slept under the stars." He walked back to the car, away from confrontation. He returned with blankets and bedding. I took my bedding from him and went into the tent. When I lay down, the embroidery of my *boubou* itched against my neck. He had jailed me and then rescued me. He had freed Bamana and then bound the country in his own chains. It was his pattern, the ying and the yang, Francis and Kofi in one person.

I woke up in the middle of the night. The tent was claustrophobic. I dragged my pallet outside and lay down a few paces from Kofi. I fell asleep to the sound of his breathing, wheezing through his nostrils. The air still smelt of burned paper.

29

I woke up with the sunrise. Birds trilled out of sight, filling the air with sound. Kofi was lying with his eyes open. He turned his head when he saw me stir.

"I've been waiting for you. There is a jar of Robb in the glove compartment. Bring it for me."

I took the keys from his outstretched hand. The SUV was shiny and unnatural in the daytime, its hard lines contrasting with the curves of the bush. I could drive off and leave him. He would either die or discover a way to survive.

I found the jar and returned to Kofi. He had struggled to his side. His eyes looked fiercely away from mine. He was like a wild bird with a broken wing.

"Help me sit up."

I slid my arm under his body and lifted him upright. It reminded me of the months I spent looking after my mother.

"My shirt."

The shirt was sewn to fit his form. For a few seconds, his chin stuck in the collar and he was trapped in fabric. He stayed still, breathing faster, while I eased the shirt over his face with my fingers.

"Now the cream on my back."

My eyes stung when I twisted the jar open. I started with his shoulders, hunched forward in rigor. He flinched and then settled to my touch. My hands ran down the discs of his spine, over scar tissue, clumped in strange shapes, comets and jagged stripes, like lightning.

"The arms now."

His biceps were still firm but the skin around them had begun to loosen.

"I'll do the rest."

I took the diary and left him alone, wandering out of sight. The bush was alive with invisible scurrying. Some trees were in bloom, others had begun fruiting: odd, green fruit, hard and round, the size of eggs. Birds had pecked at them, tearing away the skin and revealing bright pink flesh. I picked one off the ground. When I returned, Kofi was dressed and standing, fully himself.

"Try this."

He held out a twig to me.

"What is it?"

"Chewing stick. Nature's toothbrush."

He worked his twig around his teeth and over his tongue until the stick turned to pulp. When he was done, he tossed it on the ground.

"Hundred percent biodegradable. Your turn."

"Where are we going?" I asked when we had driven for an hour. The tank was full after a brief station stop.

"You ask a lot of questions. In the bush we could go a whole day without speaking because your voice might carry on the wind."

"Do you miss being a guerrilla?"

"I don't miss the hunger, but things were more straightforward then. Our clear objective was to drive the imperialists out. Of course, once that is achieved, you must then build a country. We built it well. Like this road."

We drove past pedestrians, trudging along with no obvious destination. A few tried to flag us down. They flapped their arms like large featherless birds. Kofi did not stop.

I hadn't called Rose since our last conversation. It was becoming more difficult to believe that I had ever had a life in London. How had I filled my days before I discovered Francis Aggrey's diary? Brooding over Robert's adultery, brooding over Rose's weight, dead eggs that could never hatch.

And how did I spend my days in Bamana? Waiting for Kofi to turn his attention to me. Even now, after knowing what he had done, I still could not bring myself to fear him. Papa takes care of his children. That was what Kweku had said. Not even crocodiles eat their young.

The road began to wind along a large body of water. We were too far inland for the ocean, but the water did not run like a river. A lake then, but ten times larger than the lake in Gbadolite. A bridge stretched across like a salmon leaping from shore to shore. We drove to the center of the bridge and parked to the side.

"We're here," Kofi said.

"Where?"

"Mensahkro Dam. I call it one of the seven wonders of modern Africa."

He moved stiffly when he got down from the car, shuffling instead of striding. I joined him at the bridge railings. Its metal fretwork vaulted above us, the bars finely woven as lace.

"This is one of the largest dams in the world."

They had blocked the river with a concrete wall. It could only flow through six sluice gates, six artificial waterfalls. They thundered around us, making his voice small.

"My government built this dam to bring electrical power to Bamana and our neighboring countries. Nobody believed that a tiny country like ours could have such an achievement."

"What was here before?" I asked.

"What do you mean?"

"Before you trapped the river?"

"Before we tamed and harnessed the Volta River, a few villages."

"Where are they now?"

"We resettled the villagers. Thousands were moved for the good of millions."

Kofi wanted my approval. Not me. Francis Aggrey through me. Everyone he knew from his old life was either dead, like Thomas Phiri, or distrusted, like Adrian. Only someone who knew Francis could tell Kofi if his life's work was in vain. Only me.

The villages had been destroyed for Kofi's ambition. Houses, compounds, farms swept away by a man-made flood. The hubris of my father, to so completely wipe away a civilization, to permanently bury it.

"It's a waste," I said.

"Pardon?"

"There are still power cuts in Segu."

Kofi's grip tightened on the railings. No one had cared what Anna Graham thought in years. To have even this slight power over such a powerful man: it was intoxicating.

"Why did you come to Bamana?"

"To meet you," I said.

"No. You came to meet a man in the past. There is a mythical bird we have here, Anna. We call it the sankofa. It flies forward with

281

its head facing back. It's a poetic image but it cannot work in real life."

A ferry passed below us. Smoke streamed from its funnel. Passengers crowded the deck, sinking the left side of the hull a few inches deeper than the right. I looked down at the same moment a young girl looked up. She waved. I waved back and a fluttering of palms responded, the gesture widening like a ripple.

"That is the country I created," Kofi said, when they were out of sight. "I am not proud of every single action I have taken in my life, but I created this country and there is much to be proud of. Come. Let's go."

"Wait. I want to sketch you."

"Pardon?"

"I want to paint you, but first I'd like to make a sketch. Stand still, please."

"You mentioned you were an artist."

"Yes. Don't move. The light."

I withdrew my sketchbook from my bag and braced myself against the car. It was hot. The sun seeped through the metal and into my skin. I reproduced Kofi in short, quick strokes. He stood like someone used to having his portrait taken, shoulders erect, head thrown back.

"Relax," I said. "Like you were a moment ago."

"I can't relax around you. I never know what accusation you're going to throw at me."

But he held himself less stiffly, more conversationally. He was not afraid of our eyes meeting. Despite all he had done, Kofi's gaze was open, almost innocent. My pencil traced the curve of his lips, the depression of his sockets, the wrinkles like a fine mesh thrown over his face.

"Hurry. We still have far to go."

"Thank you," I said.

"For what?"

"For this. This trip."

"I wanted to show off something I had built. Something Francis the visionary had built, but even this does not meet with your approval. It is the *obroni* way—to always find African attempts wanting. You said something earlier, that you are not my daughter in the way Afua is my daughter. What did you mean by that?"

"I didn't know you as a child. I'm not afraid of you."

"My children are not afraid of me."

"Are they not?"

He smiled. "Always stirring up trouble. You should have been a revolutionary."

"In London I'm a nobody."

"I find that hard to believe. A woman bold enough to fly all this way to meet me, to stay on alone at the request of a stranger, to challenge me at every turn."

"Sometimes I can go a week without speaking to anyone."

"It is lonely over there?"

"Yes."

"I can understand that. Before I befriended Thomas, I was very lonely in London."

"I'm done," I said.

"Let me see."

He came and stood beside me.

"It's a good likeness. Too many wrinkles but a good likeness. You have talent."

He placed his hand over mine briefly and then walked across to the driver's side.

We drove until late afternoon without stopping. Kofi put on music, a jazz hybrid with piano, double bass, and African drums.

CHIBUNDU ONUZO

"Will you tell me about the Kinnakro Five?" Despite my earlier resolution, I could not leave it alone. It was no longer about the boys. I just wanted Kofi to confide in me, to glimpse a secret part of him as I had glimpsed many secret parts of Francis Aggrey.

"Thomas Becket," he said.

"Who?"

"Archbishop of Canterbury, saint of the Anglican and Catholic Church. You didn't study him in your school history of the British Isles?"

"Yes, but I don't understand."

"His is the story of the Kinnakro Five. When one is in power, one must be careful with one's words, even those spoken in jest. There will always be those who rush to fulfill your whims out of a perverse understanding of loyalty. 'Will no one rid me of this turbulent priest?' As I remember, Henry the Second regretted his words also."

"But what—"

"It is enough, Anna. We must move forward."

It was not enough, but it would have to do. None of his other children, not even Afua, could have gotten as much. He turned up the volume and I fell asleep to the offbeat rhythm, each stroke arriving unexpectedly.

When I woke, the car had stopped. We were outside a bungalow built in the same colonial style as Kofi's show home. We were not in the bush. There were distant buildings on either side of us, but it felt isolated. The house was the lone structure on a large plot of land surrounded by trees and tall grasses. It was growing dim. No lights were on inside.

"Where are we?"

"We've come to see an old friend."

Kofi opened his door and got down. He had stiffened during the drive.

"Who is this old friend?"

"Come. You have trusted me this far."

I got down. He knocked on the front door and pushed it open. I followed into a living room with chairs upholstered in velvet, faded antimacassars draped over their headrests. There were photographs on the walls, portraits of long-dead people. I glimpsed a young man in a morning suit and top hat, holding a pipe and silver cane, his fine possessions on display for the lens. Kofi crossed the room to a doorway with no door. A rectangle of blue fabric covered the opening. The breeze blew through, swelling the fabric like a sail.

Kofi drew it aside and we walked into a courtyard. An open fire burned in the center. A woman sat beside it on a low stool. She was wrapped in a white, faintly luminous cloth. Her shoulders and chest were bare, except for a red beaded necklace, each bead the size of a pigeon egg. The fire gave off a thick smoke, heavy with fragrance, rich with bitter notes.

"*Daasebre*," she said, but did not rise.

"Wuyo," Kofi replied, and he bowed. She was the first Bamanaian to whom I had seen him show deference.

"This is Wuyo Ama. She was our spiritual guide in the bush," he whispered to me.

"What brings you here, *Daasebre*?"

"I have come with my daughter."

"The one from over the water?"

"Yes, Wuyo."

"Come, daughter," she said, beckoning to me.

Kofi nudged me forward. I crossed the steps towards her on my own. She was very old and fat. Her skin hung loose from her neck like peeling plaster. I bowed like Kofi had done.

"Daughter, what is your name?"

"Anna."

"*Daasebre*, what name did you give her?"

"Nana."

"Your new name is in the old one."

"What do you mean?" I asked.

"Have you played Scrabble before?"

"Pardon?"

"Scrabble. The game. *Daasebre*, I thought you said she is from Europe."

"Yes, I've played Scrabble before."

"If you move the tiles one way, you get A-N-N-A. If you move them another, you get N-A-N-A."

Anna was an anagram of Nana. I was close to the fire. Its smoke filled my lungs and fogged my mind. My eyes stung with tears.

"*Daasebre*, wait outside until I call you. Come, let's go," she said to me. She stood up slowly but without assistance.

"Go where?"

"Kofi, you didn't tell her?"

"Remember when I said that girls here undergo an initiation rite to become women? You are a woman already, of course, but you are not yet a woman in this culture."

"Let's go," she said again.

"I want my father to come with me."

"Men cannot take part. It is taboo. But do not be afraid. I did the rites for Kofi's other daughters. Are you coming?"

I could not refuse her. I could not refuse any experience offered to me in Bamana. There were multiple doors leading off from the courtyard and I followed her through one, into a room empty except for a bed.

"First, you must change."

A white cloth was laid out for me. There were no holes for my head or arms.

"I'm afraid I don't know how to wear this."

"Why are you afraid? Just wrap it like a towel and remove your shoes."

She sat down on the bed.

"Is there somewhere I can change?"

"What is wrong with here?"

"I'm not used to changing in front of people."

She laughed. She didn't have many teeth but the sound was not unpleasant.

"What do you have that I haven't seen before? Okay, I am closing my eyes, o."

I changed with my back to her. The cloth stopped at my knees and bunched under my armpits. I felt exposed.

"Wuyo Ama," I said when I was done. There was no answer. I drew close to her. She sat very still, like a statue in a game. Her eyes were closed. Her lips had withered away into lines as fine as wrinkles. They stretched into a faint smile. "Wuyo." I touched her arm. Her flesh was cold. She opened her eyes and looked at me blankly. I felt her body grow warm under my palm.

"Sorry, my daughter. I shouldn't have traveled. Come with me."

We stepped through another door and into a forest. It was morning. The air was fresh and crisp. Birds twittered in the canopy, piercing the silence. The grass was damp with dew.

"What's going on?"

"What do you see, my daughter?"

"Is this a trick?"

"There is no trickery here. Describe what you see."

"We're in a forest."

"What type of trees?"

"Just trees. Very tall. They look old."

"You are in Abbana's land. Abbana reveals what he chooses to reveal. We must go to the stream."

There was no stream when we arrived, only a carpet of short grass and wildflowers. Now there was a stream, freshly sprung from the earth, running fast and clear. Wuyo Ama waded up to her knees and motioned to me.

"Come, my daughter."

It was some sort of hallucination. The fire in the courtyard, the thick smoke: there must have been a drug released by the flames. I stepped in the stream. The water was cool. There were tiny pebbles on the streambed and they slid between the gaps in my toes.

"Come deeper, daughter."

It was too shallow to float but with each step I felt lighter until, when I stood in front of Wuyo Ama, it seemed I would drift away.

"Don't travel, daughter. Stay with me."

She bent and scooped water in her palm.

"Bend, please."

She drizzled the water over my head. It ran down my face like cold tears.

"Water for the washing away of childhood. We thank our mothers for bearing us, for suckling us, for teaching us strength."

She splashed water on my shoulders, on my arms, on my chest. It seeped through the cloth to my skin.

"Thank your mother," she said.

"What do you mean?"

She motioned with her head in the direction I should look.

My mother stood behind me. My mother as I had never seen her, light and unworried, on the verge of breaking into laughter. She wore a red dress, fitted at the waist, with a full flared skirt. She gave a twirl, one full revolution, so I could admire her, so I could see the pearl buttons that ran to the base of her spine. It was the dress from Francis Aggrey's diary.

"Is she real?"

"Am I real? Thank her."

"Thank you, Mum."

"For what?" Wuyo Ama asked.

"For the time you came into school and told Ms. Fenton that she couldn't stop me from auditioning to be Mary in the nativity, and you came home and cried because you were scared to do it. I didn't get the part but you stood up for me. And thanks for leaving me the flat. You did your best, Mum."

She waved.

"Why doesn't she speak?"

"The ancestors speak only when they have something to say. Face me now, please, my daughter."

But I could not turn from my mother. I took a step towards her and she took one step back.

"Do not follow her unless you want to remain in Abbana's land. Face me, my daughter. Many have gotten lost in this way."

I faced Wuyo Ama.

"At this point, usually the girls will sing a Fanti song from their childhood, but we must improvise. What song do you know from when you were a young girl?"

"'Dancing Queen.' It was always on in the flat. She never danced to it."

"That's a new one," she said. "Sing it."

I began softly, growing louder with each line until I was belting it out, then she stopped me.

"That's okay, my daughter. We must return soon. Now I will sing a song for you in Fanti. The meaning is: The season for blooming is here. Bear life in due season. Bring forth."

Wuyo Ama held my hands and sang. Her voice was feathery and weightless. The melody was high.

"Today, Nana, you have become a woman. Your ancestors congratulate you. Greet them."

I turned. There was a crowd on the bank stretching as far as the eye could see, a chain of people linked by their hands. My mother held hands with Grandpa Owen as I had never seen him, straight and broad with a full head of black hair, and Grandpa Owen held the hand of my grandmother, Esther, who I knew only from a photograph, and she held the hand of an African woman in a white blouse and blue wrapper, a headscarf covering her hair and a slim gold chain on her neck, tall and powerful, like Kofi, Kofi's mother. So they were mingled, black with white, a woman in Victorian dress in bonnet and gloves, next to a man in kente, next to a peasant in a smock and bare feet, and there were surprises, four rows deep—a petite woman in a sari. How did she come to this bank?

"Greet them," Wuyo Ama said.

"How?"

She curtsied and I copied her.

"It is time to go, Anna. Time is far spent. Come with me."

We waded to the opposite bank, away from my mother. There was a door in the forest, set in the air, standing with no support. We stepped through into the courtyard. It was dusk. The sun was setting. I gasped, and the smog of Bamana rushed into my lungs, the air as heavy as lead. I felt like a fish reeled out of water, thrashing on the shore. The fire had dwindled to embers. Red coals glittered in the low light.

"Easy, my daughter. Just breathe."

Wuyo Ama seemed unaffected. She waited until my breathing returned to normal.

"Last, it will be sealed in blood."

She held a knife in her hand firmly by the hilt. The blade was long, more dagger than knife. Its tip pointed at me.

"Papa!" I screamed.

It was over before he arrived, a swift nick on my arm, just below my biceps.

"What is it, Anna?"

Kofi was in the courtyard, approaching briskly. Wuyo Ama was laughing.

"*Daasebre*, see you daughter, o. She thought I was going to kill her." She cackled. "The knife is sterilized. I did it with alcohol myself."

I laughed unsteadily and then I began to cry.

"I'm sorry. I don't know what's come over me."

I made a fist over my mouth, but the tears came anyway, until I began to shake from the effort of trying to stop them.

"It is the river inside you that was blocked. You and your father like to build foolish dams. Cry, Nana. When Abbana cried he made the oceans."

There was nowhere to sit so I sat on the ground and wept until I was heaving air. In my mind, I saw the ancestors on the bank, stretching from my mother to the horizon. I felt a hand on my shoulder, like a large bird perching. It was Kofi. No one spoke until I had gathered myself, until I stood and dusted my white cloth, now stained with earth.

"Come, let me bless you," Wuyo Ama said. "Your going and coming is blessed. There is no split in you. Anna is in Nana. Nana is in Anna. Two streams came together and formed a mighty river."

Her palm was warm on my forehead.

"Thank you. My clothes, please?"

"You cannot take them. They are from your old life. Okay, my daughter. I must rest now from our journey. *Daasebre*, you can see yourself out."

We drove back to Segu without stopping. It was cold in the car. I was still damp from the stream.

"You called me Papa."

"You answered."

We passed a billboard with Papa's face on it, the slogan *chief servant of bamana* below his wide smile.

"Afua told me she goes with you on campaigns," I said.

"I would never expect that of you."

"What would you expect?"

"I have always left my children free to choose. Some have followed more closely in my footsteps than others."

The cut on my arm formed a scab. The trickle of blood dried up. It was night when we reached the gate of his mansion. It slid back electronically. Sule was waiting outside with a wheelchair.

"You are free to return to London now. No one will trouble you. You can go tomorrow if you want."

"What if I'm not ready?"

"You can stay also. My home is forever open to you."

"Was Sule in on the plot?"

"Yes, but you must not blame him. He was strongly opposed to the whole thing."

Sule opened Kofi's door from outside.

"Welcome back, sir."

"Thank you. Nana, go inside."

I returned to my room. My things were as I'd left them, my new clothes strewn on the bed. There was a medium-size canvas on an easel, brushes and paint in a small bucket, and more blank canvases propped against the wall. Kweku had come through.

I was not sure what had happened with Wuyo Ama, whether it was hallucination or reality, but I felt at peace, as if indeed two warring streams had finally merged. The effort of the contest, the relief that a struggle was over and that there might still be time to rebuild. Tears rose to my eyes again. Anna Nana Bain-Aggrey. She would need a new passport.

Rose. She would be waiting to hear from me. We had spoken angrily on our last call, but we were bound together in a chain that linked generation to generation. The link would not break with us.

"Mum! I knew you'd call."

"I'm fine. Everything is fine."

"We figured you wanted to be left alone. Dad said we should give you space to work things out by yourself. He said we can't understand because we've both always had a father."

"I think I'm going to stay for a bit longer."

"Take your time."

"I have a new name. My father gave it to me. Kofi. That's his name, even though everyone calls him Papa or Sir Kofi."

"Sir? Sounds distinguished."

"He is. He's complicated. He called me Nana. It means Queen."

"That's pretty. Spell it."

"N-A-N-A."

"Clever. It's an anagram of Anna."

"I want you to come. I want you to meet him."

"You think?"

"Yes. He'd love to meet you. You're his eldest grandchild."

"How many are there?"

"I'm not sure. I'm still discovering so much."

"I'm proud of you for going. I think it's really brave, and I'm sorry I didn't see things like that before."

"Thank you."

"Tired? Long day?"

"Yes."

"I'll let you go, then, but call me tomorrow."

"I will."

"Love you."

She dropped the call without saying goodbye. The door was ajar between us again. I took out my sketchbook and pencil and went to the empty canvas. It was linen, tightly woven, of very high quality. It smelled fresh, like new clothing, like a blank horizon at dawn. I made my first mark.

ACKNOWLEDGMENTS

Special thanks to:

My parents, Dr. Okey and Dr. Mariam Onuzo.

My siblings: Dilichi and Kassim Lawal, Chinaza and Uche Onuzo, Dinachi and Onu Ocholi.

Dilichi, who gave me the title *again*. Let's make it a hat trick.

Joseph Harker, for telling me his story.

My readers: Kinna Likimani, Nana Brew-Hammond, Sola Njoku, Atinuke, Onu, Chinaza, and Dinachi, who provided invaluable insights into the text, and especially to Sola, who always knows what a book needs.

My long-suffering supervisor, Professor Sarah Stockwell. The spark for this novel came from my research on the West African Students' Union.

My supportive agent, Georgina Capel.

My editors, Sarah Savitt, who always believed, Rose Tomaszewska, for pushing the story further, and Jonathan Lee, for being so thorough.

ACKNOWLEDGMENTS

My mentors, Jayne Banful for showing me new neural pathways, Ellah Allfrey for always reminding me of what I bring to the table, Oba Nsugbe for reminding me to look up and out.

The books and authors I turned to for inspiration when I was writing this novel: *Segu* by Maryse Condé, *Song of Solomon* by Toni Morrison, *The Earthsea Quartet* by Ursula K. Le Guin, the novels of Sefi Atta, in particular, *Everything Good Will Come*, and *Outline* by Rachel Cusk.

The Holy Spirit, spirit of creativity.

Chibundu Onuzo was born in Lagos, Nigeria, and lives in London. Her life so far spans two military dictatorships, one internet revolution, two boarding schools, five grandmothers, and a first book deal signed at nineteen. Onuzo's first novel, *The Spider King's Daughter*, was the winner of a Betty Trask Award, short-listed for the Dylan Thomas Prize and the Commonwealth Book Prize, and long-listed for the Desmond Elliott Prize and Etisalat Prize for Literature. Her second novel, *Welcome to Lagos*, was a Belletrist Book Pick, an American Booksellers Association Indie Next Pick, and a finalist for the RSL Encore Award. In 2018, Onuzo was elected as a fellow of the Royal Society of Literature. She contributes regularly to *The Guardian*. Her autobiographical show, *1991*, featuring narrative, music, song, and dance, premiered in a sellout show at Southbank Centre's London Literature Festival in 2018. *Sankofa* is her third novel. Find her on Twitter and Instagram @chibunduonuzo.